CONSCRIPT: BOOK 3

Scott Bartlett

Mirth Publishing

High River

Cover art by Tom Edwards (tomedwardsdesign.com)

Library and Archives Canada Cataloguing in Publication

Bartlett, Scott

Lance (Paperback Edition) ; Scott Bartlett; illustrations by Tom Edwards

ISBN 978-1-988380-77-3

Contents

Chapter 1

Po suppressed the urge to shudder as ants—or whatever the Nibiran equivalent was—crawled past the collar of his suit and down his neck.

He'd chosen an awful time to take off his helmet. Something had been caught in his eye, and it had been driving him nuts, so he'd risked taking off the helmet to dig whatever it was out.

That was when the party of Janus operatives he and the rest of Second Squad had been waiting for decided to come crashing through the jungle.

Now, Po could only lay here, perfectly still, and hope the Nibirans soon wandered close enough for his squadmates to glimpse them with their night vision and engage.

Trying to put his helmet back on would risk blowing their cover. Doing anything risked blowing their cover. So instead, he remained prone on the jungle floor while insects invaded the inside of his SERAPH suit.

You're somewhere else, he told himself. *Anywhere else. You're back on Psyche, lying in your bunk and arguing with Lorenzo. You're flying through a microgravity warehouse. You're watching the salmon swim past on the fish farm level.*

This was a technique he'd often used during bootcamp. The DIs hadn't even allowed them to move their eyes the wrong way when they were in formation, let alone scratch themselves. Now that Po was a Marine, it was moments like this that helped him realize why they'd put the recruits through such pain and torment for those thirteen weeks. If he hadn't gone through it, he seriously doubted he'd have the fortitude to just lie here while alien ants started biting him all over his neck, shoulders, and upper torso.

He gritted his teeth, and forced himself to keep his breathing quiet.

Colonel Tuffin had received an intel report that Shiv Horan, the Janus luminary the Corps had most wanted to bag during the assault on Eremus, was now operating in this region. The colonel had decided that Staff Sergeant Young's Second Squad was just the unit to pay the area a visit. An AC-900 had dropped them off miles from here, where the Sodalite Desert bordered this jungle, and they'd hiked to the perimeter of what was rumored to be a well-trafficked Janus base. Their orders were to hunker down in the bush, wait till a patrol passed, and hit them. The ultimate goal being to bring back a prisoner for a little gentle questioning at FOB Longhorn.

The patrol was getting close. Po could hear them talking and laughing in their dry, croaky voices. A squad of Marines would have been in for a chewing out from their sergeant for being so chatty, but who could expect insurgents to have any discipline?

Po's Circuit threw up a message in the corner of his vision, transparent enough to see through but opaque enough to read. It was from Staff Sergeant Young:

"*Get ready to fire on my mark.*"

Po marveled at Young's situational awareness. He'd clearly picked up on the fact Po's helmet was off and hence the suit's soundproof seal was broken, so he'd messaged his order to their implants instead of speaking over the squad channel. It was details like that made you trust a man enough to follow him into the most dangerous situations.

As quietly as the grave, Po shifted his M37C against the gnarled root he'd laid it on, peering through the scope at the spot where it sounded like the aliens were about to emerge.

Give me a flash of robe, or some of that wrinkly frog skin.

Give me anything, and then you're mine.

It was Nibiran night, without even Gnara's celestial lava flows to lighten the endless darkness. There was a good chance the others would see something before he did, using their helmets' thermal sensors. But his eyes had adjusted to the darkness by now, and he strained to watch for any changes in the otherwise motionless tapestry of the jungle wall.

Movement flickered between thick tree trunks, and he started to squeeze his trigger, when the telltale hiss of an approaching AC-900 gunship reached his ears.

"*Hold your fire.*"

Po winced as the yips in the base nearby raised a ridiculous-sounding chorus, which would have been funny if it wasn't so frustrating. The Nibiran patrol started croaking excitedly, then broke into view, pounding across the moist jungle floor, their ears bouncing against their heads as they ran.

"*Everyone sit where you are,*" Young said. "*They're running past.*"

The implant's messaging app played the sergeant's reconstructed voice through Po's auditory taps, directly into his cochlear nerve, so that there was no worry of the insurgents hearing it. The synthesized voice sounded irritated, but he was sure the reconstruction didn't sound anywhere near as irritated as Young actually felt.

More yipping and croaking rang out through the night from the direction of the insurgent base, with searchlights coming on, and the yips only growing more frantic by the second. The last Nibiran ran past, within a couple feet of where Po lay pressed against the ground, and once the alien was clear, he started breathing a little easier.

"*Get your helmet back on, Abbato.*"

As reluctant as Po was to seal legions of ants inside the suit with him, he obeyed, scooping up the helmet from the soil and lowering it over his head. The collar suctioned it into place automatically, the force getting stronger as he achieved the correct alignment.

Young spoke then, sounding less irritated than his reconstructed voice had—and again, probably a lot less than he actually felt. "This op is blown. That base is on high alert now, thanks to what I'm assuming is a serious breakdown in communication."

As always, Po admired the sergeant's professionalism. He might easily have called the gunship pilot an idiot who didn't seem to know there was a war on, but Young didn't even mention him.

The throaty rasp of a SAM being launched cut through the noise, but no one commented on it.

"We withdraw," Young said, "smooth and quiet. As soon as we have enough distance between us and them, we hike back to the jungle's edge for our ride back."

They slid backward on their bellies, and Po's night vision painted the ground green, whereas in reality he knew it was a rich red. It would have been a welcome change from the blue of the Sodalite Desert, if he could see it. Instead, he had this sickly green to look at.

Nibiru's version of the humble ant crawled down his body in ranks, on a forced march toward his feet, biting all the way. With his helmet back on, he probably could have screamed with the agony of it without alerting any Nibirans, especially with the ongoing cacophony that had obliterated the night's silence. But he wouldn't let himself. He gritted his teeth and bore it.

As they crawled, he noted the lack of anything crashing through the foliage from above to shake the jungle floor, which meant the AC-900 pilot had dodged the Nibirans' attempt to shoot it down.

Po was glad for that. Even if the idiot *had* botched Second Squad's mission.

***

Po was the last into the waiting gunship, and the second he made it to his seat he began stripping off pieces of armor.

"Whoa," Taylor said over the squad-wide as he settled into one of the crash seats. "Feeling the heat, Abbato?"

He ignored him, struggling to get as much of the armor off as he could before the pilot took off. Steam rose from his body as each piece came off. The hatch sealed a moment later, and the shuttle's jets roared. He staggered, gripping his seat's armrest for balance. Then they surged forward, soaring over the desert in the direction of FOB Longhorn.

Young stood to help him, more easily keeping his balance with all of his suit on and sealed. "You're covered in welts," Young said. "What happened?"

"Ants got inside my suit when my helmet was off. Or whatever the Nibirans call ants."

"Whatever they are, it looks like you might be allergic to them. The things are really swelling up. Check your IFAK, there should be some calamine lotion in there or something. I'd take an antihistamine, too."

Po pulled out his Individual First Aid Kit from where it was stored in a pouch in his suit's leg, dug through it for a likely looking cream, then started slathering it over the bites.

The gunship pilot's voice came over the intercom. "Staff Sergeant, did you and your boys get the alert that went out?"

Young had returned to his own seat, but now he straightened in the middle of strapping himself in. "We didn't, sir. What's up?" Ever since Janus had knocked out all of GEA's satellites in Nibiru's orbit, the Marines often missed transmissions while out in the field.

The pilot sighed. "Rin's making another move in the region, it seems. The insurgents hit Longhorn hard, coming up from the ground again in multiple spots throughout the camp. This time, they tunneled up through the floors of buildings that are empty in the night, and amassed in there before attacking. How they knew where those structures were...well, probably they had spies in Longhorn, and it's not hard to guess who. Either way, they forced everyone in camp into the bunkers—those that could make it, anyway. Last I heard, the survivors are still holding out inside them."

Po's heart was hammering in his chest. His first thought was for Navarro, and then for Zhang. But he'd come to know plenty of the Marines in FOB Longhorn.

"And that's where we're headed now?" Young asked.

"Correct. A lot of units were called back from ops—those that could be reached, anyway. Colonel Coleman requested assistance from Halberd, but it seems they came under attack around the same time."

FOB Halberd was the closest base to Longhorn. If they were under attack too, then this *was* a big move from To'sheth Rin. The biggest he'd made since removing the Marines' orbital supremacy during the Battle of Eremus. Po wondered how many other bases were under attack.

"I've been trying to raise other units converging on Longhorn—I'm gonna go back to that," the pilot said. "Hopefully we can rendezvous with at least one or two others, and figure something out for retaking the base."

The intercom fell silent, and the Marines of Second Squad just sat there, each lost in their own thoughts.

Po finished applying the calamine lotion, popped some allergy meds, and started putting his suit back on. After the pilot's news, it seemed clear he'd need it. Gomez lent him a hand from the seat beside him.

But he found himself distracted as he worked with Gomez to don the armor once more. He couldn't believe how much things had changed in the months since he'd taken a shuttle down from the S. S. *Gear Issue* down to Nibiru's surface. When he'd first arrived, the Corps had seemed invincible inside the various bases that had been set up around Basalt Country and the Sodalite Desert. A serious attack on an FOB had been virtually unheard of, then. Sure, the Nibirans had buried IEDs under all the surrounding roads, and sometimes they'd sent RPGs flying at the guard towers. But back then, any sustained assault was met with strafing runs from AC-900s. The Corps had owned the skies, and Janus had been like vermin scurrying before them.

But To'sheth Rin had apparently been playing his cards tight to his chest, waiting for the right moment to reveal them. Eremus had been that moment. While the Corps was focused on its biggest campaign yet on Nibiru, Janus had used concealed launch facilities on Maw, the planet's smaller moon, to destroy all the ships and satellites in orbit. At the same time, Rin had distributed more advanced SAM launchers to his troops, which he must have been keeping in reserve before then. The new launchers posed a much bigger threat to Marine aircraft, making even single-unit insertions dicey...let alone the large-scale bombing they'd visited on Eremus.

The Nibirans couldn't have produced all that advanced gear on their own, leading many to conclude they had to be working with outside forces. Who, no one knew...though the fact they'd had Marine-issue weaponry in Eremus, even before the satellites went down, was worrying.

Either way, the better gear hadn't been the only surprise. Janus had also clearly been concealing its numbers. The Marines got a hint of that when their checkpoints around Eremus had all been hit simultaneously, the same day they lost orbital supremacy.

But that had only been the beginning. Either Janus was a much bigger organization than GEA's intel showed, or their recruitment was skyrocketing. Po suspected it was a combination of both.

A sputtering roar reached his ears, jerking him from his thoughts. A split second later, the back of the gunship disintegrated.

A wall of intense heat crashed over Po, who'd only finished putting his suit back on seconds before. Without its cooling systems, which kicked in immediately, he probably would have been done for.

The pilot came back on the intercom. "That's our main engine gone," he said, with admirable calm. "We're going down. Brace for impact."

Chapter 2

The gunship shuddered violently as it screamed toward Nibiru's surface, and as it did, Po thought of his sister Nicky lying sick in her bed back in their unit on Psyche, looking frail but peering up at him with bright eyes.

I never wrote to her.

He couldn't have if he'd wanted to, with GEA's satellites down over Nibiru. But now it seemed he'd never get the chance.

The shuttle hit hard, then skidded for what seemed like an impossibly long time. At last, it came to rest, the hatch opening across from Po as it did. He couldn't believe it still worked—but it did, just the same as it would have if the entire back of the craft *hadn't* been choked in flame and smoke.

Young had already ripped off his restraints, and was standing in the middle of the smoky aisle. "*Move,* Marines!" he ordered over the squad-wide channel, before sprinting for the open hatch himself.

The others quickly followed, their training taking over, so that they didn't try to fight to be the first ones out. Instead, they exited single-file, in orderly fashion, their weapons and other gear in tow.

Second Squad assembled a safe distance from the shuttle, then turned back to watch it burn. The pilot was sprinting toward them, and Po's implant placed an IFF tag over his head that read "Captain Jorge Diaz." Beyond him, Po saw the deep furrow the gunship had left in the sand for hundreds of meters behind it. It seemed Captain Diaz had managed to angle their descent so that they crash-landed just past the peak of a massive sand dune, which they'd ridden most of the way down. Thanks to that, no one seemed to have been injured. Shaken up, for sure, but not seriously hurt.

"Nice flying, sir," Staff Sergeant Young said as Diaz reached them. "That could have been much worse, for all of us." They'd both lowered their visors, and the Marines of Second Squad followed suit.

The captain shrugged. "We were just lucky that dune was there. I didn't have many options."

"What do we do now, sir?" Krikorian said.

"I've already started trying to arrange another lift." Diaz glanced at the Armenian before returning to Young. "But it's not looking likely, I'm afraid. What I'm getting back is that all gunships are on lockdown until things get back under control locally." He shook his head. "Before Eremus, it was ground units that relied on air to stabilize things. But with these modern SAMs Janus seemed to pull out of nowhere, and with orbital support gone, we pilots need at least some assurance that you grunts have a handle on the ground situation before we go zipping over your heads. If the Nibirans can get those launchers in position, it makes things troublesome for us."

"Meaning, we're walking," Taylor said, ever-ready to cut to the chase.

"Seems that way," the pilot answered.

"We're sprinting, to be perfectly accurate," Young put in. "Right now, we're still about fifty-seven klicks east-northeast from FOB Longhorn, and some of it's pretty rough terrain, especially since it's best we stay clear of any roads. In our suits, we should be able to make the run in under three hours. Hopefully time enough to make a difference to the survivors at Longhorn."

Diaz was nodding. "I'll follow after you, but I'll be a lot slower, going on just my own two legs."

Young hesitated, as if reluctant to leave the captain behind. But he seemed to realize they had no choice. "Suggest finding shelter before night falls, sir. From what I understand, the desert's predators are small, but incredibly brazen when moving in packs. Apparently, their black-backed wildcats will even attack a lone Nibiran, and I doubt they'd quibble over doing the same to a human."

"I'm sure I'll find somewhere to lay my head."

"We'll keep in touch, and send someone back for you as soon as they're available."

"Somehow, I doubt anyone will be. At least, not before I make it back on my own."

"Yes, sir. Stay safe."

"And you, Staff Sergeant. And your men. As safe as it's possible to stay on this planet."

With that, Second Squad was off, sprinting across the desert in a loose group. The going was excruciatingly slow, at first. The enhanced strength their suits lent them did mean they could propel themselves forward more powerfully, but the suits also meant they weighed more, which meant they sank deeper into the sand. As team leader, Po had been assigned a Multi-Shot Grenade Launcher in addition to his M37C, and that only weighed him down more.

The ground toughened up after a while, allowing them to make better time. Young led them along a wide, looping route, one which largely avoided roads, and crossed them only when necessary. The closer they got to the FOB, the more likely they were to encounter buried IEDs on roads.

None of the Marines spoke as they ran, all of them intent on conserving their energy for the fighting that almost certainly awaited them back at Longhorn. But Zanth appeared at Po's side after an hour or so, loping effortlessly alongside him with his darting footsteps. He seemed content enough to talk.

"Are you a student of the Emancipation Doctrines, my friend?" the alien asked him.

Po wanted to laugh. He couldn't remember the Emplor ever calling him "friend." He was being sarcastic—or he wanted something.

Or maybe he's just being extra polite, to try to counter those nasty rumors that have been flying. About the Emplor being the ones to supply the Nibirans with all those missiles they used to take out our satellites. Not to mention the upgraded SAMs that stole our air superiority.

Either way, Po didn't feel like devoting any of his breath to talking, so he used the messaging app instead. Zanth had complete access to his implant, as he'd demonstrated multiple times before, and so messaging would be just as good as speaking. Po didn't even need to send the message—just inputting it was sufficient.

"*No,*" he input, in answer to Zanth's question.

"Pity. If you *were* familiar with the Doctrines, you'd know that everything is alive, including each grain of sand on which you tread. Nibiru herself is alive. Every planet has a consciousness, just like you do, though if you could experience them they would seem more alien to you than I do."

"*Do you follow Mother Nibiru too, then? Like the Nibirans?*"

"Of course not. The Nibirans do have a few pieces of the puzzle, like worship of their Giru-Giru, but their perspective is extremely limited. Just like humanity's was, before we gave you the Doctrines."

"*Not everyone follows your Doctrines.*"

"Because you do not understand them. But anyone who seeks such an understanding, and who endeavors to live according to it, soon begins to experience the rewards. The Doctrines are so valuable that it is the purpose of the Emplor to tumble through the stars and make a gift of them to every unenlightened species we find."

This part of the run was fairly monotonous, so Po decided to humor Zanth, out of boredom. "*What kind of rewards we talking about?*"

"The reward of self-knowledge, for example. The divine is found in the self, since each individual consciousness is like a cell that makes up the divine being. Therefore, to know yourself is to know the divine."

"*How can we know ourselves?*"

"Through contemplation of the self. And through its elevation, since it is obviously divine—given that it forms part of the divine body. To know yourself, you must come to know how you feel in different situations. And how you react to various stimuli. Our appetites play a central role in knowing what we should seek to experience next, you see. By indulging them, without reservation, and without condition, we come to the greater self-knowledge we were always destined to have. If we want something, we should go after it. Every time. Without exception."

Zanth's tail swished back and forth across the sand as he ran, leaving swaths that by now, Po knew none of the others would see. "*You* desire power," the alien continued, "but not for its own sake. You want it because you know the influence and control it gives might one day lead to your being able to influence and control your dear sister's future, and your little brother's. The more powerful you become, the more capable you'll be of helping them. The impulse is noble...and therefore, the power you achieve in its fulfillment is also noble. Don't you see?"

Po hated to agree with the Emplor, but he had to admit the alien *was* making some degree of sense. It also made him feel a little better about some of the choices he'd made since joining the Marines. And before.

"*If we're all a part of this 'divine being,'*" he said, "*then why am I headed to kill Nibirans right now? Is the divine being fighting itself?*"

"Of course. Just as your body will seek to eradicate cells that become cancerous. Illness and disorder can take hold in the divine body, just as in any body. Those that excise diseased cells are akin to an immune response. And those diseased cells, once destroyed, can be reincorporated into the body in other forms."

"*Reincorporated? Sounds like you're talking about reincarnation.*"

"As I said. The Nibirans *do* have part of the puzzle."

With that, the Emplor vanished, as abruptly as he always did.

"I just made contact with a unit on their way back from Eremus," Staff Sergeant Young said over the squad-wide, and Po jumped a little. He hadn't expected the sergeant to talk on the heels of his conversation with Zanth, and the timing startled him a little, even though the sergeant couldn't possibly know the alien had been there.

"It's an armored platoon, which was stationed in the city's southern outskirts to maintain order there as civilians moved back in. Now they're on their way back to push the Nibirans out of our FOB. We're altering our course to meet up with them."

The Marines responded with a few "whoops" and "oorahs." With that, Young changed direction, and they followed behind him, in scattered formation.

Within minutes, the already hardened ground gave way to the cracked and sere terrain that surrounded Longhorn.

***

The armor platoon consisted of two Polliver-4s and two Torres tanks. One of the mech pilots turned out to be none other than Second Lieutenant Karl Grieg, who'd pulled 131st platoon's bacon out of the fire during the clash across the 2-203.

He wasn't nearly as light-hearted today as he'd been that day. Everyone had gotten at least a little grimmer since the Nibirans had blown their satellites and trapped them on this planet, Po had noticed, and the second lieutenant was all business now. After a brief conference between him and Young, the two units headed south together.

Nonetheless, the lieutenant seemed happy enough to have a squad of Marines to accompany his platoon to FOB Longhorn. If there were other units available to help take back the base, none of them were answering Young's and Grieg's transmissions, and an armor platoon without infantry support was an armor platoon asking to get taken out by insurgents wielding anti-tank weapons.

After the journey south from Eremus, the mechs needed to stop and recharge from their bots. They found a natural divot in the ground where they'd be sheltered from all but aerial strikes, which Janus wasn't capable of performing anyway.

The stop worked out well, since there was still some daylight left—or rather, lava-light, from Gnara—and hitting the enemy before dark seemed like a poor way to take advantage of their technological superiority. They needed an advantage in order to have a hope of retaking the FOB from Janus, and waiting until conditions handicapped the enemy while barely affecting the Marines seemed wise.

Lieutenant Grieg got out of his Polliver-4 while it recharged, but the other mech pilot stayed inside his, for the sake of readiness. Grieg was a short Norwegian man with a mustache. Shorter than Po had expected, but he guessed that lent itself well to piloting a mech. The officer sat with his back against a rock while he used his com to try to raise Longhorn on various frequencies.

"Any station this net, this is Lima Tango Golf, Wolverines 6, how copy, over?" He said this a few more times over different channels, until finally he got some satisfaction. Po was close enough to hear Grieg's side of the conversation that ensued.

"I'm eleven klicks from Bravo Big Tree and have just rendezvoused with a squad from platoon designation Kilo Mike. We're charging our two Alaskans and will be ready to move out by nightfall, to assist the forces trapped in Bravo Big Tree. Can you tell me what the situation is in and around there?"

Grieg listened for a few seconds, his face a study in neutrality.

"I see. What kind of assistance will you be able to offer, should we gain entry into the Bravo?"

He listened a few seconds more.

"How much is 'very little?'"

More listening. A frown began to tug at the corners of the lieutenant's mouth.

"That may be, but we can't exactly let them continue to control one of our major FOBs, can we? While Marines huddle together in dim bunkers? Frankly, it's an embarrassment."

Grieg paused, long enough for his frown to deepen.

"Are you the highest-ranking person in that bunker?"

Relief washed over the lieutenant's face. "Good. Put me on with the colonel."

Grieg waited, apparently for someone else to get on the line.

"Hello, sir. Did the corporal relay what I told him?"

More silence.

"Good. And how many other units made contact with you?"

Grieg exhaled, causing his mustache to flutter.

"I see. Well, sir, I don't see any other choice. I'm sure you agree that this situation is completely unacceptable."

They talked for a few minutes more, until at last Grieg terminated the connection, slipping his com into a breast pocket.

"Was that conversation as promising as it sounded?" Staff Sergeant Young asked from the boulder he sat on nearby.

Grieg shook his head. "It seems the FOB is completely overrun with Janus. They have the surviving Marines pinned, so their mobility is obviously limited. They can fire on whatever targets they're able to see from their pillboxes and bunkers, but unless we can make a lot of headway with clearing out insurgents, it's unlikely they'll be able to leave their cover to back us up."

The sergeant nodded. "We'd better make a lot of headway, then."

"Indeed."

Nibiru's night—which was really just a darker dark—had begun to steal over the land when they set out again. The armor had four drones with them, which they launched simultaneously just under four kilometers out from the FOB. The Nibirans tended to shoot down drones as soon as they spotted them, but judging from the patter of weapons fire that was already reaching them from Longhorn, there was a decent chance they'd be distracted long enough for the Marines to collect some valuable intel. Especially considering Grieg was sending four of them at once, all of them entering the FOB's airspace from different directions.

The lieutenant gave everyone access to the four drone feeds, and Po kept them running in a semitransparent, two-by-two window off to the side, which he could look at when he wanted to but which otherwise floated unobtrusively in his peripheral vision. Darkness had fallen by now, but the drones had night vision. The cloak of night would hopefully help them stay active a little longer.

The FOB's walls looked almost completely intact on approach, without even a gate open. And yet, Nibirans now virtually owned the base. It was a testament to the fact that their ability to tunnel up into the middle of a base had rendered walls obsolete.

Po figured that was a bigger problem than most grunts realized. The Corps had a lot of gear to protect here on Nibiru, and when they'd built these mega bases, they hadn't known the aliens could bypass walls like this.

If he was Rin, he wouldn't be launching these massive, coordinated attacks on multiple bases. Not yet, at least. First, he'd continue the guerilla approach that Janus had taken before, which the tunnels would make much more effective. Rig an armor platoon with explosives, and melt away into the night. Silently kill a Marine platoon while they slept, then vanish.

That would strike even more terror into the Marines' hearts, and their war effort would fall apart all the quicker. But Rin couldn't win like this, trying to take the Corps head-on. Not without weakening them substantially first.

But maybe winning isn't his goal. Janus numbers were rising the longer this war continued, and Gunny Emery had told them before they'd ever reached Nibiru that first and foremost, Rin wanted to recruit new members.

Once most Nibirans are on his side, maybe then he'll get smart. Maybe.

The drones converged on Longhorn, climbing all the while. Before long, they'd advanced far enough to give the Marines of Second Squad and the armor platoon a good look at the entire FOB.

There were fewer combatants visible than Po had been expecting—human or Nibiran. That meant that even though they'd withdrawn into the base's bunkers, the Marines were doing a good job of keeping the enemy pinned down, too. That was important. Janus had mortars, and if they were allowed to set up a firebase, they could start cracking those bunkers.

It looked like they'd already taken out a couple, toward the center, where the angle worked out for mortars to get them from outside the base's walls. A startling number of the Containerized Housing Units were destroyed, too. The massive mess facility was a smoking, charred husk, and the stalls where Nibirans had been allowed to hawk their wares had taken perhaps the most damage, the wood burnt and the corrugated-metal huts flattened and scattered. It seemed Janus didn't take kindly to their brethren making nice with the enemy.

Or is that just to hide the fact that there were Janus spies at those stalls, mapping out the FOB for them?

"Wow," Taylor breathed over the squad channel, his voice a little unsteady. "They wrecked the place. Now what, Staff Sergeant?"

Before Young could answer, two SAMs streamed up from opposite guard towers, taking out half their drones.

"Seems they've noticed we're here," Grieg said over the channel they'd established between Second Squad and his armor platoon. "Worse, it looks like they've managed to take over the guard towers. We need to strike *now,* unless we'd like them to start taking out our armor with anti-tank weapons from those walls."

"How do you want to go about this, sir?" Young asked.

"Well, do you see any reason why we shouldn't blast ourselves an opening?"

Young was looking at the mech as they carried on their conversation. Presumably Grieg was looking back at him, but it was impossible to tell with him concealed from view by his Polliver-4.

The sergeant shrugged. "The walls don't seem to be doing us any good anymore. I say blast 'em."

"See, this is why I like working with NCOs," Grieg said. The mech's top swiveled toward the Torres tanks on the mech's right. It was a completely unnecessary movement, but it did suit Grieg's style. "You heard the sergeant, boys. Make me a hole in that wall, and see what you can do about removing that closest tower as a threat while you're at it."

Chapter 3

The tanks started out by sending high-explosive rounds at the guard tower—two for good measure. It blossomed with flame, and that seemed likely to be the end of any Nibirans sheltering inside.

Then they started in on creating an ingress through the wall itself, while the Polliver-4s ranged in opposite directions, no doubt ready to fire on any RPG-toting Janus that appeared on the wall—or worse, LAW-toting ones. The mech's mechanical wolf packs kept pace with them at their heels.

The wall withstood the tank's assault longer than any Nibiran structure had back in Eremus, which wasn't much of a surprise. Po would have been concerned if it hadn't.

But within a few minutes, a jagged, smoking breach had appeared, strewn with twisted rubble at the bottom.

"I'd say that's good enough for government work," Grieg said. "Let's move."

A rocket hissed out of the smoke from inside the base, connecting with the foremost Torres and obliterating it.

Grieg cursed, then said, "Thunder-2, get out of the breach's line of fire!"

The remaining Torres swiveled, then started moving westward, parallel to the wall. Its crew had reacted just in time: another rocket sailed from the gap, hitting the spot it had just occupied.

"Spread out and move up, Second Squad," Young ordered. "Our sensors are better than the enemy's, especially at night. Shoot at anything that shows up on thermal."

They were already pretty spaced out, but at Young's command they strung themselves out further, each advancing with M37s raised to eye level. Po was a little nervous about the order to shoot at any heat signature they saw, but he supposed their fellow Marines would all be hunkered down in bunkers. They wouldn't exactly be out strolling the grounds.

"Seeing any likely culprits, Staff Sergeant?" Grieg asked. He and the other pilot had started arcing toward the base's walls, their respective packs of bots loping along behind.

"Negative, sir. Although, there are really only a couple of buildings they could be taking cover in to hit us from at this angle. Mind taking them out?"

"Just how much paperwork are you trying to make me do, Staff Sergeant?" But Grieg didn't seem to be looking for an answer, and Young didn't bother giving one. "Hmm, let's see. Looks like a supply shed and a CHU. All right, we'll roast 'em. Are your boys ready to move into the base once we do?"

"Yes, sir."

"Good. We'll send the robo-dogs in with you. Secure the area inside the wall, and I'll bring what's left of my platoon in behind you."

The mechs had reached the wall, and now they ran alongside it, running similar to how Po imagined velociraptors would. They slowed up as they reached the breach, top halves swiveling to bring their guns to bear.

It took them maybe two seconds to shell the buildings and step back behind the cover of the still-smoking walls. Twin conflagrations rose up into the night.

"That's our part done," Grieg said. "It's all you now, Staff Sergeant."

"Me and my boys. Advance, Second Squad."

The Marines rushed the gap, reaching it just after the Polliver-4's quadruped bots converged on it and poured into the base. At least three hostiles popped up on thermal as they passed through the walls, and Po chose one in his sector, letting it have a burst from his rifle.

Then came the sound of an RPG launching, and Young gave the order: "Scatter and find cover!"

They didn't need to be told twice. The RPG detonated at Po's heels, bathing him in heat as he ran toward a pile of rubble that looked to be the closest available protection.

Gomez made it to the rubble ahead of him, but thankfully there was enough of it to offer adequate cover for them both.

Po's sensors were already integrated with the mech bots, and he kept a semi-transparent, integrated composite of what they saw in the bottom-left corner of his vision. Not only did they allow him to see clearly even while taking cover, but his implant was also good enough to make his vision flash green when there were no visible Nibirans with weapons trained on him. It also flashed yellow when one had just emerged, with the hostiles' locations superimposed as black silhouettes, visible even through obstructions like the rubble.

Relying too heavily on the function would get a Marine killed, since it could only see as much as the sensors his Circuit was integrated with. But it could become a killer edge, if its user stayed sufficiently frosty.

He was paying special attention to the open doorway which the function told him the RPG had come from. At the first flash of white there, he popped up, fired a burst that way, then took cover again.

Just in time—rounds *zinged* inches above his helmet. But his Circuit confirmed a likely kill of the Janus with the RPG.

"Good job, Abbato," Young said, which served as further confirmation.

Po was in-the-zone enough that he barely noticed the accolade. He was too focused on what the robo-dogs were showing him as they ran back and forth between the enemy and the Marines taking cover, drawing enemy fire and laying down decent suppressive fire, all while feeding Second Squad excellent visual.

He wondered whether the Nibirans knew that each of the eight mechanical quadrupeds was a walking nuclear reactor. They wouldn't explode like a nuke upon destruction—reactors weren't designed that way—but it wasn't impossible that their safeties would fail and start leaking radiation. Suitless as they were, the aliens were way more vulnerable to an outcome like that than the Marines were. That had to make contending with the support bots a little daunting.

If they know enough to be daunted.

All this flashed through his mind in less than a second. Crouched behind the rubble, he watched the sensor composite like a bird of prey.

There.

Two Nibirans were sharing a doorway to an office block, both using it as cover. But right beside them was a window that had been left open.

Stupid.

The glass was bulletproof, but that wasn't much good with the window open. A grenade seemed like a fitting gift to toss through the opening...except, Po's implant told him it was over two hundred meters away.

No way I'm making that throw, even in my SERAPH.

And so he put down his M37 and reached for his MGL, the strap going slack as he raised it.

"Need a hand?" Zanth asked, not bothering to appear this time. A ghostly red figure took shape above Po, with an arcing path stemming from it. The alien was showing him where to position the M320.

Po popped up, lined himself up with the ethereal shape, and fired.

The grenade arced true, entering the window almost dead-center.

One of the Nibirans reacted by fleeing the doorway into the open, and Paisley took him down. The grenade went off less than a second later, and the second Nibiran was heard from no more.

"Nicely done, boys," Young said over the dedicated squad channel. "Now, let's make some more room to stretch out. Echo Team, move up. You're on a roll. Delta and Foxtrot will cover you. Zapletal, stand by to advance your Foxtrot boys next."

"You got it, Staff Sergeant," Zap said.

"Let's move," Po said, using his team's channel. "And don't crowd each other. Pay attention to where you neighbor is finding cover, and make sure you spread out from him."

With that, Echo leapt up from their positions and sprinted forward, weapons swinging as they ran.

Rifle fire coughed from positions farther into the base, but as always, Staff Sergeant Young was true to his word. They laid down effective suppressive fire before it became an issue for Echo.

All of Echo Team made it to new forward positions safely, and Po breathed a sigh of relief. The memories of Eremus were too fresh, and of the men they'd lost there.

Demps. Still can't believe you're gone. He wasn't sure he could handle losing another brother, today.

Next, Echo worked with Delta to cover Foxtrot's advance, and then it was Young's turn to move with his Delta boys. They met with resistance, but not as much as Po had expected.

And not as much as we should *be meeting with. They must be keeping something up their sleeve again.*

"*Zanth?*" he input into his messaging app. "*Is there something you're not telling me?*"

But the Emplor chose this moment to stay quiet. Probably, he enjoyed watching Po fret.

Even with their newly revealed SAMs, and their neutralizing the Corps' orbital superiority, Janus was still technologically outmatched by the Marines, by a wide margin.

But Po had to admit, if he'd been To'sheth Rin, he would have attacked the Marines with everything he had from the very first battle. By keeping so much in reserve, Rin had taken a much smarter approach, employing unexpected capabilities at the moment of maximum possible devastation.

That took discipline. Whether the Nibiran commanding this force would prove as disciplined as Rin remained to be seen...but for a decentralized group, Janus seemed to stick pretty closely to Rin's playbook.

The Polliver-4s strode into the base once Second Squad had cleared a wide-enough arc centered on the rent in the wall. Behind them, the remaining Torres tank rolled in, and as it did, the insurgents succeeded in disabling one of the mechs' support bots. A second followed soon after. Po wondered if they were leaking radiation.

That's the Nibirans problem, not ours.

With the armor backing them up, Second Squad began to steamroll through FOB Longhorn. The mechs' and tank's involvement meant the destruction of a lot more base infrastructure, but what was the alternative? Let them continue to occupy the base, while Marines sat in bunkers, their supplies slowly dwindling?

They progressed steadily toward the base's center, and Po was just wondering if Grieg would try requesting backup again when the LAWs fired from the walls.

Six of them went off like giant shotguns, from positions spaced more or less evenly along the surrounding walls. Three rockets for each Polliver-4.

"Eject!" Lieutenant Grieg yelled over an open channel, but the other mech had already decided to try sidestepping the rockets.

It was the wrong move. Two missed, detonating the ground around the mech, but the third hit the cockpit dead-on.

Grieg's mech got a similar treatment, but he'd followed his own order. He was already up in the air, pushed up and sideways by the ejection seat's rockets. A green parachute deployed as he reached the top of his arc.

"Cover him!" Young rasped. Even as he spoke, the bloom of weapons fire sprouted from positions all over the base.

Second Squad returned the favor, suppressing the nearest positions, and somehow, Grieg made it to the ground safely. He landed just as six more LAWs were streaking across the base to connect with the Torres tank, obliterating it, and surely killing its crew instantly.

"That's it," Grieg screamed over the tumult as he staggered to his feet. "We get in a bunker or we're done. The base is lost."

They already had the bunker locations, and thankfully the closest one was no more than a couple dozen meters away. Hugging a row of CHUs, Second Squad hustled toward it with Second Lieutenant Grieg in their midst. Young made contact with the occupants as they ran, requesting they open it to them.

None other than Zhang was there to greet them at the bunker's hatch, waving them in, the worry plain on his broad face.

The Marines ushered Grieg in first, since he was without a combat suit, while they stood arrayed around the bunker entrance, returning Janus fire. Then it was their turn, and they hustled into the hardened shelter themselves, pulling the heavy door shut behind them.

Chapter 4

Zhang seemed in somewhat better spirits, now that Second Squad was safely inside the bunker. Even not wearing a suit, he was still taller than Po, but a little less so.

He placed a hand on Po's shoulder. "I thought you were here to pay me back for those times I saved you."

"I am," Po said.

"You call this saving me?"

"Well...I'm working on it."

Zhang snorted.

"You're not wearing a suit," Po remarked.

"Because I'm not in the box." Zhang nodded at a ladder, which Po assumed led to the squat pillbox that reared up from the center of the bunker. The rest of the space was mostly sunken, and there'd be a level under this one, too.

A harsh, accented voice spoke from Po's right, drawing both his and Zhang's attention. "Those terrorists are being supplied by someone else. They have to be." Grieg had his fists balled up, and was standing too close to Staff Sergeant Young and looked like he wanted to hit him. Young hadn't actually done anything wrong, as far as Po knew, but the second lieutenant looked mad, and keen to take it out on whoever was handy.

Young nodded soberly, apparently unaffected by the lieutenant's ire. "But who?"

Grieg seemed to rein himself in. He closed his eyes, then leaned back against the concrete wall, hands still clenched. His shoulders rose and fell with a deep breath. "The AKB, maybe? Or the Angels?"

"I don't see either having access to this kind of hardware."

"What about the Emplor, then?"

"That...would certainly complicate things."

"It would, yes. But I heard rumors about something strange that happened in Shackleton. Something unexplained, which involved a vanishing Emplor. Do you know anything about that? You were there around then, weren't you? Under Colonel Tuffin."

"Nothing I'm authorized to share, I'm afraid, sir."

"Figures." Grieg sighed, seeming to settle down. "Who expected Rin to inflict this kind of punishment on the Corps? We're already at losses no one could have predicted. I just lost my entire platoon...."

Zhang exchanged glances with Po through his visor, which he'd de-polarized. The big Marine looked awkward.

"Navarro's here," he offered, in a whisper.

Po raised his eyebrows. "Really?"

Zhang nodded, then gestured toward a narrow staircase at the other end of the chamber, leading down. "He's below. Want to see him?"

"Sure. But I guess I'll take off my suit first. Unless I can expect to be called up to shoot?"

"I would say they'll give you at least a few minutes' breather, after whatever it was you were doing out there."

"We were liberating the base."

"Somehow, I don't feel very liberated."

Po joined the rest of Second Squad near some lockers, which they'd apparently claimed for hanging their suits and stowing their gear. Most of the lockers were taken, which made Po wonder about how many Marines were in the bunker exactly...and how long their supplies would keep them in the fight.

What would happen if the food ran out while Janus still controlled the base? He didn't relish the thought of becoming To'sheth Rin's POW. GEA claimed it didn't negotiate with terrorists, but in this case, Po doubted they'd even get the opportunity to compromise their principles. Rin was pretty clear about desiring humanity's extinction, and he'd probably consider executing surrendered Marines en masse a good start.

Zhang was waiting for him with his hands in the pockets of his sweats, a posture Po was surprised they hadn't beaten out of him in bootcamp. For his part, he had a lingering fear of ever sticking his hands in his pockets, not to mention leaning against anything, or scratching, or looking at a sergeant funny.

"Did you hear about the Scourge?" the big Chinese asked.

"What about them?" Po's heart made a leap for his throat. The thought of the Scourge returning with virtually the entire Corps trapped on Nibiru wasn't a pleasant one. It had been the Marines who'd defeated them, last time. Nicky's pale face materialized in his mind's eye, and he felt a pang of guilt and sorrow. "Are they back?"

"Well...people think so."

"People have been thinking that for a while." He released the breath he'd been holding. "So they're not back, then."

"The *Parochia* missed its last scheduled transmission."

Po paused in the middle of unclasping his right bracer. "The *Parochia.* Wasn't she headed for Lalande?"

Zhang nodded. "And she only left six years ago."

"But the Scourge hit us from the opposite direction." He finished unclasping the vambrace, hung it up, then started on the other one.

"That was just a recon force. Everyone knows that."

"Everyone *speculates* that."

"Well, now they're speculating that the Scourge have a bigger presence around one of the stars past Lalande. Maybe even around Lalande itself. The math checks out, too. The Scourge hit us in 2140, and it would have taken eight years for a signal sent by their first recon force to reach Lalande. Add a couple more years to muster an assault fleet and prepare to launch it. So, 2150—one hundred and twenty-one years ago. Based on the propulsion tech they had then, it'd take a fleet around that long to reach where the *Parochia* would have been."

Po worked on removing the suit's sabatons, then the greaves. He didn't want to ask the question. But he couldn't help himself. "So, how long would that give us?"

"Four years. Less, if they've made any advances in ship propulsion."

Po finished taking off his armor at last. He hung up the final piece, then turned back to Zhang, forcing a smile. "Let's go see Navarro."

I'm sure he'll cheer me up.

Zhang led him across the chamber and down the stairs, which opened up into a space that was much bigger than Po was expecting. It was pretty open, but with closed-off sections bisected by corridors. Even the part he could see was stuffed with Marines—sitting on couches, playing cards around tables, eating, working out. It reminded him a little of being aboard the S. S. *Gear Issue*, minus the microgravity.

"What kind of supplies is this thing stocked with?" he asked, gazing around. Apparently, he couldn't stop asking questions he didn't want the answers to.

"Not enough. No one expected to actually have to use these things. We *might* have enough to last a week."

"At least they built them."

"Yeah. But the contractors had to justify their budgets somehow."

"Do all the bunkers have this many Marines?" If they did, Po had no idea why they didn't simply retake the base. Was this the FOBBITs' way of sneaking in an extended holiday?

But Zhang was shaking his head. "Some are almost empty."

"So, those bunkers have supplies to spare, then."

"But no way to get them to us."

"Do you have any good news for me, Zhang?"

The other Marine grinned. "I hear the weather's supposed to be nice tomorrow."

Po rolled his eyes. The weather in the Sodalite Desert was more or less the same every day. If you could call them days.

"There's Navarro," he muttered, heading across the room to where the Marine sat in an armchair alone, staring into space.

"Hey buddy," he said once he reached him, kicking the base of his chair. "Good to see you. Chat with any Nibirans lately?"

Navarro shot him a look. The comment had been a low blow, even Po could admit that, but not totally uncalled-for. Navarro's MOS was Linguist, and Po hadn't forgotten him bragging back in Shackleton about how he was going to talk Janus into forfeiting the war. *Something like that.*

"Weren't you supposed to be bellying through a jungle somewhere?" Navarro said.

"I was," Po answered. "And I wouldn't mind being there right now. But I came back to save your sorry hide instead."

"I don't feel very saved."

"That's what I said," Zhang put in.

"Well, maybe if our Linguists were better at winning hearts and minds, we wouldn't be fighting so many aliens."

"And maybe if you grunts weren't so brutal, the aliens wouldn't be so angry."

Po laughed, but it had a hard edge. "You're right. It didn't occur to me to try diplomacy with the terrorists who took out Cycler 3. Who tried to nuke Earth from the moon. And who killed Dempsey." His voice cracked on the last word.

Navarro looked up, his expression softening. "Hey," he said, holding up a placating hand. "Let's cool it, all right? We're all hurting."

A retort rose to Po's lips, but he choked it back. Navarro was right, which he normally hated to admit. But the other Marine had lost his wife not so long ago, to the illness that was the reason he'd enlisted in the first place.

"Yeah," he said instead, a little hoarsely.

"Anyway, I don't know if you were right before that it was dumb to try talking to the Nibirans. But it's probably not going to happen, now. Janus recruitment is skyrocketing, and what happened with that PMC didn't help."

"PMC? Private...Military Company?"

Navarro raised his eyebrows. "You didn't hear?"

"Abbato *was* out on that mission," Zhang said. "Word is, they had to hike back from a crash landing."

"Run back," Po corrected. "We ran back."

Zhang shrugged.

"Anyway," Navarro said, "a mining company hired Stellar Security Services at a huge premium, because there's been a lot of sabotage at their sites. Apparently the GEA partner corporations are all going crazy, trying to outbid each other to hire the security firms on-planet, and as things get crazier, there aren't enough to go around."

Po nodded slowly. "Right. I guess they were all stranded here too, just like us."

"Yeah. It's probably Janus running the sabotage, but after an attack on an ore hauler convoy that happened on Stellar Security's watch, which cost their client millions, they decided to take it out on the nearest village. So they went there and torched the place. I guess they figured it made it look like they were actually doing something."

Po winced. "Rin couldn't have asked for better advertising."

"Indeed."

"You still think this is a 'good war,' or whatever you said on that shuttle we took to the *Gear Issue*?"

"A *just* war. And I said you could *argue* this is a just war. Not that it is."

"Well, do *you* think it is?"

Navarro sighed. "I...might have been naive. It's true that Janus is a threat to everyone in the system, and that they need to be stopped. But I don't know if our motives are completely pure in this. I don't think this is only about stopping more terrorist attacks."

"They were *never* pure," Po said. "GEA officials have enough security around them that they're untouchable. They don't care about terrorism."

"Well, they *might* care about nukes shot at them from the moon."

"I'm sure they all stay real close to underground apocalypse condos they can flee to at a moment's notice. Trust me, Navarro. The reason GEA is coming after this planet with such a vengeance is because their partner corporations were harmed. To'sheth Rin went after the companies that keep them fat and happy. And GEA took that personally."

"I still say we can't actually know what's in their minds. But either way...things are messed up, here."

"You don't say."

The other Marine shook his head, frowning. "Janus does need to be stopped, and we're apparently the instrument God has chosen to do that. But God works through compromised people sometimes. And I'm starting to think the Corps might be pretty compromised."

"*GEA* is compromised. We just happen to work for them." Po narrowed his eyes. "And I thought you didn't believe in that stuff anymore."

"I'm working through some things, Abbato."

"We all are," Zhang said.

"Yeah. I guess we are."

***

There were enough Marines in the bunker that each enlisted only had to spend an hour in the pillbox over a twelve-hour cycle. The officer in charge, who turned out to be Colonel Tuffin, did Second Squad the mercy of letting them get a solid sleep before working them into the rotation. Even so, Po's rest felt inadequate, and his shift still felt like it came too early.

He'd barely slept, in fact. The dream was back, of the Nibiran who'd jumped him in a dusty Eremus residence and tried to stick a knife through his suit's neck seam.

As he had in real life, Po pulled the insurgent forward and over him, putting him through a coffee table and driving his own knife into its chest. But his breath caught in his throat when he noticed the Nibiran's face.

It wasn't a Nibiran at all. It was Dempsey, his green eyes locked on Po's, full of confusion.

The nightmare had jerked Po from his sleep, causing him to sit up covered in sweat. He forced himself to breathe, and to settle back onto his rack. It took him at least an hour to get back to sleep, only to be woken by the exact same dream soon after.

Within a half hour of waking for the final time, he was standing at a horizontal slit of an aperture, scanning the base outside for activity with his M37 at the ready.

It was a dull, yet necessary task. The Nibirans had diligently destroyed all the sensors in the FOB and on the exterior walls, and by now, they knew which parts of the base were covered by the pillboxes. So of course, they avoided going there. According to the colonel, they were constantly prowling the parts the Marines couldn't see, looking for spots they might set up mortars and start cracking open the remaining bunkers.

Thankfully, the base had been well-designed, and the bunkers covered almost all of it. A couple times, the Nibirans had felt confident enough to try setting up a firebase, only for the Marines to take it out from one of the bunkers.

The enemy seemed to lack direct-fire mortars, which meant firing rounds from the walls sent them too far. And while they'd managed to take out two bunkers near the center of the FOB by firing from outside the base, most of the bunkers were close to the walls, and the walls were high enough that they intercepted the rounds at that angle. The mortars weren't capable of obliterating the walls like the Torres' HE rounds had, and even those had required several hits before accomplishing it.

As for the Marines who'd been in the two destroyed bunkers—some had died, but others had been contacted by radio, and were hiding out under the rubble that had collapsed into both bunkers' upper levels. Provided they ever retook FOB Longhorn, and provided those Marines had the supplies to last long enough, then they'd dig them out when they could.

Suddenly, it felt like a cold hand had seized Po's heart.

Why couldn't the insurgents just use the breach we *made in the walls for a new firing angle on more bunkers?* Now that he'd had the thought, it seemed strange that they hadn't, in the ten hours Po had been here.

But then again, the aliens knew they were disadvantaged during Nibiru's night. And if they *did* have a place to securely set up a firebase, they'd want to make sure it was truly secure, wouldn't they? They could have worked through the night doing just that, waiting for Gnara's ghoulish light before they struck.

A hard lump formed in his throat, making it hard to swallow. The rest of his watch in the pillbox seemed to creep by. He found himself glancing at Paisley, who had the window to his right. But if the other Marine had made a similar realization, he didn't give any sign of it.

Then, with just a couple minutes left in his watch, he heard the *whoomph* of mortar fire, followed by the *snap-bang* of a round connecting with its targets. Another *whoomph* followed, then another. More impacts, each one sending minute vibrations even through the concrete walls of the pillbox where Po was stationed.

Now, Paisley did look at him, and his eyes were as wide as Po knew his must be.

Chapter 5

The next watch came up the ladder, their faces grave behind their transparent visors. Zhang was among them, and his eyes met Po's as he took his place at the aperture. "They just destroyed another bunker. Using the gap you guys blew in the walls."

Po wanted to say it had been Grieg who'd ordered the wall breached, not him. But he bit back the remark, knowing it came from a place of defensiveness and guilt. He'd been part of the unit that had blown apart the walls and then failed to liberate the base. So he shared in the responsibility.

In the military, everything that happens on your watch is your fault, and you'll do a lot better if you take responsibility for all of it. Even the things that aren't really your fault are your fault. A Marine sergeant had said that to him back on Psyche, when the bot that had custody of him escorted him late to the Mobile Induction and Processing Station. Po hadn't realized how much he'd come to internalize the sentiment.

Zanth spoke into his mind as he descended the ladder, though again, the Emplor didn't appear.

"You aren't responsible for this, Po. It's like you said yesterday. GEA is compromised, and you just work for them. The same goes for the second lieutenant who ordered that wall destroyed. *He* gave the order, and the tank crews complied. You weren't even the one to carry it out. What power did you have to stop it?"

Po didn't know why the Emplor was being so friendly, lately. But he did have a point. He had to focus on what was in front of him—on what mattered. He had his own job to do, and if he didn't do it, he'd be dishonorably discharged straight into a simjail, for a decades-long stay. That had been true when he'd started bootcamp on Cycler 3, and it was still true now.

If I went to simjail, think how Nicky would suffer. And Marco. They might never make it, if that happened.

He refused to let his younger siblings becoming hopeless victims to the system. He'd get them out of the mess Luca Abbato had put them in...even if Nicky *had* welcomed their abusive father back with open arms. And even if, because of her naiveté, Luca was able to make things even worse for their family.

The dull *whoomph* of another mortar round reached his ears, muted now that he was no longer standing at a pillbox window.

Staff Sergeant Young was waiting for them at the bottom of the ladder. He was also wearing his SERAPH suit...which meant they were going out.

"Grab your M320," he said to Po. "The rest of the squad's suiting up. Time to go fix what we broke."

"Fix what we...." Po said, trailing off. He gave his head a shake, then headed to the lockers where he'd stowed his MGL.

Everyone in the pillbox had been squadmates, which meant a third of the squad was already wearing their combat armor.

Young's words echoed through his head. *Fix what we broke.* That wasn't exactly how Po would have put it. First of all, *they* didn't break it, like Zanth had said. And there'd be no fixing the wall, with Janus controlling the FOB.

And even if we manage to destroy that firebase...even if we make it back to the bunker alive afterward...nothing will be fixed. They'll just set up another one the next night.

Assuming this worked, what they were about to do was buy the Marines in Longhorn some time. Time for what, Po had no idea. But that was the best they could hope to accomplish.

***

Second Squad advanced through the base as quickly and methodically as they could, using bounding overwatch to cover each other, but also enjoying cover from Marine bunkers along the way.

Staff Sergeant Young had mapped out their route while the others were still getting their suits on back in the bunker, a task Po hadn't envied him. Their Circuits were integrated with every other Circuit in the base, and so they had a good idea of the buildings that had Janus lurking in them, waiting to take potshots at anyone who happened by. But pretty much every path was fraught, and the routing was complicated further by the need to avoid the lines of fire created by the gap in the wall.

It meant that almost every step of the way, someone was trying to kill them. Bounding overwatch proved effective for suppressing enemy fire, since there wasn't enough of it to overwhelm them, especially in their SERAPHs. But it did make the going slow, and agonizing.

All the while, the Nibiran firebase continued sending mortar shells at bunkers throughout the base. Po didn't want any more bunkers destroyed, but he especially didn't want the one destroyed that had Navarro and Zhang in it.

By the time they reached the wall, their implants informed them that a total of three bunkers had been cracked since the attack had begun. Po could have stopped to figure out which three, so he would know how likely it was that his friends were still alive. But there was no time to do that. They needed to end this, if they could. The mortar fire wasn't stopping.

Hostiles began shooting at them as they neared the wall, from positions they'd cleared yesterday.

Second Squad dropped to the ground, taking cover behind some of the rubble the Torres tanks had created, which was out of the line of fire of the Nibiran firebase. Rounds ripped through the air over their heads, till they figured out exactly where they were coming from and began returning fire.

Young cursed. "They waited till we got here before opening up on us. Echo, I need you to accompany my Delta Team back the way we came, to see if we can find ingress into those structures. We'll clear them, and see if we can use them to fire on the firebase from there. I didn't want to do that, since the Nibirans may well redirect their mortar fire at us once we're in the buildings...but we don't have much choice, now. We need to take those structures, and once we have them, we might as well try to use them to our advantage. Foxtrot, you stay here and provide cover."

"Got it, Staff Sergeant," Zap said.

The Delta Marines went first, with Echo close behind, both teams sprinting but ready to fall into bounding overwatch if they needed to lay down additional suppressive fire.

Po knew why Young had chosen Delta and Echo for this task. Both the sergeant and Krikorian carried the only two M126 sniper rifles the squad had with them—and they were also the only ones qualified on them. They wouldn't have been much good for shooting at the firebase from the wall, but from the buildings, there was actually a chance they could take out the mortar's operators. True, the other insurgents would probably take over right away, and start redirecting rounds at Second Squad's positions...but none of them had expected this to be much fun, anyway.

They only had to suppress one enemy position in order to work their way around the buildings insurgents had been shooting at them from. It was easily done, but once Delta reached its target—a CHU—Echo was on its own. Po, Gomez, and Taylor talked their rifles at the two Nibirans trying to shoot them from the one position that was in range, while Paisley got ready to breach the office block they'd been assigned. Krikorian spent the time checking over his sniper.

Paisley had the charges in place within a minute, and he gave Krik the breaching blanket to hold.

"Ready," the Armenian said.

Paisley detonated the charges, and Krik dropped the blanket. They rushed in.

There were several rooms to check, and they took them in pairs. For a couple minutes, they found nothing. Then, as they approached the end of a hallway, a grenade hurtled out of a door to rebound against the wall and land on the floor.

"Take cover!" Po screamed, and they all dove for offices. For Po's part, he charged through a closed door, the weight of his suit splintering it.

The grenade went off, and Po reentered the hall immediately after. Paisley was already charging down the corridor toward the office the grenade had come from. Po ran after him as the other Marines reemerged from the offices they'd taken cover in.

They made short work of the two Nibirans they found, then quickly cleared the rest of the block.

"All right, Krik," Po said over the team channel. "See anywhere you can take a shot from?"

"I'm already setting up. I figure I can take out one, maybe two of the frog-dogs operating that mortar. But I expect things will get real unpleasant for us after that."

"You're probably right. Paisley, Gomez, I want you on opposite ends of this place with your eyes peeled for incoming threats. Taylor, you watch the door. If any of you see any reason we should vacate this place immediately, let us know, and we'll do that."

Po found Krikorian and crouched near his position, out of sight of the window where he'd set up his M126. "You take those shots whenever you're ready. And use your Circuit's aim assist." A lot of Marines, especially snipers, hated using their implant's aim assistance, since the question always came after an impressive shot whether the shooter had used aim assist or not. But now wasn't a time to risk letting Marine pride get them all killed.

The Armenian didn't say anything, just steadied his rifle, his shoulders rising with slow and even breaths.

Then he fell completely still, and the weapon gave a low bark, jumping in Krik's hands. He adjusted his aim ever so slightly, and the rifle coughed again. "Got 'em both," he said, his voice neutral.

"Can you take out anyone else?"

"Let's see." The rifle leapt in his hand, and he cursed, which Po took as a miss.

He fired again. "Got another one."

A round zipped into the office where they were crouched, ricocheting off a large cube of a safe. Krikorian cried out, lurching forward into his rifle, pushing it out the window.

Po quickly crab-walked to him and grabbed him by a handle on his suit, pulling him out of harm's way.

"I'm good, I'm good," Krik said, shaking free and following Po to the hallway. "Man, they reacted quick."

"I guess they were expecting it. You sure you're good?" Po motioned for him to turn around, then found the spot where the bullet had glanced off his armor, but hadn't pierced. "That'll probably bruise."

"Oh, no," Krik said, with a pretend whine.

"Mortar incoming!" Gomez shouted over the team-wide.

"Everyone get outside!" Po said, already sprinting toward the exit. He met Gomez there, and the other Marine hesitated, apparently to let Po go first.

"*Get out there!*" Po yelled, grabbing the private and shoving him out the door ahead of him.

Taylor came out last, just as the mortar was hitting the front of the building. Heat washed over them, and the explosion pelted them with debris, but the building took the brunt of the blast. No one was hurt.

Then Nibirans started firing on them from a completely different angle, and that was more of a concern.

"Taylor, Paisley, suppressive fire!" Po barked. "Gomez and Krik, follow me. We'll cover Taylor and Paisley from behind that CHU."

Rounds pattered against Paisley's suit, causing him to stagger, but Taylor sent some back, which had the intended effect. Soon, Fireteam Echo was withdrawing into a safer position.

Safer for now. Po switched over to the squad-wide. "Staff Sergeant, Krik took out the mortar operators with his sniper, but they're back at it again."

"I see that," Young said dryly. "Zap, are you making any headway from near the wall?"

"Negative, Staff Sergeant. They have us pinned."

A silence followed. Po figured he knew what was going through the sergeant's head.

The Nibirans' position outside the base was too strong, and there was no way Second Squad was going to stop them from cracking bunkers, one after another.

They might have used the guard towers on that side to try to do some damage, if the armor hadn't destroyed them yesterday.

As things were, they were left with only bad options: either huddle in a bunker and wait for it to cave in on their heads...or abandon the bunkers altogether, to face a force that badly outnumbered them.

Weapons fire came from the direction of the Nibiran position, and Po cocked his head. That sounded like...small arms fire. Which didn't make much sense, since the firebase was beyond the effective range of individual-service weapons from most of the base.

"Zap?" Young said. "What's going on? Can you see?"

Wordlessly, Zap patched a feed through to the rest of the squad's implants, which judging by the height was probably coming from a fingertip sensor he'd stuck past the wall.

The Nibirans were being engaged from *outside* the wall, getting fired on from positions that surrounded them in a wide arc. As the Marines watched, insurgent after insurgent fell, in a slaughter that was effective and brief.

As the dust settled, the first surprise attacker stood from his position, making a hand signal that looked like an order to advance on the base.

It wasn't a Marine, or even a human.

It was a Nibiran.

Chapter 6

What followed during the next hour proved a delicate situation, at least from the Marines' perspective. With Nibirans fighting Nibirans, Po and his brothers found themselves in the awkward position of wanting to help kill the aliens that had been trying to kill them, but to avoid killing the aliens who'd apparently showed up to save them for some reason.

The order was passed down through what platoon leaders were left:

"Focus on places where we know insurgents are entrenched, based on where we've been taking fire from. Shoot back at anything that shoots at you. Otherwise, don't shoot."

Thankfully, the opposing Nibiran forces weren't completely identical. The ones who'd ambushed the firebase outside the walls looked a lot more professional than the Janus insurgents. These aliens wore dappled blue uniforms, which looked kind of like the Marines' utilities, except that their awful pattern stood out against the desert sand in a way that seemed to scream "shoot me."

But their body armor was of a more consistent quality, and so was their weaponry. They also seemed to have some understanding of small unit tactics, unlike the chaotic guerilla approach of To'sheth Rin's ilk.

Thirty minutes into the fighting—not counting the time Second Squad had spent trying to take out the firebase—Po and his team found themselves heading in behind one of the Nibiran units to clear a warehouse. The aliens charged in like they were wearing something better than SERAPH armor, rifles swinging all over the place, seeking something to shoot. One of them did fire, and if Po didn't know better, he would have said the alien was shooting at nothing.

The Nibirans charged past a door leading to a hall of offices, so he took it upon himself to check that with his team.

It was a good thing they did. They found four Janus priming what looked like C4 in one of the middle offices. With their suits' superior sensors, Po and his boys had heard them jabbering in low voices the moment they entered the hallway, and they got the drop on them, killing three and taking one prisoner.

What they'd been planning to do with the explosives was anyone's guess. But it probably wouldn't have been pleasant, especially for the Nibiran team that had swept past like a bunch of hair-trigger commandos.

They met the Nibiran team coming back, and one of them blew out his floppy lips at seeing the prisoner frog-marching in front of Echo Team. Another alien, which looked a bit like a hairless dachshund, met Po's gaze with somber eyes. He didn't nod, or make any gesture at all, but Po thought he saw a flicker of gratitude in those watery browns.

The fighting was over inside of sixty minutes, at which point Colonel Coleman took it upon himself to assure the friendly Nibiran leader, through Navarro, that he didn't need to trouble himself with the ensuing cleanup. Marine teams would take care of that.

And so, while squads of Marines combed the base for any insurgents who were trying their luck with hiding, Coleman met in front of the destroyed mess facility with the leadership of the Nibirans who'd saved them, using Navarro as a translator. Echo Team was one of the units who'd been discreetly encouraged to hang out nearby, looking as non-threatening as possible, in case things turned sour.

Thanks to his helmet's sensitive speakers, Po was close enough to pick out some of the conversation, but not all of it. It was enough to figure out that the Nibirans belonged to the Gomorati Army, and that they'd already been en route to Firebase Longhorn when they received a message from another Marine base that Longhorn and Halberd were under attack, and that any help they could provide would be appreciated and handsomely repaid. If Po wasn't mistaken, the Nibiran leader took some care to emphasize that last part.

"Ask 'em why they were already on their way here from Gomorate," Coleman told Navarro.

The Nibiran head honcho, who was named Palka Oray, studied the Linguist from beneath the brim of his beige hat as Navarro relayed the message. When he'd finished, the alien went on for some time in his high-pitched, croaking voice.

Navarro gave a brisk nod when the Nibiran finished speaking, then he repeated what he'd said in English. "He said To'sheth Rin is moving troops to Gomorate, with a clear intent to besiege it. The insurgency grows every day, faster than even their government thought possible. He said they're now sure even the Gomorati Army is rotted through with traitors in their midst. Regular Nibirans know the government in Gomorate has maintained cordial communications with us, and the longer the war goes, the more that seems to anger them. They've begun to doubt they can withstand whatever Rin is about to throw at them."

"Besiege them," Coleman muttered, his eyes narrowed. "Why bother? Why doesn't Rin just dig through to the middle of Gomorate and pop up there? Attack the capital from within, just like he attacked us?"

Navarro translated the question, and Palka Oray's eyes darted as he answered.

"He says Gomorate was built on rock, to prevent exactly that. A lot of it is carved into the rock."

"Let me get this straight," the colonel said, glaring at Oray now. "All while we were building our bases, the Nibirans knew Janus would very likely just tunnel up through the middle. But they didn't bother telling us that."

Po felt himself tense up. He didn't know if he'd have it in him to be that blunt with the soldiers who'd just saved him, and the remark seemed like it could send things south in a hurry.

But apparently the colonel had read the situation right, because Oray only hung his head, ears drooping.

Him saying that probably earned us an edge in any negotiations. Didn't it?

With that, the colonel invited Oray to his office to continue their conversation, motioning for Navarro to follow, and singling out a more senior fireteam to accompany them. Apparently, Coleman was satisfied that the security situation wasn't about to deteriorate. Fireteam Echo was dismissed.

"Go back to our old lodging, in the warehouse," Young told them. "Help out with whatever cleanup is necessary there, and then get some rest."

"Yes, Staff Sergeant," Po said, then waved at his boys to follow him.

"Why do Nibirans care so much what the Gomoratis think?" Gomez asked as they crossed Longhorn, which in the wake of the fighting was almost unrecognizable from the neat and orderly base that had existed before.

Apparently, Gomez had been listening to the colonel's conversation with the Nibiran too.

"Because Gomorate's the capital, and also the most powerful city state on this continent," said Paisley, for once leaving aside the sarcasm he normally answered Gomez's questions with. "Technically, we're under their jurisdiction right now. The government in Gomorate controls Basalt Country, the Sodalite Desert, and a lot of other places besides. Even most of the city states whose territory they don't directly control answer to them in some way. For Janus to have penetrated their army in the way that Nibiran claims they have...that's a pretty big deal."

As he often did, Po stayed out of the conversation, picking over his disjointed thoughts like yesterday's leftovers.

He wondered what helping defend Gomorate would look like. Would they abandon FOB Longhorn altogether?

I guess it would make sense. This place is trashed, and Janus can just tunnel up in the middle of it again. Sure, there were probably measures the Marines could implement to improve their ability to detect tunneling invaders, but they'd take time and resources to implement. Which were both things that were becoming more and more limited.

The bigger question was, how far could they trust the Gomorati Army? It was bad enough they'd failed to properly advise the Marines on how to set up on Nibiru—even though Corps intelligence really should have picked up on the danger of tunneling Nibirans without the help.

Either way, with insurgents apparently infesting the army's ranks, the Nibirans seemed even less trustworthy than when the war began.

But what choice do we have?

They'd suffered heavy losses, while the insurgency only seemed to explode in strength. In the wake of the satellites' destruction, and the resulting loss of air and orbital superiority, every option seemed bad.

I guess it's just a matter of figuring out which one is the least bad, and making the most of it.

***

The warehouse that served as their squad bay had been virtually untouched during the fighting, and by the time Po arrived with Echo Team, the rest of 131st Platoon had finished their cursory cleanup.

When Navarro came back, Po was lying on his rack, flicking lazily through pamphlets on leadership that had been downloaded to his implant after he'd been made Echo Team leader.

He sat up when he saw the other Marine, along with pretty much everyone else in the squad bay.

"Navarro, what's up?" Paisley asked.

Taylor got to his feet and stepped forward, in front of Paisley, as if blocking him from view would deemphasize his question. "Are we rolling out to Gomorate?"

"What's the plan for Longhorn?" Zapletal asked. "We keeping this dump in operation?"

Navarro stopped in his tracks, looking harried. "I'm not authorized to tell you guys any of that stuff."

"Ah, come on," Taylor said. "We won't tell the colonel you told us."

"No, but his implant might," Krikorian said.

Po got up from his rack, and pushed through the others to grab Navarro by the shoulder. "Hey. Wanna take a walk?"

Navarro studied him for a long moment. "Yeah," he said at last. "Sure."

Some of the others got up to follow, but Po waved them back. "No one come after us. If you do, we'll just use our implants to talk."

At that, the Marines all returned to whatever they'd been doing a minute ago, most of them muttering under their breath.

Gnara was sinking below the horizon as they put some distance between them and the squad bay, walking in silence. Po didn't say anything, and Navarro kept checking over his shoulder for pursuers. After a while, he seemed to judge them far enough from the warehouse to avoid being overheard.

"So, what'd you want to talk about?" he asked. "Did you think I'd say anything to you that I wouldn't say to them?"

"I want to talk about...whatever you think is worth talking about."

"Huh." The other Marine sounded skeptical.

"Well...there was one thing I was wondering. You don't have to answer, if you think you shouldn't. But I wanted to know if you heard any news about FOB Halberd. Did they defeat the Nibirans attacking them, too?"

Navarro tilted his head as they walked, as if considering the question. "Yes," he said at last, with a sigh. "They did. Apparently the attack on Halberd wasn't as big as the one here."

"Well, that's a...blessing."

The Linguist shot him a look, but said nothing. It was another minute or so before he spoke again. "There's something else. The Gomorati leaders think they might have a lead on where To'sheth Rin is holed up. Apparently, their intel suggests he's gone to ground in some hidden compound of his, somewhere in the southeast of Gomorate's territory."

Po's heart thumped in his chest. He recalled his conversation with Paisley at the med center, when he'd promised his teammate that he'd be the one to kill Rin.

I still plan to keep that promise, he realized. As the nightmares in the wake of Eremus intensified, so had his desire to kill the Janus leader.

"They're not trying to keep that back as a bargaining chip, are they?" Po asked, his voice coming out with an edge.

"I've probably already said too much. But no, I don't think. When it comes to Rin, I think they've told us as much as they know."

Po nodded, resisting the urge to grab his M37 where it rested at his side, hanging from its strap. It would be the least professional thing in the world, to heft his weapon for no reason. But suddenly, he wanted the rifle in his hands.

"How are you doing with...everything?" Po asked, as much to distract himself as anything else.

"You mean with my wife dying? Or losing the faith?"

Po swallowed. "You really lost the faith?"

Navarro shook his head. "I lost something. In here." He brought a fist to his chest. "But also, I literally lost something. The Rosary my wife gave me...the one you put in that side-table drawer, when you visited me in the med center...I went back for it, after I got out. It was gone, and no one knew where. Just...gone." He made a spreading gesture with his fingers, as if releasing a bird.

Po tried to think up something comforting to say, or even something funny, to try to dispel some of this awful tension. But as usual in situations like this, he had nothing.

"I'm sorry, Navarro," he said at last.

"Don't be. I deserve it."

"Huh? Don't say that."

"It's true. I deserve it, and a lot worse. So do you." Navarro slapped him on the shoulder, wearing a half-smile.

"Speak for yourself."

"I did, and you disagreed." The other Marine chuckled. "But it's true. We all of us deserve it, everything that's been going on. This war, our satellites getting destroyed, losing air superiority. FOB Longhorn getting trashed. This is what happens when you live in a way that makes no sense."

Po had lost the thread of the conversation, but that happened every time he spoke to Navarro. "What do you mean by that?"

"We started convincing ourselves a long time ago that we could conform reality to our lives, rather than the other way around."

"The Marines, you mean?"

"Everyone in this system. The Marines less so, maybe. A little bit. But we've all done it. And when you try to warp existence itself to suit you, eventually it snaps back at you, like a cosmic rubber band. Thing is, it turns out existence has a name. *I am.*"

"You are what?"

"No, that's its—" Navarro sighed again. "Never mind. You ready to go back?"

It turned out the guys back at the squad bay hadn't had to wait very long for news on their situation. By the time Po and Navarro got back, the warehouse was buzzing with word that every combat unit stationed at FOB Longhorn would roll out by the end of the week. Mine clearing units would head out tomorrow, to start clearing routes between here and Gomorate.

"What about the FOBBITs?" Po asked. That was the Marine slang term for the personnel that spent their entire wartime experience within the walls of an FOB. It used to be considered a safe, cushy existence—less so, lately.

Taylor chuckled. "Poor FOBBITs. Things sure got turned upside-down for them, didn't they?"

"We're taking some of them with us, as support personnel," Zap answered Po. "The rest are being sent to Halberd. Though, I hear they're gearing up there too, to join the upcoming fight in Gomorate."

"FOBBITs are an endangered species," Krikorian said. "FOBs are useless, now."

"Not if we build them on rock," Po said.

"Yeah. Maybe. Either way, the Corps is consolidating. Pulling together. Once we're finished, I don't think it will be a good time to be an insurgent."

"Oorah."

"Fact is," Paisley said, stepping into the conversation, "We can't afford to let Janus overthrow the biggest civil authority on the planet. The system becomes a very unsafe place with To'sheth Rin in control of Nibiru. Can't let that happen."

"We need to find Rin," Taylor said. "That's what we should be doing. Make him pay for what he did to us. It'd send a message to the rest of the frog-dogs."

"First things first," Po said. He didn't disagree with what Taylor was saying...but it didn't matter what either of them thought. Command had chosen a direction, and now the rest of them would move in it. Simple as that.

Chapter 7

It felt weird to be abandoning FOB Longhorn, but maybe it was a good thing. Before Eremus, even combat Marines had started to feel invincible whenever they were back at base, protected by tall walls and taller guard towers. They'd treated it as some kind of wartime timeout, a place where the enemy magically couldn't touch them.

Well, that had proven wrongheaded. There was no safety to be had in a war. No peace. No place where you should ever feel comfortable gorging on French fries and strawberry sundaes before wandering off to your rack to slip into a food coma.

The Nibirans had taught them that, and Po thanked them for it. It only made them stronger, which made the Corps into a better implement for cutting off Janus' head.

Longhorn was emptying out gradually, convoy by convoy. Po's platoon went with one that left Thursday mid-morning. As they loaded up, he saw an AC-900 lift off from near the center of Longhorn and fly in the direction of Halberd.

We'll need to maintain at least some bases, he realized. Despite the squad-bay talk about how FOBs were obsolete now, the fact was, the Corps still needed them. How else could they maintain their gunships, and service them? Where would they keep their armor when it wasn't deployed?

I guess that's why we're consolidating. If they pulled together in the most strategic locations, they'd have personnel and resources enough to make sure nothing happened again like had happened here.

The other Marines of Second Squad were grim-faced as they filed into the APC that would take them to Gomorate, but Po found himself feeling strangely optimistic.

We have a read on you, Rin. You may have done a number on us, but we're adapting, and you're already on the run. How many cards do you have left to play? How long do you think it'll be before destiny comes knocking at your door with an assault rifle?

The convoy would stop for a resupply at a mining operation about halfway to Gomorate, which was secured by a PMC called Vigilance. RUMINT said the higher-ups were considering making every PMC on the planet an adjunct to the Corps, but Po doubted that would get authorized. GEA wasn't about to let the Marines enrage every partner corporation it had on Nibiru by stripping them of all protection. Besides, they had their uses where they were. If Vigilance Security Solutions wasn't guarding this mining company, for example, then the convoy would have nowhere to safely resupply.

As for the Gomorati Army regiment that had come to save them, they apparently had their own route, with their own supply caches they'd avail of along the way.

The APC's rear door hissed upward, meeting with its seal and blocking out Gnara's eerie mockery of daylight.

Po preferred the electric lighting to that, anyway. It felt more like home.

A couple minutes later, the APC began trundling forward. Po didn't bother patching his Circuit through to an exterior sensor. Not yet, anyway. For now, all he wanted to do was rest his head back against the APC's wall and try to snatch some shuteye. He left his helmet on, since it wasn't all that comfortable trying to sleep with it off.

***

On the second day of travel, Colonel Tuffin called a four-point short-halt for a map check. The convoy pulled off the road into a dusty, broken field just before an intersection, and Marines piled out of APCs to arrange themselves in formation to be ready to project force in the four cardinal directions.

Torres tanks positioned themselves throughout the Marines' ranks, but the Polliver-4s remained aboard the trucks that carried them. They weren't all that likely to encounter any opposition here, and unloading and loading the mechs took time.

They were nearing the edge of the desert, with vegetation becoming more frequent as they drew closer to the jungle. It was important that they not make a wrong turn, here. Once they entered the thick of the Gomorati Jungle, a few hours' more travel would bring them to the mining operation that served as their rough halfway point.

That was, if they took the right route to get there. If they didn't, there wasn't just the risk of getting lost—there was also the likelihood they'd deplete the supplies at any given stopover. There were three refueling locations along two different routes which the various convoys were planning to visit, all of them owned by GEA partner corporations.

The journey to Gomorate had been meticulously planned, and that planning would be thrown awry if too many convoys took the wrong road. It could mean units showing up late to the battle for the Nibiran capital...maybe too late.

Po was grateful for the stop. Being stuffed inside an APC with fourteen other Marines for twelve-hour days was not his idea of a good time. Second Squad had begun to irritate each other just a few hours into the journey, and Sergeant Young only intervened when roughhousing ran the risk of distracting the driver. Other than that, it seemed they were free to jostle each other all they wanted, or to do their best to drive each other nuts over the coms. Zhang had been added to Fireteam Foxtrot, to replace Corbin, and Po had found himself wedged between him and Paisley. The Chinese wasn't too annoying, but he sure took up a lot of space.

Echo Team had been assigned to watch for threats to the south during the short-halt. The south was mostly hilly terrain, and unlikely to pose much danger. An enemy unit would have had to anticipate the convoy stopping here to effectively launch an ambush from there. Otherwise, the hills were just too difficult to navigate to get organized fast enough. The convoy would be long gone by the time an attacking force from the south could make anything happen.

The other options were to attack across open fields from the north or west, or to strike along one of the roads. None of those seemed like Janus' style, and Po figured it was safe to say they likely wouldn't see any action here.

A pair of Nibiran goatherds were driving a flock across one of the nearest hills. The animals definitely weren't actually goats, but they were the closest comparison Po could come up with on the fly. Like a lot of animals around here, they looked bluish...although, that might have just been the sand reflecting off their light coats. They had horns sticking up as well as out from their heads. As he watched, one of them tossed its head threateningly from side to side, and its neighbor shuffled away from it, groaning.

Feeling idle, he used his helmet to zoom in on one of them, then told his implant to identify it.

"*Adelqo*," his implant told him. An encyclopedia entry followed, but he couldn't be bothered to read it. Besides, if he spent too much time messing around with his implant while on watch, the thing would probably tattle on him to Young.

Zanth appeared in the middle of the herd, head darting like a dinosaur's, as though stalking the animals. They took no notice of him, of course—until they did. A few of them seemed to skitter nervously away from the Emplor.

Po narrowed his eyes. *Did those things just realize Zanth was there? How is that possible?*

But the alien vanished, then, and the Adelqo continued to act skittish, so he figured it had just been a coincidence.

"Hey," Paisley said over the team channel. "One of those Nibirans is coming our way."

It was true. The goatherd, or Adelqoherd, had already left the animals behind to approach the Marines.

Po's heart hammered against his ribcage. "Where's Navarro?"

Paisley shrugged. "No idea."

Cursing, Po whipped through Circuit menus till he found the voice translation feature and cranked it up to max.

"*Halt and state your intention!*" A reconstruction of his voice boomed from his suit's speakers in mechanical-sounding Nibiran.

The alien didn't stop. He continued to totter toward the Marines, hands held up in a placating gesture. He called a response, and although Po hadn't heard it, his suit had. It displayed the translation along the top of his field of view:

"We want to give you a gift of Adelqo, for eating. Will you come look?"

"No," Po said. "Go back to your herd. We aren't interested."

The Nibiran continued toward them, advancing faster now. "Please, we want to make this gift to you, to show our gratitude for fighting To'sheth Rin."

Po brought his M37 up and planted a round in the dusty ground in front of the Nibiran's feet.

That got his attention. The alien stopped, looked down at the ground, then looked up at Po wearing a baffled expression.

"Go back to your herd, and do not approach again."

The alien's shoulders slumped, and he turned back around, looking dejected. If the alien's robes hadn't concealed his tail, it seemed probable they would have seen it stuck between his legs.

"Kinda rude, don't you think?" Gomez asked.

"Tell me you're joking," Po said.

"Uh, I'm joking."

"I know you weren't, but for your sake, we'll pretend you were."

Back in the APC a few minutes later, Young commended him on the action. "Probably, he was a harmless old goatherd, and he hoped to get something from us in exchange for his 'generosity.' Or hey—maybe he's the one Nibiran left on this planet that likes humans. But we can't take chances. There's no telling what he might have had under his robes."

"Could have been an explosive surprise," Taylor said, looking pointedly at Gomez, who looked thoughtful.

"We'll never know," Young said. "But it was definitely the right move. Besides, I heard Adelqo tastes awful."

***

With his head tilted back against the APC wall and his helmet visor polarized so he didn't have to meet anyone's gaze, Po watched the desert crawl past.

The tanks were to blame for the slow pace. There were four of them, and four mechs on trucks, totaling two armor platoons accompanying them. Aside from that, there were four APCs and four IFVs carrying 131st, 129th, and two other platoons besides.

If they had to completely unspool, they'd be a force to be reckoned with, which was probably why no Nibirans had tried their luck with an ambush. But having to go slow enough for the tanks to keep up made for a long, excruciating trip.

At last, the desert gave way to jungle. Twisted trees with sweeping branches that curled in on themselves loomed on either side of the road, interspersed with giant, pimply-looking mushrooms. It wasn't pretty, and even though the APC was supposed to be airtight, they learned quickly that it didn't smell pretty, either. A damp and fetid odor had found its way inside, and most of Second Squad kept their helmets on to filter it out. Everyone except Zhang and Paisley. Po figured Paisley was making himself suffer so he could reinforce his opinion that he was better than the others, but as for Zhang...well, he was just Zhang.

They were all thoroughly sick of each other by now, and conversation had dried up entirely. Taylor had gone from being kind-of-funny to intentionally annoying during the first two days, but even he'd apparently grown tired of talking. If he'd had to guess, Po would have said a road trip in a war zone would be anything except boring or tedious. But this...well, this was boring *and* tedious.

He'd stopped checking the time, because every time he did he was shocked by how little of it had passed. But somehow, eternity eventually drew to an end, and they came to the edge of a giant pit in the ground. "What kind of mine is it" was one of many idle questions they'd asked Sergeant Young on the first day, so they'd known for a while now that this was a uranium mine.

As they circled the pit to the cluster of buildings on the opposite side, Po peered through an exterior sensor to catch what glimpses he could of the great, tiered hole. What looked like a pond sat at the bottom. Was that just collected rainwater, or was it the chemical they used to dissolve the uranium ore? He'd read that was one way they mined it, but he didn't know enough to be sure whether that was what he was looking at.

"The security situation here is awful," Taylor said over the squad-wide.

He was right: the buildings ahead were nestled between two treed hills. It wouldn't be difficult even for Janus to put snipers up there and rain havoc on company personnel from above. RPGs would be devastating too, or worse, mortars—though the thick jungle canopy that surrounded the mining outpost would probably make their use a little more complicated.

"What do you expect?" Krikorian answered. "A PMC is like a security blanket. It makes you feel safe, and it's about as useful in a fight."

That brought a few chuckles, even from Paisley.

"There's an indoor bazaar in that long quonset hut," Young told them. "None of you are on first watch, so if you want to check it out, feel free. Just don't cause any trouble. Be nice to the locals—and *do not* pick any fights with any Vigilance personnel. That comes straight from the colonel. He said anyone causing trouble with private military will sit out the fight in Gomorate."

A couple whistles answered that, but Po had his doubts about the threat. They couldn't afford to have *anyone* sit out the coming fight. Still...whatever the consequences were, they surely wouldn't be pleasant. Best to comply with the colonel's order.

The APC came to a halt at last, but Young stopped them before they filed out. "We won't be here long enough for you to get a watch. Be ready to hustle back at a moment's notice. The colonel wants us sleeping in the APC again tonight."

That brought some muted groans, but no one seemed *too* distraught by the prospect. After all, the alternative was sharing space with PMC goons.

They headed for the quonset hut, since they didn't know where else to go, and apparently no one felt like inviting themselves into unfamiliar spaces filled with the kind of people who'd leave Earth to work on a planet like this.

It was way brighter inside the small bazaar than it was out in Nibiru's 'day,' even though the lighting was dim and inconstant. Every last stall was manned by a Nibiran, ears flopping and twitching as they haggled with customers with whom they shared not a word of the same language. Some of the customers were Nibiran, too—probably locals come from some village to take advantage of a bigger market than they were likely accustomed to. But most of the patrons were humans, either miners or private military.

The Second Squad Marines all carried their rifles, with their helmets still on, but visors open. They were effectively inside enemy territory—maybe not officially, but it might as well have been official. Young may have given them a stern warning about causing trouble, but he also wasn't about to let them leave the APC unarmed in a place like this.

"Ugh," Taylor said as they passed a stall with hunks of meat laid out in slabs, or run through with skewers. The Nibiran started at the outburst, rearing up and staring at the Marine with burning eyes.

"Is that Adelqo meat?" he went on. "I think the sergeant was right. It smells terrible."

"Doesn't smell so bad to me," Gomez said, stopping in front of the stall. "How do we pay? Oh."

The "Oh" must have been prompted by a Circuit window like the one that had just popped up for Po, informing him of a ledger system that would allow him to transfer crypto to the mining company, who would pay the Nibirans in their regional currency at the end of the day. The Nibiran had what looked like a cPad lying close at hand, which would probably allow him to see transactions come through in real time.

Gomez bought a kebab and set into it immediately, the juices flowing past his chin to trickle down his neck and into his suit. He didn't seem to mind it, or the way Paisley and Taylor were looking at him with grimaces of disgust.

"Not bad," he said.

Paisley shook his head, and they continued on down the row, stopping here and there to look over the wares on offer. There was more food, most of it better-smelling and tastier-looking than the meat Gomez had torn into. Although, watching him devour it with relish reminded Po of the tipped-over food cart they'd found in Eremus, days into the fighting. His mouth watered, in spite of how foul the Adelqo smelled.

Sausages had been spilling out of the cart onto the ground, but inside, there'd been plenty of them not covered in dirt. It struck him that it was one of his favorite memories of the war here so far. Just him and his brothers, reaching an unexpected oasis in the middle of all that chaos and death. Scarfing sausages made from some unknown alien meat, like school children finding the teacher's chocolate stash in an unlocked drawer and stuffing themselves as full as they could before they got caught.

He'd never be able to recreate a moment like that, not in a million years. As delicious as they were, the sausages hadn't even been the best part. It had been that feeling of finding an unexpected place of peace in a city ravaged by war—finding it together with his brothers. Enjoying that moment together. He wondered if the others felt the same way about it.

A lot of the stalls had homemade trinkets, of a type no Marine Po knew would ever be caught dead with, but maybe the Earthers here liked them. Others had what looked like metal charms connected to the Nibiran Earth-mother religion. There were plenty of trees inside of circles and spirals that had a single eye staring up from the middle. Gnara seemed to feature prominently on a lot of them, too. He didn't know what Gnara's relationship to Giru-Giru was supposed to be, and he didn't ask.

Looking them over, he couldn't stop thinking about the room he and Krikorian had found hidden under a tunnel floor. He hadn't thought much of it at the time. It was just weird Nibiran stuff. But seeing these hokey charms, which might as well have been key chains...how sanitized they looked...it jarred with his memory of all the little Nibiran skulls they'd seen on shelves that day. All of a sudden, he couldn't get that image out of his head.

At the third such booth he came across, he used his Circuit's translator function to speak to the proprietor, who looked like a cross between an iguana and a severely underfed Rottweiler. "Has Giru-Giru been good to you?" he asked.

The alien croaked back at him, and his helmet played the translation in his ears. "Oh, yes. Very good."

"How do you get what you want from her?"

"Something must be sacrificed. The more pain the better." The Nibiran blinked slowly, which looked almost like a wink to Po.

"You ever sacrifice any children?"

At the next booth, Taylor started, and shot him a look. "Whoa, Po."

But the stallkeeper gave him an open-mouthed grin, unleashing its pungent breath. "There are many ways to please Giru-Giru. And what is it to you? Surely it is not such a shock, to one like you." The Nibiran's eyes flicked down toward his boots, then back up, his grin remaining fixed in place. "Don't you think your species sacrifices your children to spirits, just the same as us?"

"Not where I come from."

"Oh, sure they do. They do it all over this system—I know. They sacrifice them on the altar of convenience. Or of not-suffering. The altar of self. Maybe even to some other spirit. It's just the same. Trading the blood of innocents for something wanted. Don't pretend you're so spotless, human."

Po held the alien's eyes for a long time, as emotions warred inside him. *Remember what Staff Sergeant Young said. Don't cause any trouble.* With gritted teeth, he forced himself to break eye contact and move to the next booth.

A voice crescendoed from a few stalls ahead. A man wearing thigh-high boots, body armor, and shoulder pads was leaning toward a stallkeeper with one hand planted on the alien's counter. He had what looked like a meat lollipop in the other hand, which he'd apparently plucked off a tray and was now waving in the Nibiran's face.

"This rat meat might be good food for a hunchback frog-dog, but it had *me* on the john all last night."

The alien croaked back a reply, but the merc didn't seem to have a translator, and he didn't seem to care too much what the Nibiran was saying anyway.

"What are you going to do for me?" the man said, yelling over him.

The alien answered rapidly in Nibiran, his voice carrying a whine, now.

"What are you *going* to *do* for me?" the man shouted, even louder.

The Nibiran whimpered, eyes rolling.

"Just c'mere," the mercenary said, reaching into the stall and grabbing the alien by the front of his robes. Trays fell from the counter to clatter onto the ground, sending more meat lollies flying as the man dragged the Nibiran over to his side and threw him to the ground.

Then the merc drew a pistol.

Chapter 8

"Whoa, whoa," Po found himself shouting, only barely resisting the urge to grab his own rifle up from its strap as he stepped forward. He raised his palms toward the merc instead. "Hey, let's talk this out."

The merc leered at Po from his position straddling the Nibiran, one foot on either side and the pistol aimed at the alien's head. "Get outta here, Marine."

"You don't have to do this."

"I said get outta here. How we handle the frog-dogs on this site is none of your business."

But the merc didn't shoot. Instead, he safetied the weapon and then leaned over to smash the Nibiran in the face with the butt.

Blood flew, and the alien cried out. The merc grabbed a handful of robe and hit him again, at the base of the neck. Then again, in the snout.

Po stepped forward, but Paisley's hand closed around his forearm. "Hey. The Staff Sergeant said not to get involved."

The merc grinned up at him, apparently in a much better mood now. "That's right, jarhead. You just hit the end of your leash, didn't you?" He smashed the alien in the left eye with the pistol butt, eliciting a yelp.

"*Staff Sergeant Young,*" Po messaged, his hands balled tightly together to stop himself from grabbing his M37. "*We have a situation here. Merc's pistol-whipping a native. Patching through my feed to you now. What do we do?*"

During the few seconds the sergeant took to answer, the merc continued to work on the alien. The Nibiran's howling and yelping was becoming more desperate.

"*I see it, Abbato. Stay out of that, do you understand me?*"

"*Sir, it looks like he's going to kill him.*"

"*This is not your fight. Stay. Out. Of it.*"

Po wavered, hovering nearby, feeling like his heart was being torn in two. The merc continued the beating with even more gusto, clearly enjoying the fact Po couldn't do anything about it.

Eventually, the alien stopped yelping. Its eyes rolled in its sockets, and it jerked against the floor, but it was clearly in a daze.

At last, the merc stood, picked up the Nibiran by the robe, then dropped him back onto the ground, the back of the alien's head hitting with a thud. He spat on the alien's barely stirring form, shot Po a toothy grin, then swaggered through the crowd that had gathered during the beating, which had gone completely silent a few seconds into it. People and Nibirans parted wordlessly for the merc as he strutted toward the far end of the quonset, where Gnara's unearthly light filtered through.

Gradually, people broke off, transforming from onlookers back into shoppers or shopkeeps.

Po knelt next to the Nibiran, putting a hand in front of his muzzle. According to the sensors built into his glove, the alien was still breathing.

No one was doing anything, and he sure didn't know what to do. So he just picked up the alien, lifting him easily with the SERAPH suit's power.

He turned toward the other Marines standing nearby, looked from Paisley to Taylor, Gomez to Zhang.

"Come on. There's gotta be a med center we can take him to."

***

"We're not gonna do anything, Staff Sergeant? Nothing?"

"Absolutely not." It was their APC's turn to refuel, and Young was overseeing it. He stood with his arms crossed, leaning back against the side of the vehicle while a technician inserted a fuel hose into the filler.

"We're not even gonna file a report with his superior, or anything like that?"

"What good would it do, Abbato? If that merc had the confidence to do what he did, then it's clearly a common occurrence. Which means Vigilance isn't doing anything about it, and neither is their client. It also means the Nibirans must know that this kind of thing can happen to them here. If they want to hang around despite knowing there are characters like that around, then that's their business, not ours."

Po's mouth worked for a second as he weighed what he should be saying. "They're probably here to try to get ahead a little. Doesn't seem like their lives are exactly lavish, in this jungle."

"Getting ahead always involves risks. Risks that Nibiran must have known about."

Po furrowed his brow, at a loss for what to say next.

At last, he said, "Staff Sergeant, I...I just don't understand it. Is this really it? This is the sort of thing we came here to do?"

"*We* didn't do anything. I told you to be nice to the locals, and you were. Good job."

"But, I mean...we saw an innocent Nibiran—"

"You don't know he's innocent."

"Yeah, but all the same...."

"Abbato, we have our orders, and that's all you need to think about. But if you insist on having *more* to think about, then maybe I can remind you how bad our situation on this planet has gotten. Command realizes that, and they also know we need the PMCs. Jeopardizing our relationship with them isn't worth your urge to go all vigilante on one of their employees. That's why that order was handed down. Do you understand that?"

Po's shoulders slumped. "But, not even to file a report?"

Zanth appeared at Young's side, in mimicry of the sergeant's cross-armed pose. "You're jeopardizing everything we've worked for, fool," the Emplor hissed.

Po frowned at the alien, then realized what he was doing and looked back at Young. The sergeant's eyes were narrowed, but he didn't comment on Po's wandering gaze.

Instead, he said, "I don't owe you an explanation of any order, Abbato. But I've now given you one, out of an abundance of generosity. Are you gonna let this drop now, or would you like to make it complicated?"

Complicated for me, he means, Po realized. And there wasn't any point in pursuing it any further. What was done was done, and this conversation couldn't reverse it.

"No, Staff Sergeant," he said. "I mean, I'll drop it."

"Good. Now go help the others load those ration crates aboard."

"Yes, Staff Sergeant." Po circled the APC around to the back, where others were taking crates off a pallet and carrying them to lower into the vehicle's under-floor stowage. He grabbed a crate, carried it up the ramp, and spotted the raised panel over the section they were currently filling. He headed toward it.

"Exactly what were you trying to prove back there?" Zanth asked, stalking alongside him. "Just how far do you think lecturing your direct superior is going to get you?"

Po ignored him. He dropped the crate into the hollow, then went back down the ramp for another.

The alien appeared next to the stack of crates. "Why bother questioning orders in the first place?"

"*That merc almost killed that Nibiran,*" Po input into his messaging app. He picked up another crate. With the SERAPH's strength enhancements, it was like lifting a box of pillows, not one packed with rations.

"And?" Zanth said. "You don't know what was behind the attack. Who are you to say whether he was right to do it?"

"*There have to be better ways to handle things than that.*"

"Okay. Let's assume it really was as heinous as you think. Let's assume disobeying orders would have been the right thing to do, in that case. What good would it have done you? Young already has his eye on you, from when he caught you lying to him, and when you let your team fight those EPA soldiers in the gym. If you'd gone against what he said this time, it could have meant your discharge. Then you'd spend decades in a simjail while your body turns to pudding."

Po didn't answer. He was having trouble finding anything wrong with what Zanth was saying, but something still bothered him about it. A nagging sensation from the back of his mind. But he couldn't translate it into words.

"You're a conscript, Po," the Emplor went on. You were *forced* to join the Marines, and just now you were forced to stand by while a Nibiran got a thrashing. You aren't responsible for any of this. You have a job to do. And if you land yourself in a simjail, you'll be of no use to anyone."

The Emplor vanished, and Po didn't try to call him back. Still, his mind turned over the conversation as he helped his brothers unload the last of the rations, studying the matter from different angles, like a 3D puzzle he couldn't get to click into place.

Could there ever be a situation where it would be better to go to prison than follow an order? That was the question he kept asking himself.

***

For a full day after leaving the uranium mine, the convoy passed through densest jungle. And as evening drew near on their last day of travel, they began climbing steeply. The road went up and up, and the Marines tightened their harnesses to avoid falling sideways into each other.

Through an exterior sensor patched to his Circuit, Po watched the strange twisted trees fall away, along with the enormous mushrooms, giving way to shrub-covered mountain slopes and eventually to bare mountain passes.

Just like that, they were in a desert again. The Gomorati Desert, his implant informed him. According to it, the desert stretched on for hundreds of miles north past the mountains, and it had beige-colored sand, which was more typical of the deserts humanity had experience with. As he read about this one, it occurred to him that the only desert he'd ever been in before this had blue sand. How many people could say that?

Their convoy wouldn't be traveling very far into the Gomorati Desert. The Nibiran capital sat on top of the tallest mountain in what was called the Serrate Range, and the road they were on was supposed to take them straight to it.

It struck him that climbing toward the peak brought him that much closer to space—that much closer to Nicky. He didn't actually know that, of course. This side of the planet could be facing away from Psyche right now, for all he knew. But the thought brought an unexpected and intense bout of homesickness, far greater than any he'd experienced before. They were headed to yet another fight that threatened to take more of his friends from him. It threatened to take his life, too.

It brought up the usual questions. Would he ever see Nicky again. How was she doing, since they'd stopped writing each other...and since the destruction of GEA's satellites over Nibiru cut them off altogether.

But it also made him long for the cylinders of the asteroid colony he'd grown up in. The closed-in spaces, spinning gently to simulate as closely as possible conditions humanity had always known. All the familiar faces. Even the ones he'd never spoken to, not even once, but who he ran into pretty much every day as he went about his routine.

He missed working in the docks. Operating the mech—how good he'd been at it. Teasing Dempsey whenever he saw him.

He even missed Rosa. As much as she'd angered him with the way she seemed to give up after Po had put his father up on charges after hurting her...he missed her quiet presence. Her rare, slow smile, at some silly crack Marco had made over frozen dinners.

He'd do anything to go home right now. To leave this dim, forsaken rock, so far from the sun. To leave this war. Yes, he wanted to help the Nibirans fight Janus, and free them from their tyranny. He wanted to make a difference. To do the right thing. But it was becoming harder to figure out what the right thing was anymore.

Kill Rin. That has to be the right thing. His jaw clenched involuntarily, and he forced himself to relax.

If nothing else, he could still make To'Sheth Rin pay for everything he'd taken from him. For taking Dempsey. And everyone else they'd lost.

Gnara loomed larger than life in the western sky, leering over the mountains like a one-eyed predator, contemplating its next victim.

"Whoa," Gomez said over the squad channel. "Is that Gomorate?"

Chapter 9

Peering out a sensor on the APC's nose, for a second Po could see nothing but mountain slopes and cliffs.

Then, he saw it: buildings carved from the living stone, with intricate fronts that swept back to be swallowed by the surrounding rock. Rows of half-pillars marched across their surfaces, some bordering tall, narrow windows, and others connected only by sheer rock.

As he scanned the broad mountaintop, he realized it was completely covered with such buildings, which were interspersed with lanes lined with pillars so perfectly cylindrical they looked machined. In other places sat sculptures made from blocks stacked so precariously they looked like they should fall over at a breath. Every building faced outward, overlooking the surrounding terrain, with a commanding view.

"Why aren't there any lights?" Taylor asked.

"They're completely blacked out for the coming battle," Young said. "Which is pretty impressive coordination, when you consider that Gomorate hasn't been attacked for over seven hundred years."

"Seriously?" Zhang put in. "Not even once?"

The sergeant nodded. "Generally speaking, Gomorate does the attacking. There's a reason it's the capital. Just look at the position the city occupies. According to what the Nibirans have shared with us about their history, Gomorate has existed for thousands of years. Their military history followed a trajectory analogous to ours, and before gunpowder, this place was an absolute powerhouse. Back then, they would have had the entire city ablaze with light, so that they could see and shoot an invading army as they struggled up the slopes."

"But now that mortars are a thing," Paisley said, "not so much."

"Exactly. But even today, the fact Janus would *contemplate* attacking takes a lot of guts. It's not just that the city is considered a treasure by Nibirans everywhere, which it is. It's also that the Gomorati Army is a military institution that's longer-lived than any of ours. They're not known for losing, and they're not known for mercy. They have a reputation for making a brutal example of anyone who gives the GA a reason to attack them."

Maybe Janus is so gutsy because they've riddled the Army with their own operatives. But Po didn't think he was officially supposed to know that, and it probably wouldn't do him any favors with Staff Sergeant Young to repeat to the entire squad something he'd overheard Colonel Coleman say to Palka Oray.

The city might be blacked out, but apparently the Gomorati government hadn't instituted a lockdown. Nibirans lined the streets to watch the military convoy pass. Mothers in dresses and bonnets clutched children close to them, and men wearing the same hat-with-flaps he'd seen Janus fighters wear stared at the sides of the passing vehicles with hollow eyes.

It felt strange to be showing up to a populated city to fight. Eremus had been a ghost town, other than the insurgents that had haunted her shadows and crevices, with the only signs of life the personal belongings her citizens had left behind.

In contrast, Gomorate was teeming with life. The Nibirans didn't look overly happy to see human military vehicles penetrating their city like an ax through kindling, but they'd clearly turned up for a reason. These were beings who'd lived in the lap of luxury, whatever that looked like on Nibiru. Now they were suddenly facing potential destruction...and here were these Marines, an invading army from another planet, invited in by their own government in a desperate bid to maintain Gomorate's hold on the continent.

It probably didn't sit too well with them. All the same, he thought he saw resignation in their watery eyes. They seemed to know the Marines were their last hope, like it or not.

"Whoa," Paisley said. "Check that thing out."

Apparently, hearing Paisley express wonderment at anything was enough to get the entire squad's attention, and soon the coms were alive with laughter and chatter about what was approaching the same intersection as them, visible across the open, statue-filled square that bordered it.

"How *old* is that thing?"

"Did *we* teach them to build that?"

"Nah. It's too old for that."

It was a decrepit-looking tank, painted in dappled blue, presumably for fighting in the Sodalite Desert. Po was using his Circuit to access exterior audio as well as visual, and he could hear the thing squeak as its treads labored to drag it toward the intersection.

The Nibiran tank followed the same general principles as human ones—as low to the ground as possible, with a broad dome of a turret, and a main gun sticking out the front. But the turret looked sunken, and it bobbed up and down as it went, so that it looked like it might drop through the chassis at any moment.

"The GA's armor division used to be the backbone of Gomorati power, believe it or not," Young said. "But since Janus guerillas started giving them trouble a few decades ago, they became less and less relevant. These days, they barely build any new ones."

"I wouldn't exactly call attacking a capital city a 'guerilla tactic,'" Taylor put in.

"No," Young admitted, inclining his head toward the Marine. "But that's what happens when half the planet joins your insurgency. On the bright side, the GA tank crews must be happy."

The convoy continued to trundle through Gomorate, running across several more Nibiran military units in the process. They all halted to let the Marine vehicles pass, but none of them performed anything that looked like a salute, or a greeting of any kind. They just stared at the passing convoy with dull eyes, looking just as resigned as their civilian counterparts.

"That's what it looks like when pride meets need," Zanth said, from where he'd appeared near the front of the APC. He'd opened up a digital window in the side of the vehicle, and was looking through it at the soldiers outside, waiting for the convoy to pass. "They know they need you, and they don't like it one bit."

Po had never seen the Emplor use his Circuit to open a window like that. He hadn't known he had the capability...but he supposed it made sense. If Zanth himself could appear in his vision, then why wouldn't he be able to make Po see other things?

They pulled up to a cliff face that was carved to resemble the front of a large, stately building, which ran for hundreds of meters in both directions. Entrances were spaced evenly along it, each one bordered by narrow, vertical windows that let onto chambers that looked well-lit.

Young stood up from his bucket seat. "This is us. File out, and follow the red line your implant will show you. It'll take you to your accommodations. Freshen up, and get what rest you can. You shouldn't expect to get much of it, if the Nibirans' intel is to be believed, so take advantage of what time we have."

The back of the APC opened up, and Second Squad piled out. A wrist-thick red beam popped into Po's vision the moment his boot touched the ground, floating in midair and stretching toward one of the building's otherwise identical entrances.

He ordered Echo Team to stay close on him as they made their way to wherever the Nibirans were putting them—at least until they had the lay of the land. He'd be nervous enough bedding down in the middle of an alien city *without* knowing there were Janus moles lurking in their midst.

He also didn't miss how Young hadn't ordered them to unload any of their gear from the APC.

And that wasn't just his idea. If none of us are unloading gear, then that means the higher-ups want us to stay as mobile as possible.

The sergeant spoke into his ear as they neared the entrance the red line was leading them to, as though to confirm the sentiment.

"Make sure a watch is set over anyone who goes to sleep," was all he said. But it was enough.

"Yes, Staff Sergeant," Po answered.

The building's entrance was a simple portal cut through the stone—up-close, Po could see that the rock had a reddish hue. He hadn't been sure before, seeing it from a distance in Nibiru's eternal dimness.

Past the plainly carved entrance, things got more elaborate. They found a foyer even larger than Po had expected. Two long desks stood at the far end of the room, seamless with the floor, as though they'd grown out of it. Four armed Nibirans stood behind them, looking over the Marines coldly as they filed in. There was a squad's worth of Marines here, too, and none of them were talking. A tense silence hung over the lobby, with occasional glances passed between the humans and aliens.

So this is how we're treated by the beings we're supposed to buddy up with. The open resentment didn't seem to bode well for how the upcoming battle would go.

"You gotta admire this stonework," Gomez said loudly, his voice ringing out to bounce off the high ceiling and walls. He was apparently just as oblivious to the situation in front of him as he usually was. Gomez was a stalwart companion in battle, but he read social cues like Po read Chinese.

Po enjoyed it, in a way. The fact that Gomez just never seemed to change was sort of comforting in the middle of a city where nothing was familiar.

Anyway, the other Marine had a point. The stonework *was* incredible. An intricate chandelier hung from the middle of the ceiling, the stone like thin lattice in places. It also appeared seamless with the rest of the building. And as they followed the red beam out of the foyer, they encountered rows of doors facing each other across a hallway. Not open-air portals, like the front entrance, but actual doors. It was a mundane enough thing to notice, but Po admired how straight and flush each one looked with its frame. It was a testament to how perfectly this place had been hewn out and sculpted. Something about this hall reminded him of walking past habitation modules back in Psyche, and that made him feel a little better about being here too, as irrational as that was.

Someone had propped open the door the red line led them to, and when they walked through it, Po felt vindicated in being reminded of Psyche's habitation tubes. This was an apartment. A small box of stitched dolls rested against one wall near the front room, and beyond it was what looked like a kitchen.

Paisley brushed past Po and headed down a hall that branched off of the living room. "Looks like they kicked out a Nibiran family to give us this," he remarked in a neutral tone as peered into one room after another. He looked incredibly out of place, walking around the residence in his SERAPH suit and toting his M37C. "Wonder where they are, now."

"Is every one of those doors an apartment?" Gomez asked, looking back toward the corridor they'd entered from. "Is that how many families lost their homes?"

"Only temporarily, I'm sure," Po said. "And I'm sure they have somewhere else to put them."

"You're sure that frog-dogs are humane to each other?" Paisley asked, returning from his inspection of the apartment. "Why?"

"Self-interest, for one. If a family was kicked out for every Marine team, then that's a lot of displaced Nibirans. Make that many citizens homeless all at once, and you're going to have an even bigger problem on your hands than you started with."

Paisley snorted, but said nothing else.

Krikorian volunteered for first watch, claiming he wasn't tired. Po wanted to sleep, but he was too wired for it. After taking the trouble to take his suit off and lie on a child's bed, his feet dangling off the end, he tried for less than an hour before giving up.

Swinging his legs over the side of the low bed, he brought up his implant idly and checked for battalion-wide updates. Back in FOB Longhorn, there'd always been an updated list of points of interest throughout the base. He'd had the ability to select one and have a colored line lead him straight to it, just like the red beam that had led them here.

He was surprised to find a point of interest had already been created for them in Gomorate—here in this very building, in fact. Apparently, rations had been brought to a lower level for any Marines wanting chow.

That was Po. He rose from the bed, suited back up, and grabbed his M37. Krik only nodded to him as he passed through the living room and out into the corridor.

The similarity with Psyche persisted as he descended through the strange apartment building cut into the mountain. Windows went away with just one flight of stairs, and he might as well have been in a space habitat spinning to simulate gravity. The bright yellow line leading him to chow brought him still deeper, and it wasn't long before he realized that most of Gomorate was underground.

That made him unsettled. As he understood it, one of the things that had protected the city from attacking was being built on rock. But if an underground complex like this could be carved out, then how hard would it be for Janus sympathizers to hide a new attack route in the basement of some abandoned building?

Then again, on the way in, he hadn't seen any buildings that might be called a single-family dwelling, nor had there been any of an equivalent size. If the Gomorati all lived more or less communally like this, then he supposed it would be harder for secret insurgents to pull something like that off. Plus, they'd probably have to go pretty deep, to avoid hitting any of the other underground structures around them. Unless they started digging from the outskirts, which would be of little value anyway....

Maybe it wasn't an issue. Or maybe it was. He lacked the information to properly be able to tell.

After six flights of impressively carved stairs, he exited the stairwell into a long, low space where Marines sat on the floor around hunks of stone that served as tables. Their armor was pretty form-fitting, but Po didn't see anyone sitting cross-legged. The armor was still too bulky for that. Instead, guys had their legs splayed awkwardly to the side, or some of them ate in a crouch, inserting morsels through open visors and into their mouths. The Nibirans who'd carved these things clearly hadn't been thinking of Marines in SERAPH suits.

He joined the line for chow and let his arms dangle awkwardly at his sides, one of them resting against his rifle. The suits looked cool enough running through a contested neighborhood, or sneaking through dense jungle, but for just standing around they left something to be desired. They lacked pockets, and before bootcamp Po had always relied on pockets for somewhere to put his hands. Wearing the suit, his arms always just seemed to kind of...dangle.

Some Marines at a table nearby were chatting, and he overheard them say the Gomorati Army unit that had liberated Longhorn had run into heavy resistance along their chosen route back into the city.

They might not make it back in time, then, Po reflected. He wondered what that would mean for the coming battle. Just how many insurgents did To'sheth Rin plan to hit this city with?

The Marine in front of him in line kept looking back at him and grinning. Po just raised his eyebrows in response.

"Can I do anything for you?" he asked after the fourth time the guy looked back at him.

"Nah, but...you're boot battalion too, right? I'm with 132nd." The kid twitched as he said it, his left eye spasming, and his head jerking to the side.

"Uh...yeah. I'm with 131st. Abbato."

"I know." Another twitch. "Your IFF told me." His grin widened.

"Right." Po didn't bother turning his IFF tags on, not really caring what the other's name was. "You, uh...you from Psyche, then?" he asked, mostly to try to dispel the awkwardness.

"Nah, I'm from 1950 KE. Little ice mining outfit started up fifty years ago." He gave another head toss, the most violent yet. It looked like an involuntary tic—it would be weird if it wasn't. "Population two hundred people—minus me, ha! They scooped me up right before they came to get you guys. I'm B-B-Benton, by the way. Private Maximilian Benton."

"Did they ding you with something, to make you join? Like, a crime?"

"No, I wanted to join! Wanted to." His eye twitched, and his head went sideways again, hard. "Wanted to."

"Right."

It was Benton's turn to get food, which came as something of a relief. The other Marine fingered his helmet's chin guard as he contemplated the two options on offer. Chili with beans and cheese spread...or chicken, egg noodles, and veggies in sauce. Finally, he took the chili after an irritatingly long time. Po grabbed the chicken and made for an empty slab to eat it on.

Benton plopped down across from him. "You're good if I eat with you, right?" Head toss.

"Sure. Whatever."

"Hey. Fist bump." Benton held a gloved fist toward Po, over the table.

Po stared at it for a long moment. Slowly, he brought his own fist up and touched it lightly against Benton's. Then he ripped open the MRE and started mixing it up with the sauce.

"Hey," Benton said.

"What?"

"Your brother, Lorenzo. He wanted me to tell you hi."

Chapter 10

Po scrutinized Benton's leering face, his MRE forgotten.

"What did you just say?"

"Huh? What?"

"Repeat what you just said."

Benton stared at him blankly for a few seconds. "'Fist bump,'" he said at last.

"That wasn't it."

"What did I say, then?"

"You said Lorenzo said hi."

"Who's Lorenzo?"

Po narrowed his eyes. "My brother."

"Back on Psyche? Never been to Psyche." Benton twitched.

A prolonged silence passed between them as Po stared hard at the other Marine, who'd paused with a spoonful of beans suspended just below his grinning mouth. His eyes lacked any flicker of recognition—he seemed genuinely surprised by what Po was saying.

Did I imagine it?

His first thought was to go to Staff Sergeant Young about how weird this Benton guy was acting, but the memories were still fresh of all the things he'd thought he witnessed before, which his superiors assumed were hallucinations. Back on Cycler 3, when his DIs learned he'd run screaming from an invisible Emplor, it had earned him a trip to the medical center for a psych eval. And in Shackleton, Young had managed to figure out that Po had seen another Emplor operating the HMG that had shot Paisley—even though none of the others had seen it, aside from Taylor. That had landed him in a tense meeting with Colonel Albrecht.

Benton *did* seem strange, but then, there were plenty of...*unique* individuals in the Marine Corps. Take Paisley, and Navarro. Zhang, for that matter. And probably himself, if he was being real honest. The others in Benton's squad would have to deal with him all the time, so they'd have to notice if the guy went too far from his baseline. Sure, Benton's was a weird, twitchy baseline, but it wasn't the weirdest thing Po had seen since getting conscripted. Far from it.

A message from Staff Sergeant Young told him to rouse his team and rendezvous with the rest of the squad in front of the building. Janus had been spotted on the jungle's edge.

He forked a few dripping chicken pieces and stuffed them past his lips, still studying Benton as he stood up, chewing.

His mouth was full, and he didn't have much to say to the strange boot regardless. And so, with a curt nod, he left the makeshift mess and went to muster his team.

Before leaving the room, he glanced back at Benton and saw him still sitting there motionless, with his spoonful of beans hovering just under his mouth. The only part of him that had moved was his eyes, which had tracked Po to the door.

Weird.

Po gave himself a shake, then left.

***

As he was jogging back up the stairs, which seemed way more numerous going up than down, a strident voice reached him from an upper landing

"Do *not* let me see you walking around chewing food while in uniform again." It was followed by a dull smack, as if the speaker had hit the stone wall.

The voice sounded familiar, and as Po rounded another flight of stairs, his suspicions were confirmed: it was Navarro, though he was talking in a tone Po had never heard from him before.

Navarro wore a SERAPH suit, and he was looming over a Marine in a service uniform. The Marine would have been shorter than Navarro naturally, but the suit made him loom even larger.

Navarro hit the wall again, near the other Marine's head, causing him to cringe away. "Think you're still back in the amusement park they called an FOB, FOBBIT? You want these Nibirans to disrespect us even more than they already do? Take *pride* in your membership in the Corps. Show some self-respect."

Po stepped onto the landing. "Hey, Navarro. You're the same rank as him, man. You're acting like you're his DI."

Navarro turned, and the sheer hatred in his eyes almost made Po take a step back, which would have taken him right off the landing.

"He's a *FOBBIT,*" the other Marine spat. "His rank might as well be honorary. I won't have him walking around in front of those frog-dogs making us look bad."

"Get out of here," Po said to the FOBBIT, who didn't seem to need to be told twice. He ducked under Navarro's arm and scurried up the stairs.

Po watched him go, then turned back to Navarro. "Man, what's up with you? Everything all right?"

"Nothing's all right when we have FOBBITs representing the Corps like we're a bunch of half-baked civilians."

"There are other ways to go about stuff like this."

"What do you know, Abbato? You were scum from the start. Rodriguez might have been an Obsidian Angel, but he was right about you. He and Dempsey both landed in the Corps because you couldn't stop being such a scumbag, and just look what happened to Dempsey. You ever put that together? That you basically got him killed?"

Po could feel how wide his eyes were. He'd gone from relative calm to wanting to throttle Navarro. He was definitely angrier than Navarro had been at the FOBBIT. Way angrier.

"You're a real piece of work, you know that?" Navarro went on. "I don't know why I ever bothered with you. Think you're some hero, helping out that sorry excuse for a Marine?" He nodded up the stairwell. "You'll get involved when it's me disciplining a FOBBIT for breaking protocol, but you wouldn't lift a finger to help the Nibiran that merc beat into a bloody pulp. And I'm supposed to take *moral instruction* from you?"

Po's breathing was coming heavy, his shoulders rising and falling, his hands clenched into fists. They stared at each other for a protracted moment, and it nearly came to blows there in the stairwell.

But a battle had begun overhead, and Po knew that getting into it with Navarro here would be an injustice to his brothers. Not to mention it would surely draw disciplinary action down on them both. Navarro might be fine if that happened, but for Po, the threat of discharge and subsequent simjail was always looming overhead.

"You watch your back," Po growled, before turning to continue jogging up the stairs.

"Oh, yeah," Navarro jeered after him. "I guess I'd better. With brothers like you, who else is gonna watch it?"

***

A dull rushing sound reached Po's ears as he stepped out of the apartment complex-turned-barracks, and he was accustomed enough to the SERAPH's hearing enhancements that he knew he wouldn't have heard the sound at all if it weren't for them. It was too far way.

Mortar fire.

An identical noise followed, then a third, and a fourth.

After that, explosions began to rock the city, rumbling all around Second Squad as they gathered in front of the long building. One of the mortar rounds hit a structure on the opposite side of a square to their right, obliterating it and sending rock shards flying everywhere, though none of them came anywhere near reaching their position.

By now, most of the Gomorati populace seemed to have been cleared off the streets, but nearby, some GA soldiers were gaping at the destroyed building in apparent disbelief. It seemed they truly were having a hard time fathoming that anyone would, or could, attack their precious city. Their reaction might have had something to do with Gomorate's long-standing historical and cultural importance for Nibirans, but it probably had a lot more to do with the sense of their own invincibility crumbling all around them.

The Torres crews that had come with the convoy from Longhorn didn't waste any time. They were already inside their tanks—they'd probably been in them all this time, eating and catching what shuteye they could right there in their seats—and now they returned fire, shelling the parts of the jungle canopy where the bombs had been fired from. Explosions blossomed, leaving behind burning trees in their wake. As soon as they fired, the Torres crews moved their machines to new locations, presumably uninterested in inviting the same treatment from the enemy.

"We go to wherever we're needed," Young told Second Squad as they assembled behind the APC they'd come in.

"We taking this thing, Staff Sergeant?" Taylor slapped the side of their ride from Longhorn.

"Negative. I'm not interested in all of us getting taken out by a mortar round. We'll move out on foot to wherever the insurgents are threatening to break through—and remember, stay spread out. Bounding overwatch at all times, with only one team advancing, unless I say otherwise."

A few moments of silence passed, and Paisley leaned to look around the side of the APC at the jungle below. "Think they're gonna fire any more—"

As if in answer, several *whoomph*s came from the mountain's lower slopes in quick succession, arcing upward before hurtling down toward the city like so much deadly rain.

"Check that out," Zapletal said.

Po was about to ask what he was talking about, then he saw it: long and broad rectangular shapes were emerging from between the jungle's trees, glowing dimly on thermal.

"What are those things?" Zhang asked.

Young shook his head. "I believe they're the closest thing to tanks the insurgency could come up with."

"Wait...there's frog-dogs inside those?" Taylor said. "They're carrying those things with them?"

By now, there were six of the things out in the open, and judging by the way they moved, it seemed Taylor had called it. Like armored centipedes laboring up the slopes, the 'walking tanks' crept toward the city.

"That jungle should have been cut back way farther than that," Young muttered over the squad-wide.

"Nibirans got cocky," Krikorian said.

The sergeant nodded. "And now we have to deal with that."

As mortar rounds pounded the city all around them, reducing centuries-old buildings to rubble, tracers began to emanate from multiple parts of the city, converging on the various walking tanks that were crawling up the mountain slopes. The rounds pinged harmlessly off the metal shells.

"Tell me that's not Marines doing that," Po said.

"Almost certainly not," Young answered. "Hopefully, the Nibirans figure out soon how ineffective it is."

"Maybe someone should tell them," Paisley put in.

"Well, our communications with them aren't the most...integrated, unfortunately."

As far as Po could see, the Torres tanks were busy with destroying the many fire bases Janus fighters had set up under the concealment of the jungle's canopy. That meant a different solution would need to be found to deal with the Nibirans that were hauling their own armor with them toward Gomorate.

Weapons fire came from upper-story windows of a building nearby, aimed at the closest walking tanks. Po resisted the urge to roll his eyes. Then, a thought occurred to him. "Is it all Nibirans that are holed up in buildings, sir?"

"No. We have at least some Marines at every position they've told us about."

"That's good." If there were as many turncoat Gomorati as Palka Oray had seemed to think, the last thing they wanted was to have those Nibirans at their backs, in complete control of superior firing positions.

But that still left these walking tanks, none of which had been destroyed yet.

"Man, those things just keep coming," Taylor remarked.

It was true—by Po's count, twenty of the rectangular boxes were now advancing on the city, with more emerging from the jungle all the time. All the while, tanks all over Gomorate exchanged fire with the Janus fire bases.

A new voice spoke over their squad channel—a familiar one. "You boys still interested in teaming up with a disgraced mech jockey, after my performance back at Longhorn?"

It was Second Lieutenant Karl Grieg, and as he spoke, Po's implant made his vision flash green in sync with his voice. Turning his head, he saw where the simulated radio waves were coming from: a Polliver-4 standing on the other side of the street, its support bots in various postures of stylish repose all around it. None of the machines made any motion—not that the mech could wave, or anything like that—but it had to be Grieg. His IFF tag confirmed it.

Taylor answered over the wide channel. "With all due respect, sir, they gave you another mech to pilot? After you lost an entire armor platoon?"

"*Taylor!*" Young said sharply.

"Not to worry, sergeant—the lad's question is valid. As it happens, Private, after Longhorn fell and the decision to abandon the base, there were too many spare Pollivers lying around and not enough qualified pilots. We couldn't very well leave them there for To'sheth Rin, and so I find myself back in a cockpit." Grieg sniffed. "Though I might point out, I seem to recall saving all your lives back in Eremus. I should think that makes my *overall* performance a wash."

"I'd sign off on it, sir," Young said.

"And I may need you to do just that," Grieg said, lightly enough that Po was pretty sure he was joking. "But in the meantime, I need to get closer to those encroaching Janus, and to do that safely, I need a Marine squad around me. Unless I want to find myself ejecting from yet another mech today, which as it happens, I don't."

"We got you," Young said.

"Then let's move."

Chapter 11

They advanced two city blocks down the slopes, and Po marveled at how quickly Gomorate had transformed from a quiet, historic city into a war zone. Plumes of smoke rose into the dimness all around them, and they'd already passed two buildings reduced to rubble. Gomorate had spent hundreds of years as an impregnable refuge of prosperity and calm. Now, it was just another nexus of fear and death.

The Gomorati Army was still firing uselessly at the insurgents' walking tanks from positions all over the city.

Po could understand the behavior, to an extent. When you couldn't do anything about a problem confronting you, it was sometimes tempting to do *something,* even if that something was completely useless.

Still, it was an awful waste of ammo, and an embarrassing display of incompetence. He hoped they stopped soon.

"Hey Staff Sergeant, any word on whether the GA is setting up any fire bases?" Po asked over the squad channel. "They have mortars too, right? They'd actually be effective, right now."

"I'm told they are," Young said. "None operational yet, though."

They could learn a thing or two from Janus.

Moving through Gomorate was nothing like Eremus. Sure, navigating the steep downward slopes was a factor, but it was more that the city wasn't infested with Janus like Eremus had been. In that battle, every house had been a potential warren of frog-dogs waiting to kill them. But as of now, the insurgents had barely made it to Gomorate's outskirts. And so, the buildings they passed posed little threat.

Unless the turncoats the GA's apparently full of decide to make their move. Or, unless Janus did *succeed in digging tunnels.*

Almost as soon as Po thought that, Paisley spoke up. "Hey, Staff Sergeant. Doesn't that building seem like a prime spot for the Gomorati soldiers to fire out of?" He painted it red, so that the whole squad knew which building he was talking about.

"It does," Young said slowly. "What's your point?"

Paisley gave a brisk shrug. "The GA seem to have a talent for picking excellent places to waste ammo from. That seems like a huge missed opportunity."

"Is...this a joke, Private?"

"No, Staff Sergeant. I'm suggesting you use your access to see if any Marine Circuits have footage of that building from a couple minutes ago."

A silence came over the com, then Young spoke again, sounding a lot more serious than before. "There was weapons fire coming from that location moments before we came into view of it."

Paisley nodded. "Which means they either decided to take a break in the middle of a battle..."

"Or someone stopped them," Young said. "Good eye, Paisley. As your reward, Echo Team gets to go clear that building. Delta will have your six."

But there was no need. Even as the sergeant finished speaking, insurgents began exiting the front of the building, as if leaving for their morning stroll. They were obviously Janus, since they toted similar weaponry to what they'd wielded in Eremus, and they wore robes instead of the GA uniforms.

The insurgents seemed surprised to be spotted so quickly, and even more surprised to be shot at. One of them went down, but the others hustled back inside, to fire from the safety of the entranceway.

"If you'll permit me," Lieutenant Grieg said over the squad channel as he sidestepped to get a clear shot. The Second Squad Marines dutifully got out of the way, heading toward the stony overhang of a nearby building.

An HE round launched from the Bipedal Weapons Platform, sailing directly through the front door and causing the building to collapse in on itself.

"I believe that takes care of *that* particular avenue of ingress," Grieg said.

"Sure seems to," Young agreed. "But I doubt it's the only one."

"Indeed. I'll send out an alert to our other units in the city. Shall we proceed?"

"Yes, let's."

The fact Janus had popped up so close made their descent through the sloping lanes a little more fraught. If they'd appeared there, then they could appear anywhere...but the threat didn't yet seem to justify checking every house, especially since they lacked the time for it. They had to deal with the tidal wave of insurgents, the first of which had now reached the outskirts. A few of them had already abandoned the armor they'd carried with them, melting away into the city's buildings and alleyways. Who knew where *they'd* show up next? The more insurgents they allowed to penetrate the city, the more problems they'd have.

As they continued to make their way down through the mountaintop city, Po found himself studying Paisley with narrowed eyes. How had *he* figured out that the building Grieg had destroyed with his Polliver was about to start spewing insurgents, when no one else had seen it?

Sure, it had made sense that a GA unit would have been garrisoned inside...but it hadn't been guaranteed. Plenty of buildings were empty that might have held Nibiran soldiers. So how had Paisley been so sure about that one?

There was no time to contemplate it. Grieg was apparently satisfied with how close they'd come to the approaching Janus forces, and he sent another high-explosive round into their midst, hitting one of their walking tanks dead-center and obliterating it. A couple of insurgents emerged from the flaming wreck, attempting to drag themselves to the safety of a passing Janus unit.

"Krikorian," Young said, as he unslung his sniper rifle and raised it. "Got your M126 ready?"

"Sure do," the Armenian said, raising his own sniper off its strap.

"Let's put down those two crawlers."

"Do it quickly," Grieg said, already sidestepping across the street for a broad alley on the opposite side. "If we keep moving, we can kill many insurgents, but staying still is asking to die by mortar fire."

Young and Krik wasted no time. Within seconds, both insurgents were dead, and Second Squad was moving in loose formation with the Polliver-4 toward wherever it would fire from next.

Po saw the logic in killing the insurgents trying to pull themselves to safety: demoralize the enemy as much as possible. Make them pay for ever thinking this was a good idea. It was a cold-blooded move, but war didn't call for warmth or kindness. Victory went to the lethal. The unhesitating. War created messed-up situations, where the most merciful choice was often to act with as much brutality as possible.

He never could have come to appreciate that reality, during his life back on Psyche, even with how dangerous that sometimes had been. Not even if he'd spent more time in the various war sims on offer would he have understood it. But he understood it now.

The useless Nibiran fire from the Gomorati Army started to dry up as Second Squad pushed down through the city. That was a relief, since as the insurgents got closer to the city's slopes, the angles became less workable, increasing the chance of friendly fire.

But it was also a little concerning. Had any of the GA units stopped shooting because they'd been taken out by Janus—either by secret insurgents amidst their ranks or by those who'd come by way of another concealed tunnel? So far, there was no real indication of that, but the threat was ever-present in the back of Po's mind.

Their Polliver-4 continued to blast apart enemy armor and then move, blast and move. Other units had picked up on the tactic by now, which had been disseminated over the coms as its effectiveness became apparent. Marine squads and platoons were advancing down Gomorati streets in a roughly formed front, each centered on a BWP that obliterated enemy walking tanks as they crossed the flat stretch between the jungle and the outskirts.

In answer, mortar fire began to concentrate on where those infantry-and-armor teams were pushing through the city. But that lessened the pressure on the Torres tanks, which seemed to be quickly cutting down on the fire bases hidden throughout the jungle.

It soon became clear to Po that in the coming minutes, this would become a battle fought between infantry and insurgents in the lower streets. The enemy couldn't get far into the city before being forced to abandon their rickety tanks, and so as different as this battle seemed from Eremus so far, it would quickly become much more similar.

But even before he expected it, rifle fire hammered the front of his suit from a dark doorway ahead, which was situated on a rooftop built into a cliff face below. He staggered back, then managed to wrench himself to the side, out of the stream of rounds as Paisley returned suppressive fire from beside him.

"Echo Team, keep that position suppressed while we work around," Young ordered over the com. Their mech was currently finding a way around through a side street, escorted by Foxtrot, and so wasn't able to assist.

Po, Paisley, and the rest of his team took cover behind some pillars and exchanged fire with the insurgents shooting at them from the next street down. Within minutes, the sergeant and his team had infiltrated the target building and taken down the insurgents inside. But Po still had the dents in the front of his armor, and the tender spots below where he knew bruises would already be forming. It was a good reminder to be more vigilant.

They worked their way down through the city, leaning heavily on thermal to pick up movement and quickly focus on it, in order to identify whether it was a threat. The insurgents had chosen to attack while Gnara was in the sky, which made sense, since it neutered the Marines' sensor advantage somewhat.

Another thing that affected their technological edge was the fact there was some small chance that any Nibiran they saw would turn out to be a civilian. It was normally pretty easy to tell an insurgent from a citizen—the former generally wore a dust-colored robe, carried a weapon, and liked to shoot Marines—but it took a second to discern that, and that was a second during which any Marine might lose his life.

While their communication with their GA allies was poor to non-existent, the various squad and platoon leaders maintained tight coordination with each other. The rest of 131st platoon was somewhere to the west, Po knew, commanded by Sergeant Emery and escorting a BWP of their own. None of the units advanced too far ahead of the others, so that their sweep was as thorough as it could be given the circumstances.

But their advance was slowing as they started to encounter more and more insurgents. They were coordinating too, mostly by hand radio Po knew, since they lacked the sophisticated tech of the Marines' integrated coms. Still, things were coming to a head here in the lower half of Gomorate, with both opposing forces stiffening up and doing their best to wreak maximum damage on the other.

The insurgents must know they can't win. Their mortars had been their best hope for taking out the Marines' tanks, and for destroying the mechs, but they couldn't do both at once. Only getting a shot or two off before getting obliterated by Torres fire certainly wasn't helping them any. And while Janus had clearly brought thousands of fighters to this battle, the Marines didn't just have technological superiority—they had the high ground. Plus they had the GA backing them up, and no matter how poorly trained the Nibirans were, that did count for something.

The realization didn't instill as much confidence in Po as it might have. The writing did seem to be on the wall for this battle...which meant there must be something he wasn't seeing.

If the intel is true, and Janus has enough plants throughout GA's ranks to make a difference....

If those plants managed to overpower their Gomorati counterparts, then the Marines would find themselves sandwiched between the insurgents coming out of the jungle as well as ones firing on them from behind, farther up the city's slopes.

But that hadn't happened yet, and the Marines seemed to be pushing the insurgents back—gradually, foot by foot, but it was happening. That alone would have its risks, since it would create a higher density from the ones retreating and the ones advancing from the jungle, but it still seemed like an encouraging sign.

Delta and Echo Teams were advancing down a side street, with Foxtrot moving through a nearby alley in case they needed to hook around for a flank, when a hissing sound came from the street up ahead.

It was an RPG, headed straight for their Polliver-4. Grieg sidestepped the round smartly, and it sailed past to crash into a carved cliff behind them, causing half-colonnades to come loose and crash to the ground.

This was the first Po had heard of an RPG being fired in the battle, which had made sense, since the Janus launchers tended to be clunkier and heavier than those of human make. He hadn't figured they'd be up for carrying them *and* the walking tanks they'd used to reach the city outskirts.

But now the telltale hissing came from all over the city, as if part of a coordinated strike. Another RPG screamed down the lane, its path pinning the BWP to the side of a structure. Grieg's only option for dodging was to duck awkwardly, which he did, and Gomez and Crotty barely managed to scramble out of harm's way. The round impacted the ground close to them, sending shrapnel flying, and undoubtedly turning the temperature up inside their suits a few degrees.

We should have seen this coming. Under To'sheth Rin's command, Janus seemed to have an uncanny ability to withhold a capability until the optimal time, then unleash it all at once. They'd done it with their upgraded SAMs, which they'd deployed at the same moment they destroyed all human satellites in orbit, using the missiles hidden on Maw.

Now, they were exploiting the expectation that everyone had had: that the insurgents wouldn't manage to bring many RPGs into this battle. But clearly, they'd figured it out, and now they were firing them all at once.

The next RPG caught their Polliver-4 in the legs, sending it toppling into a building and crashing through the thinly carved facade. Po figured it was down for the count, but somehow Grieg managed to get one of its charred legs under him and push back to a standing position, striding out of the rubble, torso twisting in search of a target.

It would have been better if the mech had stayed down. Another RPG connected with its torso dead-center, knocking it backward, and two more struck in quick succession.

Another round was all it took to blow the hull wide open, and the one that followed surely killed Grieg, if he hadn't been dead already.

"Lieutenant?" Young said. "*Lieutenant!*"

But as Po had expected, there was no response. Second Squad scattered for whatever cover was close at hand.

Chapter 12

The fallen mech's robotic dogs ran to confront the Nibirans that had killed it as Po sprinted inside one of four squat structures built into a low shelf. Another hissing sound came from without, and he darted around the corner—just in time to avoid a blast that impacted the entrance, caving in the ceiling and partially blocking the ingress.

He studied the obstructed doorway. *I could probably crawl over the rubble and squeeze through.* But considering a Nibiran had just fired an RPG at it, it didn't seem like the most tactical place to emerge from.

"Abbato, you good?" It was Krikorian.

"Yeah. Just hoping I'm not stuck." He called up his team's vitals and saw they were all okay, too. Krik could have done the same, but in the heat of what was happening, he probably hadn't thought to.

He began checking the place, and discovered that what had looked like four separate buildings was actually one, connected by a low hall in the back. He wasn't sure what this place was used for normally—there were tables and chairs in every section, along with what looked like rows of cabinets, and trapdoors built into floors here and there. Whatever it was, it had been completely abandoned. Maybe in the face of the impending battle.

"We're pinned, here," Young said. "Near where the Polliver went down. Lieutenant Grieg's support bots are out fighting the Nibirans, but they won't last against those numbers. Echo, can you assist?"

"I'm with Krik, Taylor, and Gomez on the next street over," Paisley answered. "If you want, we can circle back, Staff Sergeant. See if we can take some pressure off."

"If you can do it safely. But also, quickly. Polliver-4s are going down all across the city. We need to withdraw back uphill."

Safely didn't seem to apply to anything about this situation, but Po knew this wasn't the time to argue. He made his way to the westmost part of the long, connected structure. There, he found a window that gave him an angle on the building from which insurgents were keeping Young and his team pinned. He settled his rifle scope's crosshairs over one of the windows, and waited.

A Nibiran popped into view and he put a burst of rounds in its eye. The alien flew back and rose no more.

"I think you can move, Staff Sergeant. I'm covering the ones who were shooting at you."

"Good work, Abbato. Are you able to extricate yourself once we do?"

"I'll be fine. You move, then I'll move."

"Sounds good."

As Delta Team headed for the next street to the east, where they could begin their tactical withdrawal back up the mountain, Po reflected on the role that chance played in combat. The insurgent he'd just killed had no doubt been full of confidence, reveling in having the upper hand on a team of Marines.

But there'd been an angle he hadn't noticed, and a Marine had been positioned to exploit it who he hadn't anticipated. And now he was dead. Just like that.

There'd been others sharing the building with him, but they made no appearance after seeing what Po had done to their buddy. Either they were lying low until the Marines withdrew, or they'd pulled back to wait for their main force to come up. Whatever the case, decisive lethality had won out once again.

"We good to cross too, Team Leader?" Paisley asked.

"Yeah. Go. I'll be behind you."

Echo Team hustled across his firing lane, and then it was time for Po to vacate the area, before dozens of insurgents swarmed through this lane. He sprinted through the cramped hall in the back, hunched over, as far as it went to the east. And when he couldn't find a proper exit, he forced himself through a tall, narrow window, dropping to the stony ground on the other side.

He emerged onto the same hill Second Squad was climbing at a jog, and that was when things started happening in quick succession.

At least five rifles opened up on them from the south, as they were skirting the foundation of a long building whose broad face offered no cover. Barbier cried out as they turned to face the threat, falling into the dirt and pawing at his midsection, his rifle falling to dangle by its strap.

Po was at the rear—closest to the insurgents shooting at them—but somehow, he hadn't been shot. He hit the dirt, to give the Marines behind him a clear shot. For his part, he propped his elbow on his thigh, leveled his M37C at one of the Janus positions, and fired. He hit nothing, but at least he kept one insurgent suppressed.

More insurgents added their fire, and all at once hope seemed to drain from the situation, like oil through a funnel. They were all going to die on this hill, in the middle of an alien city, far from home. At least they might buy some time for the other Marines to withdraw to better positions, but for them, this war was over.

Panic seized Po's heart. It wasn't fear of death—at least, not quite. It was instead an unexplainable sense that something was incredibly wrong. That he'd left something undone, something vital. That he wasn't ready for this.

Then, someone wearing a SERAPH suit ran into the middle of the street between Second Squad and the insurgents, clutching an M37C at hip height and spraying rounds toward the enemy. He must have had his visor open, because Po could hear him screaming wordlessly as he fired—a guttural sound of resolve mixed with terror.

"Up the hill!" Young yelled over the squad-wide, his voice ragged. "Get up the hill—Krikorian, help Barbier!"

Taylor spoke up: "We can't just—"

"He made his choice," Young said. "To die for his brothers. A whole squad of them. *Get up the hill.*"

Po scrambled to his feet, but found he couldn't wrench himself away. His eyes were locked on the Marine's last stand, and as several tracers converged on him, Po's gaze only became more fixed.

"*Abbato!*" Young screamed.

The Marine went down in a heap, and at that same moment, a Polliver-4 stepped into Po's peripheral vision, from he knew not where. It opened up with twin rotary autocannons, pelting the enemy positions, ripping them up. The Nibiran fire fell away to nothing, and the BWP followed up with high-explosive rounds that obliterated the rubble, walls, and doorways behind which the insurgents had been taking cover.

Po found himself running toward the fallen Marine, falling to his knees next to where he lay on the dust-covered stone.

It was Benton, from back in the makeshift mess hall. The one who'd been twitching violently, and who'd stared at Po until he left the room. Who'd told Po that Lorenzo said hi...unless he'd imagined that.

Po opened his own visor.

Blood gushed from a bullet wound near the crown of Benton's shaved head. But somehow, his eyes still seemed to see. They found Po's face, and stayed there. Amazingly, recognition entered into them.

Then, he spoke. "Abbato, right?" he said, in a croak. "Abbato."

Young yelled something at him over the squad channel, but Po turned it off. "That's right," he said, grabbing Benton's hand as tears sprang to his eyes. *He saved us. He spent his own life to save ours. Why? I hardly knew him.* "Y-you...you—thank you, Benton. Maximilian. Yeah?"

Benton squeezed his hand back with surprising strength, and tears glistened in his eyes, too. "I'm—so—*sorry,*" he gasped. "For everything. Everything I did in this place. This...*world.*"

Po gave a jerky nod. "Nibiru brings out the worst in us." His voice was heavy with tears, too.

"Not just—*here.* This *world.* Ah-*all* of it. I'm sorry...for using *Nancy*...f-for breaking her *heart.* For...*ruining*...her *life....*" Tears streamed down Benton's face, now, mingling with the blood that had reached his chin.

Who's Nancy? Po wondered, but didn't dare interrupt.

"And f-for—for joining the Angels. I betrayed...*neighbors....*" Benton started to shudder now, and the vibration passed into Po's body as he clutched the other Marine's hand even harder, willing him to stay with him. Not to go.

"S-s-so *sorry*...for everything wrong...." Benton trembled like a leaf in the wind, from his sobbing, and from what had to be his death throes. Po couldn't believe he could still speak. "So...*selfish....*"

"*This* wasn't selfish," Po said. "What you just did wasn't selfish. You saved us, brother."

Instead of answering, Benton extended his free hand to reach around Po's neck, to draw him closer. The Marine's strength was fading fast, now, and the hand was like a fledgling's wing fluttering against Po's armor. But he leaned down closer.

"There was *something...else,*" Benton rasped. "Inside the...*meshmind....*" He gasped, and his eyes went wider. "Tell them, Abbato...." He gasped again, clearly fighting for breath. Fighting against the shadow of death being cast over him. "Something...was *in* here...*with* us...."

With that, the light went out of Benton's eyes, like someone had flipped a switch. He sagged in Po's grasp like a rapidly deflating balloon.

Po stared into the lifeless eyes, which looked peaceful, somehow. His own eyes were swollen and wet, his throat like a lump of hardened clay.

"Rest easy, brother," he managed to whisper.

Then Young spoke again, having apparently forced the squad channel to switch back on inside Po's suit. "Abbato, get up here, *now!*"

He looked up. The hill was empty, and his squad was nowhere to be seen. He glanced around and saw that the Polliver had stalked on, in an attempt to hold back the tide of insurgents for a few moments longer.

"Yes, Staff Sergeant." But before he complied, he bent over and picked up Benton, armor and all, and slung his limp frame over his shoulders.

He ran up the hill.

***

He followed his implant's promptings to a long, low building whose door his squadmates had apparently obliterated, probably by the simple expedient of ramming into it with a SERAPH suit. The suits' power was incredible, and breaching charges weren't needed for most doors. If an entrance wasn't reinforced, then simply throwing one's self into it wearing SERAPH armor would generally do the trick.

Paisley and Crotty had to lay down covering fire in order to get him safely inside. The insurgents were advancing quickly. He pushed past the two Marines, wincing as Benton's legs knocked against the door's crumbling frame.

Inside, he found a warehouse strewn with stacks of crates and a layout that reminded him of the one he'd run through back in Camp Williams, during the Nibirans' attack on Cycler 3. He'd been under Gunny Emery's command, then, and he'd been yet to kill a living, breathing being. But he'd been about to.

Not far from the entrance, Drobnic was hovering over a weak-looking Barbier, who was leaned against the wall.

Staff Sergeant Young seized Po by the shoulder, and shook him, hard. "What *was* that, Abbato?"

Po took a deep breath. "Staff Sergeant, you may wanna let this one go."

Young shook him again. "*What* did you just say?

"I said...I said you should let this one go, Staff Sergeant. Benton told me something important, about the Obsidian Angels. You can watch my Circuit footage. I think...." He cleared his throat. "I think I was meant to go down there, Staff Sergeant."

Young stared into his eyes for a protracted moment, frowning. Then, at last, he released Po's shoulder. "All right. I'll let it go."

"Thank you."

"You can't carry the body back up the city, Abbato. Look. Hide him behind that stack of pallets."

Po nodded. "We'll come back for him once we retake the city."

Young hesitated, then gave a brisk nod. "Exactly."

Paisley and Crotty were still talking their rifles as Po went to gently lower Benton's body to the concrete floor.

"We'd better fall back again, Staff Sergeant," Paisley said. "You said there's another exit?"

"Yes. Abbato, you finished?"

"I'm good."

"Then let's go." But before he started moving toward the rear of the warehouse, the sergeant stood stock-still, head cocked to one side, and Po knew he was getting a transmission from somewhere. Over a channel none of them could access.

Young's eyes found Po's, a lot wider than they were before. "The situation just changed. The turncoats have finally activated. There's Janus killing soldiers at almost every GA position."

Taylor threw up his hands. "How did we know about this, and still let it happen?"

Young shook his head, and when he spoke again, he sounded tired. "This entire thing has been like watching a vacuum train lose its brakes." He waved them toward the back of the building. "Come on."

Chapter 13

War raged noisily all around them as they filed out the back of the warehouse, with Drobnic helping the wounded Barbier limp along. The occasional mortar round still fell, mostly within the narrowing slice of city still controlled by the Marines. But they'd mostly been replaced with the crackling hiss of RPGs being fired from alleys and windows, by insurgents who melted away the moment they'd loosed their rockets.

Po could pick out the sound of Polliver-4 autocannons being fired here and there, but the tanks were barely heard from anymore.

The Torres crews were in a tough spot, now. The orders had been handed out as the battle started not to destroy any Gomorati structures unless it was strictly necessary. But they'd reached a point in the battle when any given structure was as likely as not to house Janus.

So, just how much of the city was the Corps willing to level? Clear guidance hadn't been given from higher up, that Po knew of, and the tank crews seemed to be waffling.

"Staff Sergeant Young, my First Squad is on the rooftop I'm highlighting for you now." It was Emery, speaking over the platoon-wide channel. "If you cut across, take the lane to your west and hustle, you can be here inside of three minutes. I think we should rendezvous."

"Copy," Young said. "Heading your way now."

"We'll cover you."

They enjoyed a pocket of quiet as they crossed in front of the building First Squad had hunkered down on top of, and Po sized it up as they moved. Gunny Emery had chosen well, but by now that didn't come as much of a surprise.

The building was the only one he'd seen so far that hadn't taken advantage of the entire cliff it was built into, and instead the roof jutted out several meters from the rock. The cliff face above leaned out over it, casting it in shadow, while the roof looked high enough to overlook a fair bit of the city to the south.

It felt good that Second Squad was reuniting with the other half of 131st Platoon. Staff Sergeant Young was more than competent, but he didn't have Emery's killer instinct.

The prevailing sentiment among the Marines fighting for Gomorate seemed to be an instinctive flight away from the insurgents pressuring them from the south, but that reaction didn't really hold up, under even the lightest scrutiny. If they continued with it, they risked backing into lines of fire that could very well be controlled by insurgents who'd started attacking their countrymen from inside the buildings controlled by the GA.

They needed to stand firm instead. They needed to stake a claim over some territory and start projecting force—to start making Janus respond to them. And Emery taking the rooftop seemed like a likely place to start doing that from.

"They have us pinned here," Young said the moment they encountered Emery, in a hallway one level below the rooftop.

"No, we have *them* pinned," Emery said, grabbing Young by the shoulder and embodying exactly the energy Po had hoped to see from him. He pointed out a nearby window. "This? This isn't happening. This is *not* happening. Not on my watch." His eyes moved to Po, then to Paisley behind him, and then to the rest. "This will be the cliff that tide breaks on. *We* are the rock they'll break on."

"Sounds good to me, Gunny," Taylor said.

First Squad had the rooftop, and so Second Squad moved to the windows and beheld a target-rich environment. This vantage was even better than Po had anticipated. A cliff just as sheer as the one behind this building dropped away in front of them, so that there were only two ingresses onto this level within eyesight. That means there were only two positions the insurgents could feasibly fire RPGs from. And the moment one tried, someone from First Squad took him down.

"Watch the top of that cliff, too," Emery said. "They'll likely try climbing it and shooting from there, soon enough."

The enemy's too eager. They were drunk with the prospect of taking over the unconquerable Gomorate. That, and they were spurred on by the press of the insurgents behind them. To'sheth Rin truly had mustered a horde to take the Nibiran capital...but here, it worked to their disadvantage. 131st had carved out a kill zone in the middle of the city, and it seemed to be driving the insurgents crazy. It flew in the face of their apparent success—a disturbing anomaly they were clearly keen to stamp out.

Except, they *couldn't* stamp it out. The insurgents crested the two hills in droves, and the Marines stacked bodies. Some did climb the cliff in front of them, just as Emery had predicted, and a couple of them even managed it with RPGs.

But 131st had eyes there too, and they neutralized those insurgents before they could find their footing.

Po was fully in the flow of battle, now. His M37C was alive in his hands, like a part of him. When a mag became depleted, he smoothly ejected it and grabbed another from the next pouch in the loading order he'd established back in Eremus. The customized rifle already didn't weigh much, but with the SERAPH's strength augmentation, it was featherlight in his hands. The recoil was just enough to send tremors down his wrists, which was satisfying in its own way. It was enough to know he was firing a weapon, but not enough to throw off his aim.

It felt good to unleash the M37, but the best feeling of all was being back in battle with his platoon, all of them working together to exact payback on the tide of insurgents that surged all around them. By now, they'd lost the overeagerness of Marines fresh to battle—Eremus had stamped that out of them. None of them tried to take a kill out of place. Instead, each team talked their rifles, and when one member had fired enough that there was a chance his weapon might overheat and jam, he pointed out shots to whosever turn it was rather than try to take the shot himself.

The Nibiran horde seethed around them, apparently enraged by the Marines' insolence in opposing their otherwise steady progress across Gomorate. They converged on the building like moths to a flame, almost heedless of their losses. Their obsession with taking out 131st was lessening the pressure elsewhere, enough that an armor platoon accompanied by two infantry platoons were making headway to the east, or at least so Gunny Emery relayed to them from what he'd heard on the coms.

The odds still seemed even that Po would die today, but at the moment, he found he didn't care. He'd never felt this alive. Eremus had come close, but his exhilaration then had been tempered by the endless fatigue.

Today, every odor seemed crisper than ever before—even the odors of sweat and dust emanating from his squad. Colors were more vivid, even in the deepening dark—even when he switched to night vision. Sounds were louder. His rifle felt more right in his hands.

This job was becoming more than just staying out of simjail, he realized. More than a paycheck. More, even, than the fellowship of the brothers beside him, and his desire to keep them alive. To lay down his own life to do it, if it came to that.

He *enjoyed* combat. He couldn't ever imagine explaining that to anyone back in Psyche. But all his life, he'd lacked control over anything. He'd been born a slave to Equipoise Metals—he was effectively GEA property even before they conscripted him. Almost since he'd been old enough to walk and talk, he'd been scrambling—scrambling to avoid his father's or Lorenzo's wrath, and soon after, scrambling to try to make some headway against the mountain of debt they'd buried him under. All the while with people over him, telling him to go here, do that, keep quiet, stay at home until curfew is lifted, prepare to be searched.

He still had people in authority over him, and he had no real control over where he went. But he also dealt out death en masse by means of the power he held in his hands, and by means of the training he'd been given.

His life had always been characterized by an unending tsunami of problems, but in a sense, he was solving every possible problem for each Nibiran he killed. They'd never have to think about their problems again. They were free. Maybe they were even at peace.

It was a gruesome, half-demented thought, he knew, but who cared? It rang through his head like an anthem. His Circuit wasn't sophisticated enough to read his thoughts, so what reason was there to check himself? There was none. No one could hear the dark turn of his thoughts—only him. And so he reveled in the death he doled out all around him.

If you died today, would you be at peace? a still, small voice asked, from the back of his mind.

He frowned. The voice didn't sound like him. For some reason, it reminded him of Shackleton, back on the moon. Had he spoken to someone with a voice like that?

But he shook such thoughts off. In a moment, it would be his turn to shoot, and he needed to select his next target.

"Gunny," Paisley spoke over the platoon-wide channel, without warning.

"Go ahead, Private," Emery answered.

"Shouldn't we be worried about frog-dogs coming at us from above? Grappling down the cliff from up there? By the sounds of things, if they haven't pushed that far yet, they will any second."

A brief pause, and then: "Good point. Bravo Team, keep eyes in the sky for hostiles."

"They're already coming down at us!" one of the First Squad Marines yelled, sounding strangled over the com.

There was a flurry of cursing and yelling, followed by more rifle fire—but the fire emanating outward from the rooftop dried up. That meant enough hostiles had dropped onto the roof to tie up First Squad completely. Some of the insurgents on the streets below took notice, and began directing increased fire at the rooftop, apparently unconcerned whether they hit their own fighters.

"Gunny, do you need us?" Young asked.

There was no answer. Emery was either already dead or too engaged to talk.

"If we go up there, Janus will rush this building," Taylor said. "We'll lose it. Then it's over."

Young nodded slowly, his body tense. Po could almost feel the anxiety radiating from him, could almost see it as the dreadful reality settled squarely onto his shoulders—of having to make an immediate decision that would cost lives no matter what he chose.

The sergeant's eyes settled on Po's, and through his faceplate, Po could see Young's jaw firm up.

"Echo. Get up there."

Po took a sharp breath, then nodded. "Yes, Staff Sergeant." He locked eyes with Paisley, then Taylor, and then Krik and Gomez. He nodded toward the stairwell, then took the lead.

Chapter 14

Po crept up the stairwell, leading with his rifle's muzzle, trying his best to stay ready for he knew not what.

The rooftop that came into view was one gripped by utter chaos.

The angle of the rocky overhang was such that the insurgents hadn't been able to shoot the First Squad Marines from above, so there was that to be grateful for. The Janus fighters had been forced to swing onto the rooftop from grapple lines, just as Paisley had predicted.

There were nine of them on the roof already—a number his implant had somehow managed to extract from the confusion of the melee before him—but even as he watched, two more dropped into view, planted their feet on the roof's edge, and used their lines to propel themselves toward the stony surface where Marines fought Nibirans to the death.

Across the roof, insurgents were trading shots from the roof's edge with a single Marine crouched behind a metal crate. Emery was grappling with another Janus a few meters away from Po, his combat knife inching closer to its neck. And beyond him, a Nibiran was just plunging its knife into a Marine's chest, putting its entire weight behind the blade to try to get it through the suit's para-aramid fibers. Three Marines were already laid out motionless, in postures unnatural and agonizing enough to suggest they were either dead or unconscious.

Po took in all of this in an instant, and his rifle moved almost ahead of his thoughts. He raised it to eye level as he crouched at the doorway's right side, twisting his body to plant the crosshairs over the nearest new arrival from above.

He squeezed the trigger, watched through the scope to confirm the insurgent was tumbling off the roof, then shifted smoothly to the left, to get the one just gaining his footing. His initial burst put the Nibiran down, but he was still moving, so Po gave him another. He confirmed the kill, then shifted his aim to one of the Janus that had the First Squad Marine pinned behind a crate.

Paisley was kneeling to his left, then, and together they swept the roof. Two First Squad Marines died as they fired, but together, they cleared the roof of hostiles. Po was swapping out a mag as Paisley fired his last shot.

Neither of them spoke a word of congratulation to the other. Instead, they shifted their attention to the overhang, readying themselves to greet their next visitors.

Their action gave First Squad a moment to recover, but the insurgents weren't done. Eleven pairs of cloth-wrapped feet fell into view, and these were quicker than the two Po had neutralized, who'd probably had a false sense of security from the havoc their fellows were already inflicting on the roof.

These newcomers swung onto the building almost as one, and while the Marines managed to take out five of them before they could properly gain their balance at the roof's edge, seven more were already grappling down behind them.

Po depleted another mag and swapped out a third. "Staff Sergeant," he managed as he reloaded. "Can Foxtrot come up to play?"

"Negative. Janus is rushing our position from the ground. Two of them have already made it inside."

He didn't bother answering, just gritted his teeth and kept shooting. The nine remaining First Squad Marines had backed up across the roof, gaining clearance and finding cover, but the Nibirans were half-crazed. Po wondered if To'sheth Rin might have ordered some powerful stimulant distributed to them before battle. In the insurgents descending on the rooftop, he saw his own bloodlust reflected back to him tenfold. It didn't matter how many of their fellows whose bodies they found littering the rooftop; they charged across it, brandishing knives or wildly spraying rounds at the Marines' positions. Another First Squad Marine went down.

Gomez stepped between Po and Paisley, standing in the center of the doorway to get a clear shot. He was more or less exposed to enemy fire from that position, but they needed the assistance, so Po didn't argue. Either way, for now the Nibirans were drawn to the First Squad Marines shooting at them from across the rooftop.

"This can't last," Krikorian said from behind, sounding resigned. "They keep coming. They'll overrun us."

Po shot a frown back at him. Krik had no safe line of fire from where he stood, and if Po, Paisley and Gomez moved ahead to make room, they'd be exposed to enemy fire.

"You and Taylor go meet the Nibirans that'll be coming up the stairs. Unless Young wants you somewhere else."

"Yes, Team Leader." He and Taylor turned and hustled down the stairs.

But they left Po with a pit in his stomach, and a feeling of emptiness in his chest. His earlier euphoria had evaporated, and it felt like he'd swallowed a stone that had gotten stuck halfway down his esophagus.

A Nibiran reached a First Squad Marine and dragged him out from his cover. The Marine reacted, pulling back and prevailing against even the Nibiran's obviously drug-fueled strength. But before he could withdraw behind the barrel he'd been crouching behind, two insurgents focused their fire on him, and some of the rounds got through his armor. The Marine fell to his knees, clutching at his neck as more rounds battered the front of his suit, finally felling him.

We need help. Someone, please help us.

Po didn't want to die, and to his shame, he found himself trembling slightly at the prospect. He took a moment to breathe, and steady himself.

He wanted to survive—to do what he could for Nicky and Marco. Even if he was basically estranged from them now. He realized that he still wanted to live, if only for them...and for his brothers still alive, in front of him, in the next level down, and in the streets below.

He aimed at one of the Nibirans charging across and missed, even though his target was just a couple meters away. The insurgent almost reached another First Squad Marine, but fell to a burst from Emery, fired crosswise.

A hissing sound reached his ears through the din, probably singled out and amplified a little by his implant, as it sometimes did with battle sounds the AI identified as worth bringing to his attention. The sound grew louder, and Po took a moment to wonder what it was before refocusing on another Nibiran landing on the roof's edge.

"AC-900s incoming," Young said over the platoon channel. "A lot of them."

Po's heart leapt. *There's a chance, then.* The Corps hadn't tried a dedicated bombing and strafing run since Eremus, where Janus had employed much better surface-to-air launchers than they'd been known to have.

But it had become a fact of the war on Nibiru that the Marines had abandoned such runs...and hopefully, that had lulled Rin into a false sense of security. Maybe the insurgents hadn't brought many SAMs with them to Gomorate. *Probably* they hadn't, since they would have been next to impossible to transport with them under their makeshift, walking tanks.

The building vibrated and then shook beneath them as the gunships dropped their deadly payloads closer and closer, illuminating the night with flashes and punctuating the din of combat with explosions. Few fires sprang up, since Gomorate lacked much that was combustible, but Janus had to be feeling the effects of such punishment. Even if they were hopped up on amphetamines, or whatever Rin had fed them.

The Marines fought on for control of the rooftop, but with renewed vigor. At first, the insurgents came at them just as furiously as before, in the same numbers. But then, little by little, the assault from above tapered off. Until all at once, it fell away completely.

Their work was far from done. The streets below still teemed with insurgents, and now they were desperate. No SAMs had gone up, which had to mean that Po had been right about the insurgents not having them. With the arrival of the gunships, their fate had been all but sealed, and they had to know it. Some of them might escape Gomorate, but most likely wouldn't. They fought like wild animals trapped in a corner. Wild animals on drugs.

As Second Squad and the remnants of First Squad defended the building chosen by Gunny Emery, the news came over the coms that the secret insurgents had had minimal success against the Gomorati Army soldiers they'd turned on. Now that the GA had either killed or captured the moles that had popped up in their ranks, they became the anvil to the Corps' hammer, against which many a frog-dog was struck.

It still took an eternity, but a moment finally arrived when the shooting in the street in front of their building dried up. They'd kept a watch on the rocky overhang above, but no more Janus had tried to rappel down it. Fighting still raged in parts of the city, with the cough of rifle fire reaching them intermittently, occasionally punctuated by the hiss of an RPG. But the stronghold that was this apartment building had held firm, and now 131st Platoon enjoyed an oasis of calm amidst all the carnage.

For now, they were forced to stay here. With all their wounded and dead, there would be no sallying forth to make the remaining Janus pay even harder than they already were. No one in either squad suggested abandoning their brothers, not for any reason. If the thought crossed anyone's mind, they kept it to themselves.

"I'm out of bandages," came Drobnic's cry over the platoon-wide, mere minutes after the fighting died down. "Bring me whatever rags you can find."

Po started rifling through bins and drawers in the apartment they'd been shooting from. The first two places he checked held nothing—the occupants had either cleared them out before fleeing, or they'd never held anything in the first place.

The third place he checked was the drawer of a bedside table, and when he opened it he froze in place, staring at the sole object it contained for a long time.

It was a Rosary, with beads of marbled blue stone, plus a medal, and a golden cross that dangled from it.

His hand shaking, he picked up the beads and brought them close to his visor. They were the very same Rosary beads he'd left in the drawer at Navarro's bedside, back in his room at the med center in FOB Longhorn. The beads Navarro had said he'd lost. Po would have staked his life on these being the exact same ones...though he couldn't begin to form an explanation for how they could possibly be here, in the middle of a Nibiran city, thousands of miles from the FOB.

It defied any explanation. Nevertheless, it seemed they'd been here with him all along.

He opened a pouch on his suit's hip, dropped the beads in, and closed it up again.

Chapter 15

What was left of 131st made their way back to the apartment complex the Marines had claimed as a barracks. Gomorate's inhabitants had yet to reemerge from their hiding places.

It was shocking, how radically the city had been transformed. A battle that had lasted a day and half of a night had turned Nibiru's prosperous capital into a smoking waste strewn with rubble and bodies. Looking behind him, out over the mountain's slopes, Po's eyes snagged on multiple buildings that had been flattened by Marine gunships, after eyes on the ground had painted them as probable insurgent shelters.

Few Janus had surrendered—and more had escaped. But most had fought to the death. As such, Marine casualties were heavy too. There were plenty being carried past on stretchers, including members of their own platoon.

Thin, tan bags lay in rows along certain streets. These were the ultra-portable body bags the Corps carried with them into battle, hoping not to have to use them. But they were ready if they were needed.

Today, they were needed. The bags laid out in rows were all full.

131st's wounded had already been carried to quickly erected field hospitals, and their dead had been taken, too. But the still able-bodied Marines trudged back toward their barracks.

Somehow, Po felt almost as tired as he had after the weeks he'd spent fighting in Eremus. He wasn't sure how that worked—all he knew was that he barely had the energy to keep pushing forward.

But there was something he needed to settle, so he dug deep inside himself, to try to summon energy he doubted he had.

He opened up a two-way channel with Paisley.

"Hey. Wait up."

The other Marine stopped, turning. His shoulders slumped, and he wavered a little on his feet. He looked just as exhausted as Po felt. The others continued uphill, either not noticing they'd stopped or not caring.

"Open your visor," Po said.

"Why?"

"Just do it." Po didn't want to talk over a channel, which might be monitored. But then, what difference did it make? Their implants could be monitored too, and their helmets might also transmit their conversation to any superior who cared to listen in.

I need to be careful how I say this.

"What?" Paisley said with his visor opened.

"You have one too, don't you?"

"Have one what?"

"A...helper."

Paisley's face remained expressionless. "What are you talking about, Abbato?"

"You know what I'm talking about. You're being *fed*. By someone. Things you shouldn't know. Aren't you?"

The other Marine studied his face for a long time. "You should get some sleep," he said at last.

Po narrowed his eyes. He knew he couldn't get any more specific than he already was. Either he was wrong, and saying anymore would expose the assistance he himself had been getting from Zanth, or Paisley was stonewalling him.

Of course he is. Wouldn't I do the same? Haven't I been?

"Yeah," Po said, nodding. "Fine." He waved toward the hill, indicating they should keep going. "Forget I said anything."

***

Po was sure he fell unconscious the instant his head hit the pillow, back in the apartment Echo Team had claimed for its temporary home in Gomorate. It also felt like he slept for about five minutes before someone was shaking him awake for his watch.

The fireteam was tasked with patrolling the city's upper streets, where the least fighting had occurred, or was likely to occur going forward. It was also the part of town where the highest-ranking Marine officers present were currently meeting with Nibiran government officials and GA generals. The risk was low, but the stakes were high. Best to stay alert.

He'd put Gomez on point, and the other Marine was unusually focused on the task of patrolling and surveying the lanes and alleys for any sign of a threat. Not that he was normally negligent, but he generally devoted at least some of his bandwidth to gawking at new things, and making naive, amazed statements that would pin him immediately as a back-system yokel to anyone who happened to overhear.

But today, he was strangely quiet.

Gomorate was slowly coming to life, and up here near the mountain's peak, you could almost believe there had never been a battle at all. As long as you were facing away from the lower slopes, anyway.

The Gomorati citizens that lived in these parts seemed amazingly resilient. They were trickling into the roadways, and that trickle quickly became a flood, which parted around the Marines patrolling in single file but otherwise showed barely any sign of registering their presence. They didn't stare, hollow-eyed, like the Nibirans had at the convoy. In fact, they didn't look at the Marines at all. Neither did they offer a word of thanks—not that Po would know it if they did. He could have turned on his Circuit's translation function, but why bother? What did humans have to say to Nibirans?

The aliens might have shown a little gratitude for saving their city, but their lack of it didn't surprise him. Anti-Marine sentiment was prevalent all across the planet, and now these beings' city had been totaled—shortly after the Marines had arrived. There was no denying that the Marines had done most of the work in totaling it.

Sure, they'd destroyed Gomorate defending it from insurgents. But they'd still destroyed it. And maybe that was part of To'sheth Rin's plan, too. Maybe the assault on the capital was, at least in part, another recruitment drive for Janus.

A sigh came over the team channel, and Gomez's name lit up in the com interface, indicating it had come from him.

"What's eating you, Gomez?" Po asked him.

The Marine shook his head without turning back. "Just thinking about how First Squad lost three men. That might have been us. Could just as easily have been us on that rooftop, instead of in the apartment one level down."

"You're right. It could have been."

"They died for us."

Po hesitated, automatically reaching mentally for a qualification—to correct some slight inaccuracy in what Gomez had said. To adjust his statement, and bring it closer to truth.

But there was nothing to correct. "Yeah," he said. "They did."

He glanced over his shoulder, not really knowing why. His eyes met Taylor's through transparent visors, and he saw the fatigue there, and the sorrow. The longing. For what, Po didn't know. Maybe, to fill the same hole Po carried around with him in his own chest.

The shared look was too much. He quickly turned back, to hide the emotions that were welling up. It was incredible to consider how bonded to his team he was, and how intertwined their fates were. And yet, inside his armor, he was still so utterly cut off from them. Still so utterly alone.

It felt like a miracle that he hadn't lost any of his team, yet. All at once, he felt like a brittle reed that might break at the slightest disturbance. If he'd lost any of them—Taylor, Gomez, Krik, or yes, even Paisley—it would have broken him. He knew that beyond any doubt.

If that's true, how do I continue?

It had all suddenly become too much. He was running on nothing. They'd been fighting for months now, and the constant stress, the killing...it was eating him from the inside out. When could he expect to find rest, or peace? Was peace a possibility for him anymore?

"*Zanth,*" he typed into the message app. "*Zanth, are you there?*"

But the Emplor didn't answer him, didn't appear. He felt like he needed his alien helper more than he ever had, right then, and it was at that moment of greatest need when he failed to show up.

It's all becoming too much. The weight on his shoulders was too great, and he felt like he'd lost the ability to make sense of anything.

What did it mean that Benton had broken down, and then sacrificed himself to save the Second Squad Marines? Or that Paisley abruptly seemed to know things he shouldn't—the kind of things Po had benefited from before?

Or, what did it mean that he'd found Navarro's Rosary in a drawer in a Nibiran apartment?

He'd give it back to its owner, except for the exchange they'd had in the stairwell. Navarro had always annoyed him, but Po had to admit, throughout bootcamp and even on the moon, he'd always been there for him. But Nibiru seemed to have broken him, too. Yet another thing in Po's life that had once seemed reliable, but wasn't anymore.

He missed Nicky. He missed Dempsey. He even missed Lorenzo, who he'd been sure Benton had mentioned in the hours before his death...but then, why couldn't that have been a hallucination? It seemed as likely as anything else.

What else is left, for me? What else is there?

He felt like he was trying to catch a fistful of air. To catch his balance atop quicksand. Objectively speaking, he hadn't been at war for that long, but he already felt like it had picked him up and wrung him out, every drop.

The urge was strong just to drop to his knees on the stone Gomorate was built on. To drop, and stay there. How pathetic he would look, a big tough Marine in a SERAPH suit, kneeling there with his head hung while his team exchanged worried looks over him. But that was what he wanted to do.

What kept him putting one foot in front of the other, scanning for threats, clutching his M37 at the ready...he didn't know.

Well, he did know. He did.

It was the same thing that had made First Squad put their lives down for him.

And so he mentally shoved his thoughts to one side and focused on forcing himself to trudge onward.

One foot in front of the other.

***

Staff Sergeant Young sat on an ottoman across the Nibiran living room from Po while the rest of Echo Team was getting chow. Po sat on a couch. Both of them looked utterly out of place in their SERAPH suits, surrounded as they were by domestic, cozy furniture, all in warm colors.

Cozy for a frog-dog, anyway.

"I wanted to let you know what's going on with your Circuit footage," Young said. "From Private Benton's last moments."

Po nodded.

"I can't tell you much. All I can say is, I've passed it on, and from the little I'm given to understand, GEA's intel agencies have been putting in overtime trying to figure out what's going on in the system. Starting with you and Taylor seeing an Emplor behind the heavy machine gun that shot Paisley, and ending with this latest piece. Obviously, there's more to all of this than we're seeing. If that wasn't true, then the Nibirans could never have surprised us like they did with their attack on Cycler 3. It's also safe to say that GEA knows way more than you and I do."

"Whatever it is, it seems like it must be big. If GEA's drawing connections between the Emplor, Nibirans, the Obsidian Angels...."

"Yeah. Seems like it must be."

"I actually had another conversation with Benton," Po said. "Before the one on that street—I didn't think to tell you about it before, but you should probably pass that one up the chain too."

"Your conversation with him here, downstairs, in the temporary mess? Don't worry, it's already been identified and passed on."

Po raised his eyebrows. "Right. Good, then." An idea occurred to him, but he hesitated, fearing to say it. But he decided he needed to know. "Did you hear him say anything about Lorenzo? About my brother?"

"I did," Young said, and some of the weight dropped from Po's shoulders. Not much, but some. "He told you your brother says hi. Lorenzo was found to be a member of the Angels too, correct?"

"That's what my sister said. In one of her letters."

"Well, this seems to corroborate that. Why a member of the Obsidian Angels would say something like that, I can't say for sure. It doesn't seem advantageous to mention a known Angel when you're one yourself, and no doubt trying to keep a low profile. But Benton's behavior was erratic to begin with. It seems like something's going on with the meshmind, and his final words certainly pointed that way."

"Any ideas what that might be?"

Young shook his head. "It'd be useless to speculate."

"Yeah." Po figured the sergeant knew more than he was letting on, but it wasn't a surprise he'd want to keep it close to his chest. Young still didn't seem to fully trust Po, not after he'd lied to them, and then pulled that dumb stunt back on the moon, in the MMP's gym. His distrust apparently hadn't grown enough to warrant disciplinary action, but Po still sensed a gulf between them.

Then again, maybe it wouldn't have mattered. Generally speaking, even NCOs didn't share intel with subordinates for no reason. Not in the Marines. Not in Po's experience.

Better ask something I have a reason for wanting to know, then.

"So what's next, Staff Sergeant?"

Young waved his hand through the air. "I have as much as you do, that's confirmed. The brass doesn't invite me to their meetings with the Gomorati officials either."

"What do you have that's unconfirmed?"

At first, the sergeant only answered the question with a sardonic-looking half-smile. But after a few seconds' pause, he spoke, and the smile faded away. "Apparently, the GA expects another assault on Gomorate, hard on the heels of this one. A bigger one."

"Are you kidding me?"

"I wish I were. And I do have this from a pretty good source, actually. If the GA's intel is to be believed, Janus' new recruits are coming in waves. They don't seem to appreciate that Gomorate has teamed up with the likes of us. And there's no getting around the fact that we're responsible for most of the rubble that used to be Gomorate's historic buildings."

"Janus started it."

"And we finished it. With gusto. As usual." Young's smirk returned, but this time, there didn't seem to be much mirth behind it. "I'm sure we'll do it again. The Corps isn't taking this sitting down. Reinforcements are on the way—the higher-ups recognize how important this city is becoming. But it looks like we won't be here to enjoy round two."

"We? You mean, the boot brigade?"

"Just 131st."

"Where will we be?"

"We'll be...." Young frowned. "Put your visor down. We'll discuss it via com."

Po glanced over his shoulder, then back at his superior. "They swept this place twice, Staff Sergeant."

"Still. Can't be too careful." Young raised his own visor.

"What is it, Staff Sergeant?" Po asked over the two-way channel.

Young exhaled before answering, long and low. "My contact, who will remain unnamed, tells me the Nibirans have lost touch with two of their best agents. Agents who were tasked with uncovering To'sheth Rin's whereabouts. Their last known location was a known Janus base to the south, which the GA figures was one of their staging areas for the attack. They think the missing agents might have been getting close to locating Rin, before they got caught and disappeared."

Po sat up a little straighter. "And?"

"And, Colonel Coleman apparently wants to send the unit that's least likely to be missed by the Nibirans to investigate."

"That's us?"

"That's us. The colonel doesn't seem quick to trust the GA, for obvious reasons. So he's sending the greenest infantry platoon he can find, to go hit that base and see what we can dig up."

"The same green platoon that just turned the tide against a Janus horde, you mean? Plus a couple other things I seem to remember us doing."

"The Nibirans probably don't know about that. They were too busy getting killed by their fellow soldiers during the battle, and I doubt their intel is good enough to know about what we did back in Eremus. It's definitely not good enough for them to know what we did on the moon. Let's not kid ourselves—the colonel is probably right that sending us is his most discreet option."

"Hm."

"Plus, he knows we have a couple tricks up our sleeve. That may have factored into his decision, too."

Who can say. Po was probably being more prickly than he needed to be about 131st's standing in the Corps, but maybe that was to be expected in the wake of First Squad losing three Marines. "Well," he said, "this is all assuming any of this is more than rumor. Right?"

"Right," Young said, after only a moment's hesitation.

But Po had a feeling the sergeant was a lot more sure about this info than he was letting on.

Chapter 16

A pack of yips followed a few meters behind the remaining Marines of 131st, each one taking a turn to run to the front, bark its own name at the marching platoon, then fall back to the rear of their formation while the next took took its place at the front to bark.

"Can I shoot 'em, Gunny?" Taylor asked Emery, hefting his M37 for emphasis.

"Definitely not." The Gunny didn't bother glancing back as he answered.

"Why not? Look how much attention they're drawing to us. Isn't this supposed to be a discreet exit? It'd only take one burst to scatter 'em."

"Doing that would draw way more attention. Now cut it out."

They progressed toward the southeastern edge of the city in silence. That was the part where Gomorate's outskirts came the closest to the surrounding jungle, and the thinking was that they'd spend the least time out in the open that way. With any luck, anyone who did see them would assume they were merely headed out to patrol the surrounding area. And hopefully they wouldn't be watching for them to come back.

It'd also be good if they didn't take too much notice of our rucksacks, or all the gear we're carrying.

Whoever Staff Sergeant Young's contact had been with the inside scoop on the brass meetings with the Nibirans, he'd been dead-on about everything. It made Po think back to his meeting with Young and Colonel Albrecht, and how buddy-buddy the two had seemed. There was no question Young had connections. He was a good leader, and Po respected him, but he also clearly knew how to play the game. He'd done his share of sucking up to the higher-ups—Po had no doubt of that. It showed. He seemed to have the goods before anyone else. Which also meant his connections trusted him to keep his mouth shut, Po knew.

Then why did he tell me? That seemed to be a gesture of some kind. An olive branch, maybe. It was possible Young was actually coming to trust Po more.

And really, how could he not? Po trusted Young more, too. The sergeant had led them in and out of situations that should have killed half their number. He'd never messed up—never let anything bad happen that he could have prevented. All of Second Squad trusted Young more now than they had the day they'd arrived on Nibiru, and it had brought them closer together. Made them into a tighter fist. A deadlier weapon.

Today, though, no one was very talkative. Po hadn't known the Marines that First Squad lost as well as he knew the boys in his own squad. But he felt the loss keenly all the same.

Rogers. Philman. Ross.

Their names had been marching through his head on a parade loop. There were gaping holes where those Marines had once stood. Tears in the fabric of the family that 131st had become. Every one of these Marines would die for each other. If that hadn't been true back on *Gear Issue*, it was now. They'd proved it to each other time and time again, and the bonds that resulted from that glued a unit together closer than any group of men would ever find themselves, out in civilian life. These were bonds of life and death, closer in some ways than blood.

Closer than Lorenzo ever was to me, that's for sure. Closer than Luca.

Someone might as well have stabbed him through the heart for each Marine lost, and he knew his brothers felt the same. They were silent in their grief, but they were also silent in their lust for vengeance. More than ever, they all wanted Rin. They each wanted to be the one to kill him. Not just for the glory. Not just for the notoriety.

Yes, those things. But most of all, to avenge the oceans of Marine blood that monster had spilled.

131st was down seven Marines in total. Four more First Squad men had been injured too badly to come on this mission, making seven casualties...but Navarro *had* joined them, bringing their total to twenty-four.

Po found himself glaring through his visor at the back of Navarro's helmet. The linguist had been attached to 131st in case any talking with the enemy needed to be done, though Po certainly didn't plan to do any.

He still hadn't settled things with the other Marine. And he hadn't yet given his Rosary back, whose strange appearance he still couldn't make sense of. Either way, he and

Navarro hadn't had the chance to talk since right before the battle for Gomorate, in that stairwell.

But we will.

Navarro's words from that day echoed in his head, crowding out the repeating names of the fallen Marines for a moment: *You'll get involved when it's me disciplining a FOBBIT for breaking protocol, but you wouldn't lift a finger to help the Nibiran that merc beat into a bloody pulp. And I'm supposed to take* moral instruction *from you?*

Those words still rankled. Mostly because they were true.

"Hey, Paisley," he said over a private channel. "Why'd you stop me from getting involved that day?"

Paisley glanced sideways at him, confusion showing through his visor. "Huh? What are you talking about?"

"Back at the mining outpost. When you held me back from stopping that merc."

"Oh." Paisley shook his head dismissively. "Get over it, Abbato. Man, how you hold onto stuff."

"Seriously. Why'd you hold me back?"

"For your own good."

Po sniffed. "I could have taken the merc."

"Yeah? And then what? Get discharged? Kiss your freedom goodbye?"

"Freedom? How much freedom do we have in the Corps, exactly?"

"A lot more than you'd have in simjail."

"And what about the one the merc was beating?"

"The frog-dog? What about him?"

"Would have made a difference to him."

Paisley turned to look at him again, smirking. "So what? Why would you even *think* about throwing away your career for a frog-dog?"

"Because it was the right thing to do."

"From whose perspective? Don't you think you'll have the chance to do a lot more good out here in the Marines than you would have in jail?"

Po fell silent. Paisley had a point, he knew, but it also didn't seem like the whole story. Sure, Po knew he was doing good in this war. But there was bad, too. And when higher-ups were willing to turn a blind eye when people like that merc did what he did...well, that could only lead to more of the same.

"You really need to brush up on the Emancipation Doctrines," Paisley said. "If what other people are doing doesn't affect you, then you shouldn't interfere. Sometimes it's hard to watch others do what they do, sure, but it's actually a spiritual crime not to grow into everything you were meant to be. That means accomplishing all things, *experiencing* all things, enjoying all things. Landing yourself in a jail cell is the opposite of that."

Po continued not to speak, and Paisley didn't add anything else. Normally, this would be the perfect time for Zanth to appear, stalking beside him and affirming everything Paisley had said, but for some reason the Emplor was absent, and had been since before the fight for Gomorate.

***

It was the first time Po ever had to sleep outside in his armor. The cave system where the GA claimed Janus had established itself was almost a two-day march south, and taking an APC or getting a lift from an AC-900 would have drawn too much attention. So they were hoofing it, and Po and his fellow boots were getting a taste of what it was like to try to catch some shuteye on the jungle floor while wearing a SERAPH suit.

Sure, he'd slept in his suit before—inside the APC they'd taken from Longhorn to Gomorate, with his head leaned back against the wall. Like in the APC, he left his helmet on now, both for comfort and for fear of ants crawling inside his suit again.

He'd figured stretching out on the ground would be better than sleeping sitting up in an APC bucket seat, but he was wrong. The suits really just weren't designed for it. They were too stiff, and they wouldn't let his back settle onto the ground the way it wanted to. Then there was the constant fear of an enemy patrol coming across them. And the reluctance to ever let himself go completely, in case he needed to be up, alert, and shooting in seconds.

When Crotty shook him awake for his watch, it almost came as a relief.

"Hey," Po said to the other Marine as Crotty settled down where he'd been lying. "This is reminding me of something. Remember back in Cycler 3? With you making the fire watch schedule?"

Crotty chuckled. "What a thankless job that was."

Po nodded. "Good prep for becoming a Marine, then."

He checked over his M37, then started doing circuits around the perimeter of the camp. It was him, Drobnic, Zapletal, and Taylor on patrol, and they exchanged nods whenever their paths crossed.

On Po's third lap, he came across Navarro sitting on a trunk of one of the jungle's giant mushrooms, which had fallen, its enormous top half-buried in the damp ground. In his suit, Navarro was heavy enough that he'd sunken into the trunk's spongy material. He had his helmet off, and his head was in his hands.

Po kicked the base of the mushroom's trunk on his way back, making the whole thing wobble and jostling Navarro even more than he'd meant to. It brought a smile to his lips.

"Whoa," the other Marine said, hands flung out as he used his feet to steady himself. "You want something? You could have just spoken."

Po raised his visor and shot him a vicious grin. "Oh, don't mind me. Just doing scumbag stuff."

Navarro squinted at him. "Okay...."

"You having trouble sleeping?" Po kicked the enormous mushroom again, harder. His boot sank deeper into the thing, and it shook hard enough that Navarro was bounced to his feet.

He turned to face Po. "Do you wanna talk about something?"

"Well, you wouldn't listen anyway, would you? I know you're not interested in taking any *moral instruction* from me."

"Am I missing something, here?"

"I don't think you miss much, Navarro. You sure don't miss that FOBBIT walking and eating. Jumped all over 'em like you thought you were Colonel Coleman."

"What FOBBIT?"

Po stared at him. "The one you were chewing out in the stairwell. Making out like you were gonna beat him."

Navarro shook his head. "Po, I honestly have no idea what you're talking about."

Eyes narrowed, Po walked over to the other Marine, stopping just a few inches away from him. "Right before the battle," he ground out. "In that apartment building we took over for a barracks. In the stairs leading down to the mess."

"I wasn't at any apartment building, Po. I was with the colonel, translating for him as he planned out the battle with Janus."

Po watched Navarro's face carefully for some sign he was lying. "Prove it," he said after a few seconds. "Send me the Circuit footage."

"I can't," Navarro said slowly. "It's classified. You know I can't share a conversation the colonel had with a GA general."

"Of course you can't. Liar."

"You can ask the colonel yourself, once we get back. I don't know what you saw, Abbato, but that wasn't me."

Po found his breathing coming faster and shallower as he stared at Navarro's face, waiting for him to break, to let on he was lying through his teeth. But he wasn't breaking. And Navarro was studying him right back, wearing an expression of increasing concern.

"How have you been feeling lately?" he asked.

"Feeling?"

"Yeah. Are you feeling...down, at all? Like you're losing hope? Are you getting any intrusive thoughts?"

Po turned away abruptly, wincing. "You sound like the quacks in the med center back in Cycler 3. You trying to diagnose me, now?"

"No, actually. I think you might be under attack."

"Attack?" Po said. "Obviously I am. We're always under attack. Janus is lurking behind every rock, under the shadow of every tree, or they might as well be. Waiting to try and kill us."

"That's not what I mean. Janus is not the greatest danger on Nibiru, Po. I'm talking about spiritual attack."

Suddenly, Po didn't want to hear what Navarro was saying. "Don't bother me with this stuff again. It drives me nuts."

"Me too...just, in a different way." He sighed. "I haven't seen a priest in months. I don't know where they all went—I guess the Corps moved a lot of the chaplains to a more peaceful base when things got hairy. But I haven't made a confession since I rejected the faith, while I was recovering in the Longhorn med center." Navarro winced too, but he looked even more miserable than Po felt. "I'm in the exact same danger you are, Po. We both need His mercy right now. Our lives are utterly dependent on Him."

"My life is completely dependent on this." Po raised his M37C.

The remark made Navarro look even sadder. "That's not the kind of life I'm talking about."

Po felt so done with this conversation. So done with Navarro. He pulled the Rosary from the pouch where he'd been keeping it, holding it out to the other Marine, the beads dangling from his gloved hand.

Navarro stared at it with furrowed brow, then turned his gaze to Po's face. "You're the one who took it? From my med center room? Why?"

"I didn't take it," Po spat. "I found it in Gomorate. In the building where Janus attacked us on the roof, where we lost the Marines from First Squad. "

A long silence followed. "I don't believe you," Navarro said at last.

"And I don't believe you weren't in the stairwell that day. I also don't care whether *you* believe me. Just take it. I don't want it."

Navarro reached out his hand, which trembled slightly. His fingers closed tenderly around the beads. His eyes met Po's again. "You're on your way, Po. On your way to Him. That's why they're attacking you. That's *when* they attack. When they sense you might finally depart from the broad path that leads to destruction."

"Give me a break," Po said, turning to stalk away from Navarro, switching to the team channel as he did. "Hey, Zap. Switch places with me."

"Why?"

"Just do it, would you?"

"Yeah, okay. Fine."

On his new route, Po ran into Zanth, who sat cradled by a thick, twisting branch that snaked from near the base of one of the strange trees.

"Did he really say you're dependent on *mercy*?" the Emplor asked, a mocking smile stretching his lips. "Really? Out here? This far out in the solar system? Surrounded by insurgents thirsty for your blood?" He chuckled.

Po narrowed his eyes at the alien, partly in suspicion, partly out of resentment for another prolonged absence. "Yeah, actually. He did."

"Don't tell me you take him seriously. Don't tell me you think *Navarro* has the answers. He's just another foolish human who thinks he's in touch with something deeper."

Po didn't answer. He knew he should continue on his circuit around the camp, continue patrolling, but he was afraid Zanth would go away again. As much as he hated to admit it, the Emplor's keeping away for so long had scared him.

"Why do you think we came to this backwater system?" the Emplor asked. "For the good of our own health? For our amusement? Trust me, there's *nothing* about this system that is to our liking. We've come because we *are* in touch with something deeper. The prince sent us to you. To lift you up. So that you monkeys can start actually living."

"The *prince?* Who's that?"

"The one who sent us with the Emancipation Doctrines. He even sent me to you. Because you're talented, and because you have the potential to have an impact on your species' destiny. But also because you're apparently too thick to get what you need from the Doctrines on your own. That's why I'm here, to hold your hand, to *drag* you if necessary—to the truth that will serve you best. Navarro thinks you need to be all things to all people, but it's exactly the reverse. All people can and should be all things to *you*. The world can be made all things to you, and for you. But you must make it so. And I'm here to help with that. If only you'll let me in."

Po's breathing was coming faster again. His tongue felt tied. He didn't know what to say.

Zanth sneered. "Navarro said to ask the *colonel* whether he was with him, when you get back to Gomorate. Because of *course* Coleman will be happy to take time to provide an alibi for a *private* to a *PFC*. Perhaps he'll invite you to tea so that he can do this, yes?" The Emplor laughed again, so loudly that Po cringed instinctively, fearful the others would hear. But of course they wouldn't. "There's an easier way to confirm whether Navarro is a filthy liar or not. Simply watch your Circuit footage."

Zanth vanished the instant he finished uttering his final word, and Po started, fear suddenly filling his chest.

Still standing there, he took the Emplor's advice. He navigated to the moments before the battle for Gomorate, in the stairwell, just after speaking to Benton in the temporary mess.

And there was Navarro, berating the FOBBIT, whose fear was plain and real on his face.

But Navarro had seemed so earnest in insisting that he *hadn't* been there.

As for Po...

...he had absolutely no idea what was going on.

All he knew for sure was that anxiety was raging within him now, threatening to tear up his insides.

Chapter 17

Courtesy of the agents the GA had lost track of, 131st had a roughed-in layout of the Janus cave base—a drawing which someone had scanned into the platoon's closed Circuit network. Apparently one of the two super-spies had managed to send the sketch back to Gomorate before they'd gotten themselves captured or killed.

Delta Team was taking on the base's front door with what remained of First Squad, and Staff Sergeant Young had ordered Po to take Echo and Foxtrot around to the southeast, to stake out a hole in the ground which intel suggested the insurgents had been using to bring in supplies without attracting too much notice.

Well, they failed at that. Po was pretty sure a platoon of Marines showing up on your doorstep qualified as "attracting too much notice."

"What are the chances we get to do anything on this op?" Taylor asked from his position behind a fallen tree to Po's right. His M37's muzzle poked through a gap in the tangle of branches.

"Coms discipline," Po said, without much emotion. He wasn't in the mood to chat, and he hadn't established a channel between his team and Foxtrot so he could listen to the other Marine whine.

Young's voice broke over the platoon-wide. "The Nibirans are pushing back hard on our end," the sergeant said, sounding a little breathless over the chatter of weapons fire in the background. "Now would probably be a good time to poke your nose in for a look, Abbato."

"Copy, Staff Sergeant," Po said. "Foxtrot, you're up. Echo will cover."

"Aw, come on," Taylor said.

"Shut up. Last time I say that."

Foxtrot emerged from their position, with Zap on point, which his team had learned to yield to him automatically by now.

"Heads on a swivel," Po told his team, and followed his own advice. He ignored the cave mouth, confident Zapletal's team had that covered, and instead scanned the surrounding jungle for any sentries Janus might have posted.

If they *did* have any sentries nearby, then that didn't say much for Nibiran situational awareness. Sure, Po had led his team to this back entrance as stealthily as he could manage, but if a sentry had failed to notice them by now, then that wasn't an insurgent whose career prospects looked very bright.

Foxtrot crossed to the ingress without incident, but Po still wasn't willing to take that at face value.

"Taylor and Krik, you're staying out here to watch our six." Po maintained eye contact with Taylor as he gave the order, silently daring him to complain. But for once, his teammate kept quiet. Not that he looked happy about it.

Po, Paisley, and Gomez joined Foxtrot inside the cave, which ran north-northwest from the mouth, opening up into a tunnel wide enough for three Marines in SERAPH suits to walk abreast.

"Hey, Zap."

"Yeah, Abbato?"

"If you lend me Holmes, I'll let you keep point. At least until this thing opens up more."

Zapletal chuckled. "You got it."

Holmes fell back, evening up the two units to four each. Po didn't need to tell the Foxtrot boys leading the way to be ready to drop if they encountered resistance. They would if they did, likely without thinking, and then together they'd unleash havoc on the cave system's defenders.

Except, resistance was minimal as they moved through the base, clearing branching tunnels as they went to make sure no one came at them from behind. And the GA agents' intel was proving good. They found multiple 'supply rooms' in a row, just as the map said they would, each one a shallow protrusion off of the main branch of the ingress tunnel.

"The tunnel narrows up ahead, Abbato," Zapletal said. "Right before opening up into a cavern."

"Copy. Stack up as if you were breaching a room, then move in. Slow is smooth is fast. But we're also not looking to waste any time."

"Understood."

Foxtrot came under a smattering of fire as they moved into the cave, but their armor deflected all of it, and Zapletal and another of his Marines pincered the offending Nibiran's position behind a stalagmite, neutralizing him.

"Seriously?" Holmes said. "That's all they left to guard this end?"

"Guess they really didn't expect us to find the back entrance."

Po nodded. "It *was* pretty tiny. If we didn't know to look for it, we probably wouldn't have." He swung his head to peer into the dimness to his left, using thermal to scan for hostiles. "Stay alert. There's some chance that'll draw some Janus away from trading shots with the sergeants at the main entrance."

He posted Foxtrot to watch for insurgents coming from that direction. But as he and the others cleared chambers that projected from the rear of the big cave, they met with no further pushback.

Back here, there were sleeping areas, including a spacious one with only one cot, presumably reserved for the enemy commander. There were rough wooden tables, gnarled and twisted and clearly made from trees the aliens had felled nearby. They were low enough for them to sit on the ground on ragged, filthy-looking mats to eat. No food had been left out, at least.

In the last chamber they checked, they found sections blocked off by iron bars driven straight into the rock to create cells. Most of them were empty, but behind one, they found a haggard-looking Nibiran who stirred from where it lay on the floor to rise unsteadily and stare at them with bloodshot eyes. It resembled a dachshund to Po, with its long, elegant nose and triangular head.

"This is new," it said in a feminine-sounding voice, looking Po up and down. "Humans?"

Po willed his visor to lower and met the Nibiran's gaze. "That's right. Are you Ara Darshim?"

"I am," the alien said hesitantly, clutching an iron bar for support. "How did you know that?"

"I've been using your map to get through this place."

Darshim paused. "Humans working with Nibiran intel. Much has changed, I see, since my captivity."

"Yeah," Po said, glancing over his shoulder, knowing he needed to keep moving. "I find it hard keeping up too, and I haven't been locked in a cave."

"The map was Omal's handiwork. He has a talent, does he not?"

"Omal Rin. Right? Your fellow super-spy." Rin seemed like an unfortunate name to bear, and apparently Omal was indeed a distant relation of To'sheth's. The Nibirans claimed he was ashamed of his fourth cousin or whatever, and all the more motivated to help track him down for the blood relation. Po was surprised the GA had trusted a Rin, but he supposed it had been working out well enough so far for them.

Darshim wasn't answering, and Po narrowed his eyes at her. "They didn't mention you could speak English."

"No? And does GEA make a habit of publicizing the entire resumes of *its* intelligence agents?"

"Honestly, nothing would surprise me. Is there an easy way to get you out of here?"

Darshim shrugged. "Kill enough Janus, and you might find the key." Her moist eyes fell on the giant, medieval-looking lock.

"Understood. Well, I'll be back." Po turned, lowering his visor and speaking over the Echo-Foxtrot channel as soon as it was closed. "Holmes, stay here and watch her." *No reason to be naive.*

Holmes nodded, then positioned himself against the cave wall next to the entrance, facing the captive Nibiran but focused on the entry into the jail. Satisfied, Po motioned for Paisley and Gomez to follow as he rejoined the Foxtrot boys in the larger cave.

Reunited, the seven Marines advanced through the darkness, rifles up and footfalls light as they rounded a bend into an even larger section which began to ascend steadily.

Already, the SERAPH suit's enhanced sensors were bringing Po the sounds of combat up ahead.

"Easy," he told the others. "Nobody advance past my position."

He came to a divot in the cave floor, which allowed him to stay concealed while he eased a finger over the rise. Micro-cameras built into the fingertip patched a feed through to his implant, which showed him sixteen entrenched Nibirans firing out of a broad cave mouth at Marine positions scattered through the dimness outside. He forwarded the feed to the others.

"Get up here, quick and quiet," he ordered the six Marines at his back. "Find cover and concealment you can shoot at them from behind, and send my Circuit a ready-signal once you're good to go."

Inside five minutes, six green lights flooded his implant from six eager Marines. The signals came complete with which insurgent each of his squadmates was aiming at. There was no inefficient overlap.

And so, he gave the order. "Fire, then neutralize the next target to the right."

Muzzles flashed, and tracers crisscrossed the cave. Nibirans hit the ground in rapid succession, clawing with futility at bullet wounds all up their backs.

The next volley all but decimated the entrenched insurgents. Emery and Young needed no further invitation. The rest of 131st Platoon converged on the cave, mopping up the remaining defenders.

With that, the cave system was theirs.

"Good work, Marines," Emery said, clapping Po on the back as he passed by.

"Thanks, Gunny," Po said. "By the way—there's someone out back you might want to have a chat with."

***

Once he understood who it was waiting for them at the back of the cave complex, Staff Sergeant Young turned and headed in that direction right away, without preamble.

"Hold up," Emery said softly, and Young stopped and turned around.

"What's up?" he asked. "You, uh...thinking it might be a trap?"

"I left Holmes behind to watch her," Po put in.

"Anything's possible," the gunny said, as if Po hadn't spoken. "But I was moreso saying we should think about how we'll handle this conversation, *before* we charge into it like a squad of half-cocked jarheads."

"Oh," Young said. "Right. Sorry. Diplomacy's not my strong suit."

"Mine neither," Emery admitted.

Young cast his gaze across some of the other 131st Marines who'd gathered nearby. "Where's Navarro?"

"We don't need him," Po said, a little more roughly than he'd intended. "She speaks English."

The gunny raised an eyebrow. "That's a first. All right." His eyes seemed to unfocus as he stared past the other Marines into the cave's dimness. Then, his gaze snapped onto Po's face. "You spoke to her already, then?"

"Briefly." Po shifted his stance, suddenly conscious of how long he *had* spoken to her, while his brothers fought Janus at the cave mouth.

"What did she say?"

"Said she's Ara Darshim...that the other spy, Omal, drew the map we have of this place." Po nodded into the dim recesses of the cavern they stood in. "And she hinted we could expect to find the key to her cell on one of these Janus."

"That'd be this," Crotty said, holding out a rusty hunk of metal. He'd just stepped into earshot, from the direction where some of the others were searching the felled insurgents.

"Convenient," Emery said, plucking it from the private's open palm.

"Too convenient?" Young said.

Emery shrugged. "At a certain point, we have to trust that things are what they appear to be."

"Easier said than done, dealing with the Nibirans. Especially after seeing their own brothers turn on them. Think they won't do the same to us?"

"A lot of them would," Emery said. "Maybe most. But I also think a lot of this system's problems come from how suspicious we've become. Of each other, of what we're told...of what our fathers tried to hand down to us. Sure, a lot of it is bunk, but...."

"Aliens seem like something it might pay to be suspicious of," Young said slowly.

"I don't disagree. But I also know that, if we can't take Ara Darshim at her word, then we can't take any advantage from this. The whole op was pointless, and we might as well have stayed in Gomorate."

"So, we proceed, then?"

"We proceed. My boys will come too." Emery tapped Po on the shoulder. "And I want Abbato with us."

His chest swelling with a sudden pride that was probably unearned, Po followed behind the two NCOs, clutching his rifle like he was marching into battle.

"Paisley, too," Emery said, and Po deflated a little. "Never hurts to have sharp minds on deck, especially in uncharted waters."

Chapter 18

They found Ara Darshim in repose atop a pile of filthy straw the insurgents had apparently given her for a bed. Maybe that was standard furniture for Nibirans, but Po didn't think so. He hadn't seen anything so degrading to its user anywhere on Nibiru, not even in the poorest quarter of Eremus.

But she seemed unashamed by it as she tracked the approaching Marines with cool eyes. Holmes stood nearby, looking bored, and Darshim seemed fine with availing of her substandard accommodations in front of him. The presence of a couple of NCOs didn't appear to prompt any self-consciousness, either.

Even so, she rose smoothly to her feet as Emery approached the bars of her cell, holding the huge iron key so she could plainly see it.

"Well," Darshim said. She looked more steady on her feet than before. Had Holmes found her something to eat? "That was kind of the terrorists, Gunnery Sergeant Emery, to lend you the only key to my cell. Only, I don't know them to be so magnanimous. I hope nothing unfortunate befell them in the exchange?"

"She's funny," Young said. "A funny frog-dog."

"Who knows what 'magnanimous' means," the gunny mused. "Hm. Good English." He stepped closer, eyes locked onto the Nibiran. "My chevrons told you my rank, but what told you my name?"

"Your face," Ara Darshim said. "Which I matched with your entry in the extensive dossier my agency has compiled on your...organization. GA's intelligence agents have all memorized it. We don't have Circuits to rely on, and so we must use our brains instead. And how did you know I was a frog-dog?"

In the wake of the sarcastic remark, Emery exchanged looks with Young.

"Your smell," Sergeant Young said after a pause.

Darshim nodded slowly, apparently unfazed. "Is this a negotiation, or...what is this, exactly, Sergeants? Using slurs seems like an odd way to begin *fruitful* negotiations, but I'm not sure what else this exchange is likely to be. Surely you didn't come here merely to rescue me, so you must have some inkling of what I'm able to offer you."

"What are you able to offer us?" Emery asked.

"You need me to spell it out? Is it truly possible you're in the dark? That you stumbled upon this nest of Janus and decided to play exterminator for the fun of it?"

"I want to hear what you think you have," the gunny said, his voice just as level as the Nibiran's. "And how valuable you believe it is."

"I know where To'Sheth Rin is hiding. And I know *exactly* how valuable that information would be to you. You believe it could turn the tide of this war. And that it might mean the difference between survival and destruction for the Marines here on Nibiru."

"Lying about something like that could carry a hefty price tag, frog-dog," Young growled, and Emery held up a placating hand.

"What good would it do to lie to someone who doesn't trust me?" Darshim asked, some emotion entering her voice for the first time. "To do so would be to spit into the wind. Lying is only effective when one's listener expects one to tell the truth. Otherwise, it's pointless. But as it happens, I'm not lying. And so that should be our starting point."

"Mind games," Paisley muttered, from just behind Young.

Emery shot him a look, then returned his gaze to the Nibiran. "What guarantee can you give for your words? Anything?"

"Only the guarantee that believing them is your only real option."

Po exhaled sharply through his nostrils. That sounded a lot like what Emery had said, back in the cavern. But there was no way Darshim could have heard that, was there? So she really must see the Marines' situation as clearly as she claimed to.

"And what do you want from us in exchange for Rin's location?" the gunny asked. "I'm sure you're not offering the information for free, just like we didn't come here simply to spring you from jail."

Ara Darshim tossed her triangular head. "When Janus uncovered our true identities, they treated us brutally. Especially Omal. Him, they tortured, much worse than they did me. When he wouldn't talk, they brought him to Karakata, to be subject to one of their...specialists."

"Karakata?"

"You don't know it? Karakata is an underground city, Janus controlled. But then, I suppose your intel must break down, beyond the planet's surface. Even your satellites couldn't penetrate Nibiru's depths, and I doubt many of my countrymen were eager to divulge much to you."

"Omal Rin means something to you," Gunny Emery said. "Doesn't he?"

"He is the father of my child."

"Child?"

"Yes. I am *with* child, Gunnery Sergeant. That's why the Janus here didn't torture me as badly. I suppose I got lucky, there. Many Janus wouldn't let such a thing hold them back."

Emery's eyes flicked down, then back at Ara Darshim's face. "You don't look pregnant."

The Nibiran hummed, then left her cell's bars to dig through the straw at the back, carefully displacing it clump by damp clump.

There was a faint *splash*, and Po realized a small, stagnant pool lay at the back of Darshim's cell. A fishy odor permeated through the air as she approached the bars once more, carefully cradling an orange translucent orb about twice the size of a baseball. Inside, a frail-looking shadow stirred.

"There is much you don't seem to know about Nibirans, Gunnery Sergeant," Ara Darshim said. "Apparently, our intel on you is much better than yours on us. Or maybe there are certain things you simply don't care to know. Either way...in fact, I *am* with child. And this child is my everything." She held it aloft, as if displaying a jewel of inestimable value.

***

There was a prolonged silence. Several First Squad Marines traded glances with each other, shifting their stances uncomfortably. Paisley spat through his open visor onto the cave's stony floor.

Emery's eyes were on the gelatinous sphere, and his expression was as neutral as ever. "If that's your everything, then what else do you need?"

Darshim lowered the giant egg—or whatever the proper term for it was. "A child needs its father just as much as its mother. Especially, he will need him later in life, once adulthood begins to call."

"Ah," Emery said, nodding. "I see. So you want us to get Omal Rin back."

"And I don't pretend that will be easy, Gunnery Sergeant Emery. Karakata is not like this place. This base of Janus', it seems you took for yourself easily enough. But an incursion into Karakata will cost you something. Nevertheless, it is the price I demand for To'sheth Rin's whereabouts."

Paisley stepped forward, raising his M37 to eye level, aimed at the Nibiran. "How 'bout we just kill you where you stand, unless you tell us where he is right now?"

"Stand down," Emery barked, pushing Paisley's rifle toward the ground himself. "We don't operate like that, Marine."

Paisley stared at Emery in disbelief. "What are you talking about, Gunny? That's exactly how we operate."

"You're mistaken."

"It's how GEA operates."

"But it's not how we do. Safety your weapon, or I'll take it from you."

Shaking his head, Paisley complied. "Sorry Gunny, but I don't get why you'd risk Marine lives to protect a frog-dog."

Another leader might have struck Paisley, then. But Emery remained just as cool as before. "This isn't about protecting *her*. It's about what we do, and what we don't do. You took an oath to discharge your duties 'well and faithfully,' Private. I hope you thought about what those words meant before you spoke them."

Apparently Paisley had nothing else to say, and Emery turned back to Darshim. "What can you tell us about Karakata?"

"I can give you a chance of infiltrating it without drawing the enemy's notice. It's a slim chance...but it's your best one, and it could mean survival for many of your men."

"Then I'll hear of it, and everything else you have to tell." With that, Emery slid the iron key into the rusted slot, jiggling and turning it. The tumblers resisted for a second, but even the most stubborn lock couldn't withstand the SERAPH suit's strength. It would either yield, or the key would snap in half.

This time, the former happened, and Ara Darshim emerged on legs that looked shakier than they'd seemed before, as she cradled her offspring with both arms. Eying Paisley, she kept as much distance from him as she could.

Emery's gloved fingers closed around her upper arm, gently but firmly. "This way," he said. "Let's talk."

***

Dragging the bodies of Nibiran insurgents through dense foliage wasn't Po's preferred way to spend his evenings, but he supposed it was better than simjail.

Gunny Emery wanted no trace left of their fight here with Janus. That meant collecting spent shell casings, as many as their suits' sensors picked up, and dragging bodies into the jungle for burial in a mass grave.

Burying terrorists felt odd, but Po saw the logic in it. Leaving them in a pile would draw carrion feeders, which would offer a pretty massive clue as to what had occurred here to any insurgent forces that happened along. Plus, if the wind was blowing in the wrong direction, there'd be the stench to tip them off, and lead them straight to the corpses of their fallen comrades.

Burning them wasn't an option either. If they burnt them out in the open, the enemy could easily stumble upon the leftover evidence of such a large fire—not to mention the risk of drawing them a lot earlier than that, with the resulting smoke. Incinerating the bodies in the middle of dense foliage carried the same risk, with the added danger of setting the jungle ablaze as well.

And so, Po and his team, along with Fireteam Foxtrot, had been tasked with carrying the dead Janus through thick jungle and burying them.

Well actually, Echo Team was doing the carrying, and Foxtrot the burying. As Po arrived with his second insurgent over his shoulder, the alien's robes torn and tattered from catching on branches on the way in here, he paused to survey the other team's progress.

The ground was soft, with few rocks. The reddish hue of what stone there was reminded Po of Gomorate.

The SERAPH suits were as good for manual labor as they were for killing, maybe better. Zapletal and Holmes were both wielding e-tools, tossing shovelful after shovelful of maroon dirt over their shoulders and out of the hip-height hole they'd already managed to dig.

Zhang stood nearby, with an e-tool that looked like a pickax, except the 'ax' part was a shovel. It looked like a useful implement, except that the big Chinese Marine was just standing there, staring into Nibiru's dimness, which was even deeper here beneath the jungle canopy. Foxtrot's two remaining Marines were taking a breather nearby, waiting for their turn to dig again.

Po had his visor closed—the suit's climate control worked better sealed, and the jungle air was hot and muggy—and he decided not to chide Zhang over the squad channel. He opened up a two-way instead.

"Hey, Zhang, you gonna do something with that?" he asked as he lowered his insurgent onto the pile of those awaiting burial.

Zhang gave a start.

"Gunny's going to want to get moving soon," Po continued. "If you're not working, you'd better hand that e-tool off to a Marine who will."

"Sorry, Abbato." Zhang immediately began attacking the dirt, wielding the e-tool with big swings that sent dirt cascading up and over the side of the hole.

Po was going to turn back to collect the next body, but he hesitated. "Everything all right, big guy?"

Zhang paused again, drawing looks from Zap and Holmes. He shrugged. "I'm just...worried."

"Yeah? About what?"

"That little baby."

"Huh? Baby?"

"The Nibiran lady's."

Po stared at him for a second, still uncomprehending. Then, he got it. "Oh! That. That's not a baby, Zhang, it's an egg." He'd never heard a Nibiran called a lady, either—that had thrown him off for a moment.

"It has a baby inside it."

"No..." Po said slowly. "It won't be a baby till it hatches, or whatever it is Nibiran eggs do."

"What is it right now, then? If it's not a baby?"

Po stared harder, his brow furrowed. "It's...just a bunch of cells, basically."

"Okay. Well, I'm worried about that lady's bunch of cells that she has inside that egg."

"Why? It's fine."

"But we're going to attack Janus, in a city they control."

"Yeah. Just like we did in Eremus."

Zhang shook his head. "But we didn't have a baby with us, then."

"Egg."

"Whatever. What I'm saying is, we're heading into danger, and we have a mother with—"

"She's not really technically a mother yet. She won't be until she has a baby."

The Chinese Marine sighed. "Well, I don't like the way some of the others have been talking about it. Calling it names like 'frog-dog spawn.'"

"Is that inaccurate?"

"I just...I'm not sure anyone cares whether it lives or dies."

"Oh, I think they do. If it dies, Ara Darshim might not cooperate anymore."

"Abbato...we have a responsibility to her, you know. And to her...egg. Just because she's not human doesn't mean it's right to mistreat her."

"Who's mistreated her?"

"No one, yet. Aside from calling her frog-dog."

"I'm sure they have plenty of names for us, too."

"Have you heard her use any of them?"

"No. That wouldn't be very smart of her, and I think she's pretty smart."

"Hm. Well...." Zhang returned to swinging the e-tool at the ground, and dirt flew even faster than before.

Po began to make his way through the thick jungle foliage again, and back to the scene of the recent battle. He pushed branches out of the way, trying not to snap too many off.

Zhang's just a big softie. Great guy, but.... Po wondered sometimes if Zhang actually would have made it through bootcamp, if GEA hadn't been leaning so heavily on the DIs to whisk recruits through.

Still, he couldn't get the Chinese's words out of his head. He hated that. He found he was most content when his mind was essentially blank, and when he couldn't get something out of his head—whether his own thoughts or someone else's words—it drove him nuts.

Chapter 19

The journey from the cave-system base to Karakata was slow-going. Ara Darshim seemed to have a pretty good idea of where Janus was operating in the region, and the route Emery chose to minimize contact with them was long and circuitous.

"How long were you embedded with that Janus cell?" Staff Sergeant Young asked Darshim, barely bothering to conceal his suspicion.

They were trekking through a fairly open area, though one with a dense canopy far above, which let in little of Nibiru's already scant light. Emery insisted they only travel when Gnara was down, and so the Marines leaned heavily on night vision. Po wasn't sure how the Nibiran was managing not to trip, but she was, her egg nestled protectively against her hip in a sling made of cloth.

"Fourteen months," Darshim answered.

"Longer than we've been here. I see. And how much contact did you have with your GA handlers during that time?" Young's words left his mouth and fell dead onto the moist jungle floor. There was no echo here, like there had been when they'd conversed back in the caves. There was the opposite of an echo. The jungle seemed to devour every sound the instant it was produced.

"I made contact with them twice during that time. It's hard to do that, as an embedded agent. Have you ever been one?" She asked the question innocently, and her expression was innocent, too. But Po could hear the hidden implication in it.

Young ignored the question. "The GA had plenty of traitors in its ranks. We learned that when they turned on us, after Janus attacked Gomorate. I wonder how much more likely an embedded agent might be to turn coat?"

Darshim kept her peace, which seemed wise to Po. 131st Platoon trudged on in silence, their footfalls inaudible atop the living bed on which they trod.

They made camp just before Gnara-rise each day, with multiple sentries posted around the perimeter, as opposed to patrols walking circuits around it. Emery deemed that sending patrols moving about might easily attract the attention of passing insurgents, while the Marines' dark gray SERAPH suits allowed them to remain fairly hidden in the shadowed jungle, so long as they kept still.

Their progress was further slowed by Darshim's need to find pools and streams to immerse her egg in, for hours on end. Sometimes they were able to make camp where there was water, but not always, which meant they had to stop the next time they found some—for hours.

On the third day, they found no water to make their camp near, and none the following night either. The Nibiran became increasingly agitated as they walked, until at last she complained to Gunny Emery. Within minutes, the gunny had Marines digging a hole with their e-tools, three feet deep, to where the soil was so wet as to nearly be muddy. Darshim carefully lowered her egg to the bottom, then gently scooped more sodden soil on top of it. With that, they waited four hours, until she was finally content to fish it out and keep going.

Much to most of the Marines' irritation, Emery seemed to be doing everything he could to accommodate Darshim. This deep inside insurgent country, everyone was already on edge, and sitting around while the Nibiran soaked her egg wasn't helping. There were a lot of dark looks exchanged, though not a lot of open complaining. Po wasn't sure how much was being done over private channels, exactly. He would have thought the knowledge that their implant feeds could be reviewed any time might prevent that altogether, but he was wrong, given that Taylor and Krikorian both complained to him directly over two-way channels.

"Remind me again how this frog-dog getting knocked up on the job became our problem?" Taylor asked, meeting Po's eyes through their transparent visors one morning, as they were once again making camp.

Po tried his best to conceal his sigh. He felt his teammate's frustration, but it was his job to represent his superiors' interests to his subordinates—and that's what anyone reviewing *his* Circuit footage would be looking for.

"Do I really need to put this together for you?" he said.

"Please," Taylor answered.

"The whole reason we're going to Karakata is to save Darshim's boyfriend, so that she'll tell us where To'sheth Rin is. Do you really think she'll do us that favor if her baby dies because we were in a rush?"

"Her *baby?* Thing's a fetus encased in Jell-O, Abbato."

Po paused, then gave himself a shake. "Her fetus, then. Her egg. Whatever. Either way, you know she wouldn't be happy if it died."

On their fourth day, near the start of the march, Young drew up beside him. "How you holding up, Abbato?"

Po glanced at his squad leader. "Huh? As well as anyone, I guess."

"Yeah. I reckon you are." Young offered a grin through his visor, which looked a little forced—or stiff, or something.

"Uh...thanks? Thanks, Staff Sergeant."

"Listen, I wanted to say...you've been doing good work, here on Nibiru. Gunny's been talking you up a lot, ever since we left Gomorate, and you know what, he's right. After the thing on the moon, I wasn't sure about you, and I still haven't changed my mind about what happened there. But you've shaped up, since then. So, good work."

Po nodded slowly. "Thank you, Staff Sergeant. That means a lot. Seriously."

"Don't let it go to your head too much. But, well, the colonel's been pushing us to start handing out some field promotions. He's worried that we have so few men who can step into squad and platoon leader positions, if the need arises. I'm putting your name in for lance, and I have zero doubt Gunny Emery will back me up. Just wanted you to know that."

Young clapped him on the back, and moved away, leaving Po with a smile spreading slowly across his face.

Well then, he thought, already willing himself to stop grinning like an idiot. *How about that.*

***

Until now, Po hadn't thought it was possible for a stench to be so fetid that it defeated his suit's filtration and seeped inside. But the trench 131st Platoon currently waded through, filled with chest-high Nibiran sewage, had finally destroyed that assumption.

This was Ara Darshim's "secret" for infiltrating Karakata. The original architects of the cave city had planned for its inhabitants' effluent to ooze down several enclosed pipes and open, smaller trenches, to a larger trench at Karakata's lower end. The big trench fed into a broad tunnel that eventually spewed into a swift-moving underground river, which sprayed into a large lake a kilometer away.

Works well enough, I guess.

At least, it seemed a lot better than letting refuse collect in large piles throughout the city. But it also seemed less automatic, less out-of-sight than the waste reclamation system he was used to from growing up on Psyche. He knew it kind of came with the territory of being a less-advanced species, but that was harder to fully appreciate while he was covered in the reeking byproduct.

The SERAPH suits truly were designed to operate in any environment. Accessing the underground river had required diving into the lake it fed into, and right before that, Po learned the suits had built-in buoyancy compensator.

Well, he hadn't *learned* it then, technically. The fact *did* ring a faint bell from the countless classes he'd endured on the suits, back in School of Infantry. But he'd definitely forgotten about it, and the inflatable bladders, fed from the suit's air supply, were unobtrusive enough that he hadn't had cause to think about them until today.

With the bladders deflated, the suit had negative buoyancy—which was to say, it sank like a stone, heavily enough that Po had been able to trudge along the lake bottom, with excruciating slowness.

At partial-inflation, he became very aware of the air sacks' presence. The function allowed for a sliding scale of buoyancy, and the ability to float at any depth.

But with them fully inflated, the bladders pressed uncomfortably against him, and he rocketed toward the surface. Thankfully, he managed to deflate them to negative buoyancy again before he actually broke the surface. Splashing around in a lake was the kind of thing that might attract unwanted attention, and which seemed certain to attract the wrath of one of the sergeants.

Once they'd passed the mouth of the underground river, varying levels of buoyancy were called for. Sometimes, it made sense to fully inflate the bladders, to bob along the roof of the underwater cave, pushing himself along by natural handholds he found in the rocky ceiling. Other times, he fully deflated them, to use the suit's weight to hold fast to the floor of the swift-moving river while he crawled along it, finding purchase with his hands and feet wherever he could.

Eventually, the current became weak enough that he could swim against it, under negative buoyancy.

Meanwhile, the sewage system became progressively more disgusting the closer to Karakata they got. The lake bed where the river fed into it was covered in brown and green, which glistened softly in what fading Gnara-light reached it, and the water that flushed into the lake was particle-filled and foul-looking.

Shortly after entering the underground river, they were greeted by loosely held-together lumps that smacked them in the chest, arms, and faceplate.

Things only got denser and browner from there.

Then they passed the point where the enclosed tunnel fed into the river, and things reached a whole new level of disgusting.

Before, most of the foul matter had been dispersed throughout the river's swift-moving water. But here, it was a thick bog of liquid and solid waste, the latter like turgid leeches that oozed and slid around their suits. The tunnel was big enough for them to go three-abreast, and they helped each other along the uphill slog, using night vision to spot when a Marine was about to lose his footing and go under.

Here, it wasn't the current that made the going tough, but the waste's solidity. It slid against them like a thick porridge being squeezed along a giant's straw.

By then, Po had begun to appreciate the brilliance and value of the intel Ara Darshim had provided, and also to question whether acting on it was worth it.

The tunnel let into the first, main trench, and here they added the need for stealth to the challenge of pushing against the slow-moving tide of filth. Po's limbs had begun to ache deeply, even with the assistance of his suit's added strength, and he longed for the enemy to notice their incursion, so that they could climb out and engage them already.

They began encountering rusted pipes of various sizes, which crossed the trench at random intervals. Several times, the pipes were big enough—and positioned inconveniently enough—to force them to duck underneath, completely submerging themselves in the ripe muck.

As for Ara Darshim herself, she was lounging inside a concealed shelter the Marines had erected on the leeward side of a cliff near the lake. Taylor had been assigned to watch her, and Po had already cursed him multiple times for the lucky jarhead he was. When Emery had ordered Taylor to stay and watch Darshim, he'd gotten the same disappointed look he'd worn when Po had ordered him to wait and watch outside the Janus cave complex. Remembering it now, Po experienced an urge to punch that look right off his teammate's face.

They left the main trench and began wading up one of its tributaries. Po found himself studying the buildings they passed, partly to distract himself. He'd long ago turned off his night vision, since Karakata was lit by some kind of bioluminescent lichen, which had either crept across the cave's roof itself or been cultivated there by the city's inhabitants.

Many of the structures were little more than shacks, and looked likely to topple over from a stiff gale—which he supposed they didn't get too many of, down here. Surprisingly, many of the creaky-looking structures had what looked like lean-tos built against them. Nibirans were apparently so desperate to live in this insurgent-infested hole that they'd sleep under low roofs that looked far from waterproof.

But then again, there wouldn't be any rain here either—maybe just the occasional dripping stalactite. The only reasons he could think of for having structures at all in a cave city were privacy and protection—and also for increasing floor space, though most of the homes they passed looked to be just one story.

On the other hand, many buildings had far more than one story. These were the giant stalagmites Darshim had talked about—or maybe they were stalactites. It was difficult to tell. They were meters-thick pillars of rock that stretched from the great cave's ceiling to its floor. Their new Nibiran spy friend had called them cave-scrapers, and now that Po thought about it, they had to be stalactites, since they would have had to form over a long period by sediment-filled water dripping from the ceiling.

Unless the Nibirans had carved this entire place out of solid rock? Darshim hadn't given any indication either way, but considering some other things Po had seen them do, he supposed it was possible.

There was no question that Darshim had done the best she could to make this op a success. In addition to tipping them off about the sewage system, she'd given them extensive intelligence on Karakata, its population and layout, and also what public sentiment was like here. Basically, they loved Janus and hated the Gomorati government. Eremus had been divided against itself, which had made it less of a known quantity. But to hear Darshim tell it, Karakata was most definitely an insurgent hotbed.

As for the sewage system, Po had to admit that it really was the perfect ingress into the city. That a platoon of Marines would enter that way *had* to be the last thing Janus would expect. That anyone would enter that way—that they'd have either the capability or the will—couldn't possibly have entered into the insurgents' minds.

Which didn't mean it had no downsides, even aside from the gag-inducing stench. The crisscrossing pipes were also becoming more of a problem.

They came to an especially thick one, which cut across the trench and whose girth reared well above the sewage.

Gunnery Sergeant Emery felt out the bottom with his foot. "It's low enough we'd have to practically crawl to get under it."

"Any chance of crawling over?" Young asked. He grabbed a ridge where one pipe joined another and pulled himself up.

A high-pitched *creak* pierced the night, and a chorus of *yips* rose up all around them. Po froze, wincing. They all froze, and he figured they probably all wore similar expressions, too.

The sounds the Nibirans' favorite animal made always struck him as completely ludicrous, like someone with a warbling voice actually saying the word "yip." But as usual, the furry ensemble was a lot less funny than it might have been, since it was almost invariably accompanied by the worry that insurgents were being alerted of something the Marines would rather they stayed ignorant of.

Such as, for example a platoon of Marines infiltrating an underground city they held in an iron grip.

A croaking Nibiran voice called out something in the local dialect, and the yips quieted down some. The Marines all stayed rooted in place, their helmets peeking out of the vile sludge. The visors were hydrophobic, and so submerging the suits entirely wouldn't be a big deal, from a visibility perspective.

Nevertheless, not one of them seemed eager to do it.

But it seemed they would have to.

Gunny Emery seemed to relax a little, the tension visibly leaking from his body—visible even through his SERAPH suit.

"All right," he said over the platoon-wide, turning back toward the pipe. "Who's first?"

Chapter 20

The Marines of 131st Platoon ghosted through Karakata's industrial sector, which Ara Darshim had assured them would have been largely vacant for hours by now. They were prepared to hog-tie and gag anyone they could get away with not killing, and to kill anyone they needed to. But their luck seemed to have improved since the yip-provoking incident with the pipe, and so far they hadn't met anyone.

Industrial sectors always produced byproducts, and Po wondered how those were dealt with. Probably, he didn't want to know—probably, he'd just waded through a whole bunch of them, and considering the stench made it inside his suit, he wondered what other off-gases might have.

Doesn't bear thinking about, he decided.

As for smoke—well, his suit had already signaled to him that the air quality down here wasn't the best. But if the Nibirans were emitting smoke at industrial levels, that surely would have rendered Karakata's air unbreathable. So he figured they might have cut ventilation shafts through the rock, to the surface above.

Why didn't Darshim mention those? But maybe they were too narrow for a Marine in combat gear.

Or, maybe she *had* mentioned them, and they *were* big enough, and Emery had still opted for the sewer.

That also didn't bear thinking about. He liked Emery too much to let himself dwell on it.

Echo Team found itself paired up with First Squad's Bravo, bringing up the rear. Delta and Foxtrot were paired too, and so were Emery's Alpha and Charlie. Those two teams were leapfrogging each other, clearing the way, while Echo and Bravo acted as reserve, to watch the others' backs and also to move up fast if they became engaged.

Together, they were making for a thick, rock spire at the center of the industrial sector—one of the cave-scrapers, which Darshim knew to be Janus-controlled, and which she seemed sure was where they'd be holding Omal Rin.

The sergeants had tried their best to downplay it, but this was where the Nibiran's intel became a lot less certain. She'd been separated from Rin back in that cave complex, after their capture, and her conviction that he'd be in this cave-scraper was little more than guesswork. But she refused to point them to *To'sheth* Rin unless they rescued the father of her child. And so here they were, taking an enormous risk.

Had Emery made the right call, here? Would it have actually been better to try to force Darshim to give up the Janus leader's whereabouts?

Po didn't know. Ara Darshim seemed pretty tough, if he was being honest, and he wasn't sure she'd have given up Rin's location even if they tortured her. Either way, Po had to agree with Emery's thinking. They *weren't* torturers, or even interrogators. They were Marines. Darshim had proposed a trade, and now here they were. Doing what they knew, and not what they didn't.

That felt a lot better, somehow.

"I have eyes on the entrance," Young said over the wide channel. "Looks like they have just the one guard posted. Incredible. They really do think they're invincible, down here."

"Any shot at getting the drop on him?" Emery asked.

"Negative. He probably has a radio—he'd alert others for sure. But I can get him with my M126, no problem."

"And hope the silencer does its job."

"Exactly."

"There'll probably still be an echo, off the ceiling."

"Well, hopefully we're far enough away from anyone equipped to do anything about it."

A silence came over the line. "Yeah," Emery said at last. "I guess this is our play. Take the shot."

As predicted, even with the silencer, the sniper's report bounced off the cave's roof. True, their helmets' sensitive hearing meant they'd hear it before a Nibiran would, but Po still cringed and waited, half-expecting a fresh chorus of yips to break out.

Nothing came, and he was sure he heard several sighs of relief come over the com.

"Target neutralized," Young said. "Shall we?"

"You shall. Take Echo and Bravo in with you, and have them secure the back entrance. I'll keep Alpha and Charlie with me, and set up a kill box on this side."

"Copy."

By the time Po reached the lane the cave-scraper was on, Young's boys had concealed the guard's body somewhere, and Emery had his Marines positioned in windows and on rooftops surrounding the spire's entrance, each one with a line of sight on the area in front of the looming building. Po mentally took notes as he passed through, memorizing each Marine's location as best he could, a task their IFF tags made fairly easy. He'd be responsible for setting up a similar kill box in the back, after all.

"No one's come out to say hi yet?" he asked, checking over his mags in their contracting slots a final time.

"None," Emery said. "Best get in there."

Staff Sergeant Young's Delta Team was already moving, even as Emery spoke. The cave-scraper's front entrance was a simple metal door, unlocked. Young yanked it open, and his team began moving through, weapons raised.

Rifles coughed immediately—three terse bursts, followed by silence.

"Clear," Crotty said.

"Come on in, Foxtrot," Young added. "And Echo and Bravo. Water's warm."

Po entered the building hard on Zapletal's heels, feeling hyped up and ready for a fight. But the fighting was over—on the ground level, at least. Three insurgents were laid out, one for each rifle burst Po had heard.

According to Ara Darshim, the insurgents liked to keep prisoners on the top level of cave-scrapers, inside windowless chambers of stone. It was meant to induce claustrophobia, and helplessness.

Po could imagine it being pretty effective at that. Even after months on Nibiru, he still hated wide open spaces, but being cramped up this far underground didn't sound all that appealing either. Especially not at the top of an insurgent-filled tower. Even if Rin managed to escape from that, he'd still be in the middle of a Janus hotbed.

Not a cozy situation.

Wishing he were ascending the tower with Young and the others, he made his way through the ground level, feeling deflated. The building's layout was more elaborate than he expected, with sweeping, symmetrical stairs leading in opposite directions, and precision-carved doorways that led through a succession of curved rooms. It reminded him of the launch facility they'd discovered on the moon, somehow.

"Stay frosty," he told the others, and then immediately failed to take his own advice. He emerged out the cave-scraper's back entrance, where an insurgent was waiting for him with a shotgun.

Po had no time to line up a shot. He pulled back as he saw the weapon's muzzle swinging toward him, but the blast still caught his shoulder, knocking him backward and forcing him to pivot.

Growling, he used the targeting data his Circuit called up instantly to finally line up his shot, sidestep back into the entrance, and fire at the Janus who'd shot him. The insurgent staggered backward, the satisfied expression it had been wearing vanishing from its face.

He helped his enemy to another few rounds, to make sure he stayed down, then scanned the area for more hostiles as Paisley stepped confidently past him.

"You good, Abbato?" he asked, not turning to look at him.

"Yeah. Suit absorbed it." He could count on heavy bruising to come, and his shoulder already felt stiff, but he was definitely still in the fight. "We just had contact out here," he reported over the platoon channel.

"So did we," Emery answered, sounding grim. "If they didn't know we were here before, they do now. Staff Sergeant, what's your progress looking like up that thing?"

"Moving fast. We're on the third level. Encountering minimal resistance, and all from frog-dogs who look surprised to see us."

"Just how I like my frog-dogs," Krikorian muttered.

"Coms discipline," Po said, even though Krik had only spoken over the Echo channel. Po switched to the one that encompassed Bravo, too, and began directing them to the best vantage points he could see to cover the cave-scraper's back entrance—doorways, balconies, windows, and rooftops. "Buddy pairs, people. Every shooter needs someone to watch for Janus trying to sneak up on him."

Po stayed just inside the cave-scraper's rear entrance with Paisley, and they neutralized two more insurgents as the others were still taking their positions.

This is going to get heated fast, isn't it?

The idea of an entire city's worth of Janus descending on them was...concerning. A platoon's worth of Marines in SERAPH suits could do a lot of damage, but even so...trying to face an insurgent force big enough to control Karakata would mean serious losses, if not outright annihilation.

"Status, Staff Sergeant?" Emery asked over the platoon-wide, his voice sounding strained. Weapons fire came over the coms behind his voice—from extremely nearby, by the sounds of it. "We need to grab Omal Rin and go."

"Just hitting level six," Young said, and Po heard the undercurrent of annoyance in his voice. That seemed fair enough—the sergeant needed to focus on coordinating his men as they cleared room after room, each one with the potential of holding hostiles lying in ambush. "We're moving as fast as we can, Gunny."

"Understood. Move faster."

The staccato of weapons fire reached Po from what sounded like a couple streets over, and Gomez's voice followed over the com. "We can't get to the rooftop you assigned us, Team Leader. Taking heavy fire on the street which has the only entrance to that building that I can see."

"Then pull back and help secure the other positions. We're probably going to need a reserve force anyway. Sterling and Hindley, I want you ready to leave your position too, to back up another if needed."

The Bravo Marines acknowledged his order, and Po exchanges glances with Paisley. The other Marine's jaw was set through his transparent visor. They both knew what was coming.

"At least they can't use mortars," Paisley said. "They'd bounce off the roof of the cave."

Po nodded. "Silver linings."

RPGs would work fine, though. He decided not to say it out loud, for morale reasons. He was sure his Marines knew to expect RPGs.

"Rin is dead," Young said flatly over the platoon-wide.

A silence came over the line in response. For his part, Po's heart sank right to his boots. *Our reason for coming here. Our whole reason for sticking out our necks like this.*

"Dead?" Emery said, sounding as shocked as Po's felt.

"A Janus torturer must have gotten too enthusiastic. Or too frustrated. That, or they decided he'd outlived his usefulness...maybe they got what they needed from him, and decided to dispose of him."

"And they left his body in the cell?" Emery said. "You're sure he's dead?"

"He's dead, Gunny. Body looks fresh, actually—maybe they were planning to clean him up soon. But he's gone, for sure, for sure."

Emery's sigh was loud and sharp. "Very good, then. Get back down here. We need to push out."

Pressure mounted on Po's position while they waited for Young's team to descend the cave-scraper. The positions he'd assigned the others were meant to give them firing angles on the entrance, to take down an unsuspecting group of Janus come to investigate what was going on. But the Nibirans knew they were here, and his Marines found themselves shooting the other way, to pin down insurgents trying to get inside the buildings they'd set up in.

Even so, hostiles made it through, and Po and Paisley soon found themselves in a shootout with a trio of them.

"Krik, where are you?" he said. "Your position is perfect for taking out these frog-dogs me and Paisley are mixing it up with."

"Yeah, but I'm tangled up with a team of 'em trying to storm the front of *my* position."

Right. Po made a snap decision to bring his boys back to the tower, and he was about to give the order when he decided he'd better check with the gunny first.

Might mess up his plan. If he still has one.

"Go ahead," Emery said. "We won't be withdrawing in that direction. I'll keep Alpha and Charlie where they are—stand by to come and back me up if I tell you."

"Yes, Gunny." With that, Po switched over to his team's channel. "Everyone pull back to the tower. If we don't withdraw now, we're gonna find ourselves separated from each other. Krik, let those insurgents in to wander around your building. Come help us mop up these insurgents, then drop out the window and get over here."

"You got it, Team Leader."

Within a minute, two of the enemies Po and Paisley had been fighting were dead, with the other retreating.

Not for long, I'm sure. Janus members got cocky when numbers were in their favor, and Po couldn't remember a time when numbers had been *more* in their favor than they were right now.

By the time his boys were all inside, Young and his team were pounding down the last curving flight of stairs to ground level. They'd apparently done a great job of clearing the spire on their way up, and coming down had been much faster.

"We going for another dip, Gunny?" Young asked, sounding like his old calm self again—not irritated like he'd been during his ascent through the cave-scraper.

"Negative. We'd be too exposed if we all tried to jump back into that tunnel, and we'd probably swim through the river to find Janus waiting for us at the lake. Now that they know we're here, we'll use the front door."

Chapter 21

Emery's Alpha and Charlie Marines proved to be positioned as well as Po had thought they were. The area in front of the cave-scraper was completely secure—for now. Po felt confident this whole sector would be crawling with Janus inside ten minutes. They didn't want to be here for that.

"I want each team to split up and find a direction to push out in," the gunny said. "We'll all go in the direction we're getting the least pushback from. We've lost the luxury of carefully evaluating our options today."

The teams fanned out into the surrounding streets, and Po's team ended up being shot at the least. "This lane's completely peaceful," he said. "Straight, too, and narrow. Might be we can risk running along it without worrying too much about insurgents shooting at us from upstairs windows. Not seeing many windows, anyway—looks like the backs of warehouses to me."

"I'll take it," gunny said. "Everyone move on Abbato's position. Abbato, see if you can find a good spot for overwatch."

"On it, Gunny."

As it turned out, there *was* no good overwatch position...but it didn't matter. 131st Platoon charged down the lane and came out into an open plaza between hulking factories and warehouses, with another cave-scraper towering off to the left.

Emery had sent the exit's location to all of their implants as a waypoint, and their only way of making meaningful progress toward it was to cross this open space. Hugging the structures on either side would only take them perpendicular to the direction they needed to go.

"Do we backtrack, Gunny?" Young asked.

"Right into a wave of Janus? No way. We're committed, now. Spread out in buddy pairs and everyone watch your side. Be ready to meet force with force. Everyone with an M320 or M126, get 'em ready."

The platoon unfolded like a paper fan, spreading out across the plaza and jogging across, muzzles up and sweeping in all directions.

The insurgents didn't bother with small arms fire. Their opener was an RPG aimed at the platoon's left flank.

Zapletal and Holmes went down in the ensuing blast. Most of the platoon kept running, but Zhang lingered, running through the smoke toward the downed Marines.

Cursing, Po sprinted after, laying down suppressive fire in the direction the RPG round had come from. Paisley was right behind him.

Po checked the two Marines' vitals, and all at once he felt like a rapidly deflating balloon. Holmes had died instantly, and Zap was barely clinging to life, with what looked like multiple internal injuries throughout his torso and head.

"Holmes is gone," he told Zhang, pushing him away from the dead Marine's smoking body. "Grab Zap."

The big Marine bent down and lifted Zapletal onto his shoulders. Then, he hesitated. "What about Holmes' body?" he asked, his voice sounding choked.

"We can't take it right now. But we'll come back, Zhang. The Corps will come back. And if Holmes is still here, we'll get him out, just as soon as we make these frog-dogs pay."

"But—"

Rifle fire flared up, tracers *zinging* past in the dimness, and then came the hiss of another RPG being launched.

"*Run!*"

This time, Zhang listened. They sprinted after the withdrawing platoon, Po running backwards to return fire at the insurgents harassing them. At first, rounds *pinged* off his armor, each one sending a jolt through him. But that stopped as he zeroed in on the insurgents shooting at him. When Paisley saw what he was doing, he did the same.

More fire came, from more Janus positions, but by then the platoon was in place on the other side and able to return fire. Po, Paisley, and Zhang made it past the mouth of the alley 131st had secured.

Zapletal died just as they did.

"Leave him," Emery said, eyes locked on Zhang's, his voice stern.

Again, Zhang hesitated. But slowly, he lowered Zapletal's battered body to rest against the side of a building. Everything about his bearing said it was the last thing he wanted to do. But he did it.

"Let's keep moving," the gunny said.

They advanced through an intersection, then past another block of what looked like factories. According to the map Darshim had helped Emery and Young construct of Karakata, they were nearing the edge of the industrial sector, and would soon enter residential streets.

Would the fact they'd be moving through an area where civilians lived limit the insurgents' actions against them? Po didn't know, but he had his doubts. Janus recruitment did depend on public sentiment, but news took longer to cross Planet Nibiru's surface than it took humanity's rumors to span the solar system, and by the time it did, it was generally jumbled and seasoned with uncertainty.

That was his understanding, at least. Either way, the insurgents were ruthless, and apparently willing to go to great lengths to kill Marines.

But other than some harrying fire from their flanks and behind, and two RPG rounds that did minimal damage beyond causing some uncomfortably raised internal suit temperatures, the pressure from Karakata's insurgents was minimal.

"Are they holding back because of the civilians around here?" Crotty asked, his head on a swivel. So far, Po hadn't seen any Nibirans peeking out through windows, and certainly none were in the streets. But he supposed they had to be here.

"I doubt it," Emery answered. "By now, Janus knows not to take two squads of Marines in SERAPH suits lightly. My guess is they're coordinating with each other by radio to organize a larger attack."

No one had anything to comment on that, it seemed. But Po noticed his fellow Marines' movements becoming even snappier, and more efficient. The now-familiar signal had gone off in all their brains: that danger was upon them. That it was time to dig deep, and to fall back on the actions and responses training had ingrained in them. And to rise to the highest point that training would allow.

At least, the signal had gone off in Po's brain. He and his fellow boot battalioners had been in plenty of hairy situations before, and pulled through. Maybe they'd even do it again today. But there was no guarantee of that. All they could do was fall back on their training.

The harrying fire and occasional RPGs continued, coming from the same directions, as if in confirmation of Emery's analysis. They crossed much of the city this way—coming almost to the western outskirts, which wasn't far from the main tunnel that led up and outside, to freedom.

Then an RPG came from the window of a house at the end of the street they were on.

The ground ruptured in front of Gomez, throwing him back off his feet. Po stepped forward, and the rest of Echo Team followed without needing to be ordered, rifles raised and raking the offending building's windows with suppressive fire.

"Zhang, grab Gomez!" Po choked out. Zhang wasn't on Echo Team, he was on Foxtrot, under Zapletal. But Zap was dead. So Po gave him the order, and Zhang sprang readily into action.

Rifle fire came from a different building, at a more oblique angle. Some of the rounds peppered Gomez where he lay, others tore up the dirt around him. He jerked, and lay still.

Young's Delta Team maneuvered around Echo for a clear firing angle at the new enemy position, returning fire while Emery ushered the rest of the Marines off the street and into surrounding lots and alleys.

Zhang got Gomez up onto his shoulders. The latter's vitals were on the wane, with red splotches all across his back and chest, but he was still alive, and Po figured he had to continue living. He couldn't imagine a world without dumb, kindly Gomez in it. He didn't *want* to imagine it. So Gomez had to live.

Echo and Delta melted away, covering each other, and covering Zhang with Gomez while they retreated to better cover.

"Each team find a safe route around that red zone and rendezvous at the point I've highlighted on your maps," Emery said. "We're almost through, boys. Give 'em pain."

"Gunny, can I fold what's left of Foxtrot into Echo for now?" Po asked over the platoon-wide.

A moment's pause, then: "Your call, Abbato."

At those words, Po's heart swelled three sizes.

"You heard the Gunny," he said after switching to a new channel, which his implant had automatically put together after gleaning the need for it from the conversation. "Patrice, cover Zhang. Windham, take point with Paisley, keep your eyes peeled, and be ready to treat any insurgent positions to your M320. Krik, you're with me."

They made good progress down an alley, then had to hop a fence when they came to a solid rock wall. After that, they had to leap over low dividing walls between lots.

Occasionally, the ground *squished* under their feet.

"What did they do to the ground here?" Zhang asked, apparently filling in for Gomez by asking dumb, obvious questions, since Gomez was down for the count.

"Looks like they brought in organic matter from outside," Paisley said, and he sounded a lot more tolerant of Zhang's obtuseness than Po would have expected.

"Why?" There was a little strain in Zhang's voice as he passed the unconscious Gomez to Patrice, who'd already hopped over the divider they were trying to get on the other side of. Once Patrice had him, Zhang jumped into the next yard himself, then took the downed Marine back.

A glance at Gomez's vitals brought a frown to Po's lips. He was in bad shape.

"A little horticulture, I guess?" Paisley answered. "Or just making it a homier property for frog-dogs? Hey, maybe this is their spawning pool. I bet *our* frog-dog would kill to soak her spawn in one of these for an hour or two. I bet there's lots of nutrients in here for growing little terrorists."

"That's enough," Po said. "Focus."

Staff Sergeant Young spoke over the 131st channel, cutting across their chatter. "We're pinned in a covered stairwell that leads down from ground level to a locked door. Two frog-dog positions firing on us. Anyone in a place to help us out?"

Po checked the map, where Young had marked Delta's location, as well as the buildings where the insurgents were entrenched. Thankfully, their Circuits filled in the map as they went using input from every Marine's feed. If it wasn't for that, he'd be working with a lot less intel right now.

"We got you, Staff Sergeant," he said. "Sit tight." He switched over to his new team channel. "Paisley and Windham, start alternating with each other to head between houses and check the street out front for a decent place to cross."

It was a minute before Windham found one—a dip in the lane that offered any rooftop shooters only limited visibility. It wasn't perfect, but it was the best they were likely to get in enough time to help Delta Team.

"Spread out and cross. Krik, you and I are the outermost elements. Keep your head on a swivel and be ready to return fire. *Before* they shoot at us would be best."

"Hm. What you just said carries some interesting philosophical implications," Krikorian said.

"Shut up and keep a look out."

"Copy, Team Leader."

They crossed the lane without incident and cut across to the next before backtracking toward Po's position.

"Stop here," Po said at the mouth of an alley. "We have eyes on the target structure from here. Krik, set up behind that bin and scope that place with your M126, would you? See if you can spot anyone who might be about to cause us trouble."

"You got it." Krikorian stood behind the dumpster-looking object Po had indicated, which stuck out of the alley and into the street, enough that he could rest his rifle on top of it and still see the house through it.

The rifle bucked, coughing louder than Po would have liked, just as Young's had earlier, when he'd taken out the Janus guarding the cave-scraper.

"One troublemaker down," Krik reported. "I suggest we rush that place, in case anyone overheard my handiwork." He shrugged as he reslung his M126. "Seems likely enough."

Unfortunately, Po agreed. "Good idea. Let's move, Marines. Not you, Zhang. Or you, Patrice. Stay here with Gomez."

Po rested a hand briefly on the unconscious Marine's back, and with that he sprinted toward the target house with the others.

Chapter 22

There was no time for finesse.

Po had borrowed his personal motto from centuries of hard-won military experience:

Slow is smooth and smooth is fast.

But today, fast was fast, and slow was dead. They crashed into the house, pounding up a set of stairs into an open area where eight Nibirans were taking turns firing at the pinned Marines below.

Eight weapons turned toward them. Some of them went off, sending rounds ricocheting off SERAPH armor, leaving dents and the promise of bruises, but not slowing the wearer down. They could nurse bruises and lick wounds later, but right now they had brothers to save.

Spreading out, they neutralized three Janus in the first second, and two more in the next. By then, the remaining three were opening up on the approaching Marines, their bodies rigid with fear as they emitted high-pitched yelps.

Paisley spent the rest of his mag and got his target with his knife, driving it into the insurgent's chest. Windham ignored the rounds impacting his torso to approach his opponent head-on, raking the alien with his M37 until it stopped firing at him. Po felled his next target with two clean rounds to the head, before it could hit him with more than one.

"Ten seconds to clear this place," Po said as he moved to the window to check what Staff Sergeant Young's situation looked like now. He cursed. From here, they had no good firing angle on the other position keeping Delta pinned.

He patched what he was seeing through to his teammates' Circuits. "We hug the buildings to the left, then see about entering the front door of that nest. Could be we'll have to breach it." He shook his head. *What a mess.*

"All clear?" he asked. He had meant it when he'd given them just ten seconds.

"Clear as it's going to get, I guess," Paisley said.

"Then let's go."

They'd just left the house and begun to make their way along the lane Young was on when PFC Bozzelli got in touch—leader of Charlie Team.

"We just took care of that for you, Abbato. That position's neutralized. You and Delta can withdraw the way you came."

Po gave a sigh of relief. *Finally, something goes our way.* Things were getting dicey enough without needing to spend time clearing *another* house. "Thanks, Bozz. Staff Sergeant, you copy?"

"On our way."

Po led his team to meet Young's Delta boys, and then they covered for each other as they withdrew to the house he'd just had Echo clear, Delta's rifles up and sweeping while Echo moved, and vice versa.

Echo Team filed into the house they'd come from, quickly scanning the place to make sure no one new had arrived to set up shop. They took just a few seconds to make sure it was still clear, then began moving toward the back stairs they'd initially used to enter the place.

They reached the open area that made up the bulk of the upstairs floor plan. "The rendezvous point gunny set is just another couple streets ahead," Young said as he passed a large open closet, which Paisley had rechecked on his way past.

A Nibiran emerged from the closet's depths, stepping swiftly around one of two large tanks at the back, where the alien had apparently been hiding. It was holding a grenade in each hand.

"Staff Sergeant!" Po managed to yell, bringing his rifle up.

Too late.

Young began to turn to answer the threat...

But it was too late.

The Nibiran barreled into the sergeant, and the grenades went off, sending Po staggering backward.

The unarmored insurgent was ripped to pieces, and Young fell back onto the floor, with the front of his suit blackened and punctured in several places.

A ragged syllable of negation tore from Po's throat, and he stumbled forward to fall to his knees at the side of the sergeant's smoking form, hands hovering uselessly over his ravaged torso.

The SERAPH suits were incredible, and they'd produced some incredible results—like when Paisley had survived an HMG burst at close range.

But the grenades' twin blasts had been enough to kill Young instantly. His vitals confirmed it: all black. Staff Sergeant Young was gone.

All the times he'd wished for Emery instead of Young as squad leader came rushing back to him, unbidden. All the times he'd taken Young for granted. And the times he'd bucked him—caused trouble for him.

Young was a great leader. You didn't appreciate him. And now he's gone.

The temptation to give in to numbness and fatigue was strong, but he had to force himself to go through the motions of what needed to happen next.

"Gunny," he croaked over the platoon channel. "Staff Sergeant Young...he's gone, Gunny. Insurgent got him with two grenades."

A silence came over the com—one longer than Po ever would have expected from an NCO like Emery, in a situation like this.

"Then you have to leave him and push to the rendezvous point," the gunny said, again surprising Po with how level his voice was after the long pause.

"Yes, Gunny," Po said. Because there was really nothing else to say. Moments like this tested whether one really deserved a leadership role, he knew.

Young would want me to get his boys to safety.

"Let's go," he said in his best impression of Emery's calmness as he rose to his feet clutching his rifle once more. "Nothing's changed about the mission." It was a harsh thing to say, and the harshness was calculated to snap the others out of their shock at Young's fall.

It seemed to work. It got the others moving again. They hustled to the back of the house then filed down the stairs there, heads up and looking for the next insurgent willing to throw away his life to take out a Marine in a SERAPH suit.

***

Gomez was in even worse shape when they returned to the alley where they'd left him with Zhang and Patrice.

The Chinese Marine was clearly fretting about it, but to his credit, he held his peace. Talking about what they had no control over right now would only slow them down and lead to more casualties.

They reached the rendezvous point without incident. Po didn't count insurgent rifle fire and RPG rounds as "incidents," since they didn't succeed in killing or wounding any more Marines.

"The tunnel leading to the surface is just ahead," Emery said from where he crouched in the middle of the broad alley they'd met him in. "We're almost there. One more push."

"It's there according to the frog-dog's map, you mean Gunny?" Paisley said.

"That's right."

"Why are we still trusting her again?"

Emery rose to his feet, tilting his head forward a degree, as if to get a better look at the private. "The map's been one hundred percent accurate so far. And I've seen no evidence she meant to lead us to a trap. Her lover really was in that cave-scraper. Dead."

"Just feels dirty, trusting our lives to a frog-dog."

"We have literally no other option than to head up that tunnel." The gunny made a cutting gesture with a gloved hand. "Enough chatter. We cross the last open area in one big staggered line. Return fire at anything that tries to stop us."

The surviving Marines left the alley from both ends, in case one of them was being suppressed by Nibirans. Leaving from both directions allowed them to set up a quick flank if needed, but thankfully, it wasn't. Everyone made it to the open area without getting shot at, and there, they quickly fanned out into the formation Emery had ordered them to cross in.

Incredibly, they reached the broad tunnel without losing anyone else. Nothing about the tunnel's mouth suggested it led to safety, but Emery was right. They were down to their last option, and so they needed to make it work.

"This is their turf," Emery said over the platoon-wide as the Marines began to move in formation up the tunnel. "But keep in mind, they're subject to serious disadvantages. They might as well be blind and deaf compared to our suits' sensors. You'll hear them coming before you see them. When you see them, shoot them."

As always, the sergeant's words were like a shot of caffeine. Taking up the rear with what was left of Second Squad, Po found himself moving with more sureness, and scanning the receding tunnel before him with greater vigilance.

The Nibirans also seemed to appreciate the import of Emery's words, without needing to hear them. While Po *could* hear the skitter of their sandaled feet on the stone, and even their robes rubbing together—all magnified by his suit to a level that was audible, but which didn't distract—he saw no sign of the aliens. They were clearly pushing them up the tunnel, but they seemed to know better than to engage while the Marines had the higher ground.

I don't like that they're pushing us. Did the Nibirans expect to have a better chance at the cave's mouth? What was to stop the Marines from staking it out and shooting anything that emerged?

The fact the aliens were getting just close enough to keep the pressure on didn't exactly inspire him with confidence.

But as before, they were out of options. They'd been caught out in the middle of an insurgent-controlled cave city, and those still alive were lucky to be.

He realized the tunnel was lightening, but not by much. He supposed that made sense—Gnara had been going down as they entered Karakata through its sewer tunnels, and it hadn't had enough time to come back up, even if their time in the city had felt like an eternity.

Either way, suddenly, they were out of the tunnel and emerging from a cliff face onto a field where the jungle had been cut back for hundreds of feet.

For defense, Po realized. It made perfect sense. But it also suggested—

The *hiss* of multiple RPG rounds came from above.

"*Scatter!*" Emery yelled, right before one of the hurtling grenades came down right in front of him, blowing him off his feet and onto his back, three meters from where he'd been standing.

No further word came from the gunny. "You heard him!" Po yelled. "Break, and make for the trees!"

For his part, he shrugged off his rucksack and dropped it onto the ground as he ran to the gunny's side. He fell to his knees, then hoisted Emery up and over his shoulders. Even with the suit, he'd expected to strain, but with adrenaline flooding his system it felt like he'd picked up a dummy filled with straw.

RPG rounds continued to detonate all around him, but the Marines had already made themselves harder to hit by splitting up and sprinting as fast as the SERAPH suits' strength augmentations would carry them.

A round came down next to Navarro, throwing him through the air and onto his face.

Everything seemed to slow to a crawl, and for some reason Po felt too frightened even to call up the downed Marine's vitals. Despite how mad he'd been at Navarro lately, he realized he couldn't bear the thought of losing him, either.

Krikorian was the only one anywhere near close enough to help.

"Krik—"

"Don't worry," the Armenian said, already turning and running back for Navarro. "I've got him. He's going to be fine."

That was far from certain, but Krikorian scooped up Navarro anyway, and together they ran with their burdens toward the jungle as insurgents continued to rain RPGs down all around them.

How they weren't hit was anyone's guess. Maybe he'd find some answers by watching his suit's footage later. If he got the chance.

But for now, they were deep in enemy territory, completely exposed, and being chased by an enemy that already had a taste for their blood. They carried three of their wounded on their backs.

At a time like this, he reflected as he breached the treeline at last, a Marine could be forgiven for wondering if a simjail cell might have been preferable.

Chapter 23

Po forced himself to continue pushing through the jungle, his feet like lead as he lifted them from the soft, mossy ground only to plant them down again. Climbing over the gnarled, twisting trunks that often blocked his way took an effort of will each time.

The adrenaline had left his system as quickly as it had flooded it. Draped over his shoulders, Gunny Emery now felt like he was cast in bronze.

Mortar fire whistled softly overhead before crashing into the foliage all around him. Sometimes, he saw the burst of flame with his own eyes—saw the fallen twigs it set alight. Other times, the impact was nowhere near him. Did the Nibirans actually still have a bead on them, or were they firing blind?

The crackle of rifle fire sounded in the distance. A firefight between Marines fending off pursuers, he assumed. Superior sensors didn't count for much when you were fleeing for your life, and the aliens seemed to understand that. They were doing their best to press the advantage.

Back in Cycler 3, Po had been subjected to more than one surprise night march. At the time, it had seemed like just another fit of sadism on the part of the DIs, in their neverending quest to come up with creative ways to torture their charges.

But ever since he'd left the O'Neill colony—ever since the surprise attack had forced him and his fellow Marines to flee aboard the S.S. *Gear Issue*—the purpose of his old instructors' behavior had become increasingly clear. What he'd once seen as wanton cruelty, he now considered necessary preparation for a solar system that was big and ugly, and which confronted the men sent out into it with danger in limitless, unending configurations.

He hadn't even enjoyed the benefit of a SERAPH suit, during his time in the now-destroyed training base. Now he did...but the suit's strength enhancements didn't count for much in the face of exhaustion built up over days of long marches through an unforgiving jungle, punctuated by a battle and then a rout in an underground insurgent city.

He found that he didn't have much energy left over to flee in panic through that same jungle, with his only surviving sergeant on his back. From what he observed of the other Marines around him, they were feeling much the same. Many of them stumbled as they ran, their feet catching on roots and trunks, a product of being too tired to lift them high enough.

And most of them weren't carrying anyone.

"Look alive, Marines." Somehow, Po managed to keep his own fatigue out of his voice. "Dig deep and lift your legs high. The jungle isn't going to get out of your way, so you need to stay out of its."

It felt like a dumb thing to say, but it also seemed that the time for saying dumb things had arrived. They were all of them stupid-tired, and clearly shaken by what had happened in Karakata. Marines had grown accustomed to viewing themselves as superior to Nibirans in every way, even after Janus had managed to wipe out their satellites and do serious damage to their air supremacy. Watching so many of their platoonmates die—men who'd been wearing the SERAPH armor that helped make the Marines the fearsome fighting force they were—it had been a rude slap across the face. It didn't seem like it was supposed to happen.

And yet it had. It had happened back in Gomorate, mostly to First Squad's Marines, and now both squads had been ravaged.

The carnage creeps closer and closer. And it's anyone's guess who will be next.

Now they were fleeing before Janus' wrath, in the wrong direction. Running blindly through enemy territory, with only their suits' short-range coms to keep them together and pointed in the same direction, scattered as they were.

We need to be making our way back to where we left Taylor and Ara Darshim.

Or did they? Was there any point in going back there now, other than to reunite with the Marine? Would Darshim do anything for them, now that her child's father was confirmed dead?

Their end of the bargain had been to bring her lover back to her. They'd failed to do that. So what reason would she have for spending any more energy helping them?

The mortar fire fell away abruptly—first, with the rounds impacting somewhere behind him with greater and greater frequency, and then tapering to nothing as the Nibirans seemed to realize the Marines had drawn out of range. After the last mortar burst, Po also didn't hear the chatter of rifle fire anymore.

The ground angled upward before him, gradually, then more sharply. That was bad for energy levels...but maybe good for something else.

"Let's regroup on that rise," Po said, flagging it for highlighting by the others' Circuits. "Form a welcoming party for any terrorists still dumb enough to be chasing us."

The words felt hollow, in the wake of their panicked flight. But they seemed to do something for the others. Several of them appeared to step a little more smartly after he spoke.

As the others sought out firing angles along the rise, Po gave his next order. "Windham, you still have everything for the troposcatter unit?"

"Sure do." The Marine adjusted his rucksack on his back, as if in confirmation.

"Good. Take Patrice and scout ahead, check out the terrain. Have an eye for a decent spot to set up the system. If you can get above the canopy, that'd be ideal. Set it up and try to raise any other units in the area. If we get lucky, might even be an AC-900 flying somewhere in range. We need an exfil."

The two Marines nodded, then resumed their climb up the hill. For his part, Po gently lowered the gunny onto a dark patch of exposed soil, then picked up his M37C from where it hung on its strap. He scanned the trees below, his right eye looking through the scope while keeping the other open for a wider view of what was in front of him.

So far, that was nothing except many-branched trees, giant mushrooms, and the natural mulch of the jungle floor.

Were the Nibirans brazen enough to chase them beyond the range of their mortars?

If they come in enough numbers, they might be.

They couldn't stay here. Not for long.

We can't stay anywhere *in this country. Not if our wounded are going to make it.*

"Can't give you a field promotion," Emery muttered.

Po frowned down at the gunny. His vitals were still pretty messed up from the RPG round detonating a couple meters from him, and fevered mumbling seemed par for the course. Except, he wouldn't have expected Emery to transmit said mumbling over a two-way channel.

"You okay, Gunny?" It was another dumb thing to say, but apparently he was committed to saying dumb things, now.

"I'm not a commissioned officer," Emery said, sounding like he was forcing each word. "So I can't give you a battlefield promotion. But you're already acting like a lance corporal, Abbato. Already taking the lead when there's no one else left to do it."

"Uh. Thanks, Gunny."

"I'm gonna ask you to continue acting like one," Emery said through audibly gritted teeth. "This mission isn't over. I want you to take these Marines and go find Darshim again. Have her take you to Rin. And kill him."

"I'm not leaving you, Gunny. Not like you are. Same for Gomez. And Navarro."

"Get us that exfil. Then go."

Po almost snorted. He knew it was important for a leader to stay positive, but Emery's optimism bordered on the absurd. The number of things that would need to go right was staggering.

He settled on one of them. "How do we know Darshim's still going to cooperate with us?"

"She will."

"Oh. All right." *That settles that, then,* Po thought sardonically.

"A lot of the higher-ups were against this mission from the get-go," Emery said. "Colonel Coleman authorized it, but enough brass disagreed that we're all going to be in a lot of trouble if you mess this up. No pressure."

"Thanks, Gunny."

"One of their fears has already come true. We left fallen Marines behind today in SERAPH suits, for the Nibirans to study, maybe even to reverse-engineer. But we haven't left anyone for them to interrogate yet. That was their other worry. Marines know lots of things that would hurt the Corps, if an enemy tortured them out of us."

"Sounds like we're going to be in trouble no matter how this goes."

"Not if you succeed. Not if you win. Like I said, Abbato, no pressure...but killing Rin might be the only way the Corps survives this war in any recognizable form. We need to cut the head off the snake."

This time, Po didn't answer. He was too focused on the terrain in front of him, where insurgents could appear at any second. Too worried about the Marines who would probably die, if they couldn't get them help soon. Right now, talk of killing Rin seemed about as useful as wishing for a unicorn for his birthday.

But Emery wasn't deterred. "Aim to capture or kill him. He won't surrender. If he does...you must accept. But he won't."

"Yes, Gunny." Since there seemed to be no reasoning with Emery, he defaulted to humoring him.

"When you kill Rin and make it back, I'm going to do whatever it takes to get you that promotion," Emery said. "So don't screw up. And don't die on your way back."

Po found himself grinning behind his visor. Emery's irrepressibility, as ludicrous as it was, truly was contagious. He couldn't help catching it, in spite of himself.

That's what it takes to be a leader. Isn't it? Believing in your men's success, even when that belief is ridiculous.

"Abbato." It was Windham, speaking over the platoon-wide. "We contacted a gunship."

"*What?*"

"This hill tops out above the jungle roof. We set up the troposcatter and contacted an AC-900 flying almost a hundred klicks west of here. It's on its way."

"Is there...enough room up there for it to land?"

"Plenty."

Emery was looking at Po through his transparent visor, grinning much wider than Po had been. "Step one," the gunny said.

He still couldn't walk, so Po knelt and hoisted him over his shoulders once more to begin the laborious trek to the top of the jungle. The gunny didn't make a sound, even though his vitals made clear the pain from his injuries had to be excruciating.

As Po trudged upward, Navarro opened a private channel with him, sounding little better than the gunny.

"She's watching over you, my friend."

"Who is?"

"Our Lady. God's mother."

"What are you talking about?"

"How else do you explain finding my Rosary, hundreds of miles from where it should have been? God doesn't do stuff like that without a good reason. I want you to take it with you again."

"No way. You're keeping it." *Last time I took it, it didn't seem to work out too well for you.*

"I'm sending you another prayer, then. Act of Contrition. I know you've done stuff. We all have. But God is merciful, and we can't get to a priest out here. Don't go into battle again without getting right with Him first. If you're truly sorry...."

The Marine trailed off, and Po didn't answer. This hardly felt like the time to argue with Navarro, who might well be dead before they met again.

"I'm also sending you some basic phrases in Nibiran. You won't have a translator with you anymore, after this. Got a feeling I'll be taking a ride on that AC-900."

"I'd think, yeah."

"So, I highly recommend you spend some time memorizing these phrases."

"My implant knows Nibiran."

"Haven't you figured out yet that relying on your implant is a handicap? Memorize the phrases, Abbato. Trust me."

Po would have shaken his head in exasperation, if he wasn't occupied with bearing the gunnery sergeant up a thickly treed hill. "Sure thing. I can do that while I enjoy my usual snifter of brandy by the fireplace tonight."

"Funny."

A data packet hit Po's implant, and Navarro stopped talking. Either he had nothing else to say, or his injuries had dragged him down into unconsciousness.

Chapter 24

The AC-900 touched down on the hilltop in a roar of thrusters and swirling bits of foliage and dust.

Windham had said there was "plenty" of room for the gunship to land, and Po assumed he'd told the pilot the same thing on his approach, but as he watched the craft touch down he saw that the private's assessment was highly debatable.

Maybe he caught some of Emery's sunny outlook too. The fact was, the remnants of 131st Platoon *needed* the gunship to be able to land, and so Windham had apparently gone with a rather generous portrayal of the situation.

As things stood, the gunship looked none too steady, with one of its landing struts hovering in the air over nothing. The craft teetered alarmingly for a few seconds on touchdown, before settling into place with a groan.

The pilot got out in a sour mood, though he was less irate than Po probably would have been in his position.

"Who's the joker who told me I had plenty of room to land?" were the first words out of his mouth.

Yep. Windham told him the same thing he told me.

The Marine kept quiet, and so did Po, but the gunship jockey quickly moved past his irritation, probably because he'd had plenty of time to assess the LZ on descent, and the decision to land had ultimately been his.

"Consider yourselves extremely lucky that you managed to raise a gunship at all, especially on *troposcatter,*" he said. "AC-900s are barely running any missions now, because we're running out of fuel on this planet."

"Why were you out on one, sir?" Po asked.

"That's need-to-know. Do you need to know?" After a few seconds' silence, the pilot added, "Didn't think so."

"Well, we'd better get these wounded loaded, sir," Po said. "And I'd recommend that you get out of here. I doubt your approach went unnoticed, and there's a good chance this spot will be crawling with Janus soon."

The pilot had no disagreement there, and he opened a side hatch for his passengers to be carried aboard. Thankfully, their suits' iatric capabilities, though limited, seemed to have stabilized their conditions—even Gomez's, who was still unconscious but breathing. It was worrying for him to be out this long, but at least he was alive.

While Emery, Gomez, and Navarro were loaded aboard the AC-900, Po was already preparing for attack from below. He distributed the Marines who weren't busy carrying the injured around the crown of the hill, just below it. The gunship's presence was complicating the tactical situation, but they had the high ground, and they'd at least be able to hold out a while here.

It depended on how many fighters the Nibirans sent at them. If they came in overwhelming numbers, they'd have to withdraw...but he wasn't keen to find out what retreating down the hill's far side looked like. The jungle looked particularly thick there, and for all he knew it concealed a sheer drop. He hadn't gotten that far in his planning yet, and even as he had the thought, he sent Krikorian to check it out.

"Carefully," he admonished.

"Yes, Team Leader."

"I lead the platoon now, or what's left of it. Emery said he wants me to do what a lance corporal would in this situation."

"What do we call you, then? Platoon Leader?"

"Um...yeah, I guess." It was a bit clunky, but it wouldn't be right to call him lance corporal since he hadn't actually been given the rank. And it certainly wouldn't do to call him "sergeant," even though leading a platoon was properly a sergeant's job.

The gunship departed into the sky, and Po finished directing his Marines around the hilltop to await an impending Nibiran attack. As he did, he took stock of how much of 131st was left standing.

The battle for Gomorate had already cut them down to twenty-four, and with the men they'd lost today, they were down to eighteen, in a platoon that began with thirty. They also lacked anyone with actual experience commanding a platoon, and while Po was determined to do his best, he was horrified of screwing up and costing men their lives.

"Zanth," he breathed, after making sure he wasn't transmitting over coms. "You there?"

No reply. The Emplor had apparently gone on another one of his hiatuses. Po hadn't heard from him since before they'd taken the base where they'd found Ara Darshim.

On top of everything, their supplies were dwindling—the gunship pilot had been flying light, and he hadn't had anything to share to help pad things out.

Depending on where we're supposed to go next, we could be in real trouble. Gunny's optimism was all well and good, and Po was trying his level best to emulate it. But they couldn't eat optimism.

Krikorian returned, and crouched next to Po, where he'd nestled his rifle's muzzle in the crook of a twisted branch.

"It's actually a pretty easy descent, with good concealment," the Armenian said.

Po glanced at him, then back at the terrain in front of him, which had remained empty of signs of enemy activity. He focused on breathing as he fit this new information into their situation.

"Okay," he said in reply. "Okay." He switched over to the platoon-wide. "Windham, you're with Second Squad now, to even up our numbers. First Squad, withdraw down the hill behind us while Second holds this hilltop. Once you're in a secure position, we'll join you at the bottom, and we'll all go from there. We need to get back to Taylor and Darshim, which means looping around to give Karakata a wide berth. Stay extremely frosty, everyone. We can't afford another disaster."

He winced as soon as he'd said the last words, sure that Gunny Emery wouldn't have phrased it like that.

***

Traveling with his fellow Marines was rarely just a walk in the woods, Po had come to realize.

Every trek had its own unique challenges, and they always seemed to be under some sort of time pressure, along with a mountain of worries to carry, along with their weapons and supplies.

On this particular journey, Po had to not only worry about when an army of insurgents out of Karakata might descend on them with RPGs and other toys they'd somehow liberated from the Corps itself, but also whether Taylor and Darshim would be where they'd left them.

Emery had given the private strict orders to sit tight with the Nibiran, since without satellites, coms were too limited for getting back in touch to be a sure thing.

But the land surrounding Karakata had probably been crawling with Janus ever since they'd discovered 131st Platoon in the middle of their city, and even Emery's orders wouldn't keep Taylor in place if he was in danger of being flushed out by an insurgent patrol.

There was also the fact that every single Marine now under Po's command was in desperate need of sleep, and none of them were likely to get it any time soon. Assuming they rendezvoused with Taylor without any hiccups, they'd still have to put a safe distance between them and Karakata before thinking about bedding down for the night.

Po's eyelids felt like weights, and his eyes were grainy, but he didn't permit himself to open his visor to rub at them. For one, his gloves were filthy, and he'd probably just make them worse. For another, he couldn't have the others see him compromising his own vigilance by fussing with his visor and eyes. Survival could very well mean split-second decisions, and if men died while he was trying to make himself more comfortable, he'd spend the rest of his life berating himself.

The Marines' tiredness was manifesting as irritation, and Po had to admonish them to keep coms discipline more than once. Emery had handed command to him in more than just name: he'd also granted him a platoon commander's level of authorization over his Marines' implants, which let him see which men were contacting each other over private channels.

"Cut the coms chatter, Paisley," who'd been talking to Crotty about something for the last two minutes. "Stay focused."

A shocked silence followed. Then: "Yes, Platoon Leader."

There were two close brushes with Nibiran patrols, but both times they were able to stay hidden while the insurgents passed. And then, at last, they were nearing the cliff where they'd left Taylor guarding Darshim. Amazingly, they'd reached the location without incident...and there were no signs of Janus anywhere around here, that Po could see.

Can we really be so lucky?

The concealed shelter they'd erected before heading into Karakata was still where they'd left it...

...and so were Taylor and Darshim.

Darshim looked exactly as she had when they'd left, as though it had been five minutes instead of hours. As for Taylor, he looked up as soon as Po entered, his visor lowered. "About time. Where's the sergeant?"

"Young is dead. Emery just got medevaced out of here."

The other Marine's mouth hung open, the color draining from his face. "Who else?"

"They got Zap and Holmes, too. Gomez and Navarro were wounded, and went in the gunship. Gomez was pretty...well, he was unconscious since before we left Karakata."

"I am sorry for these losses," Darshim said.

Po nodded brusquely in response.

"Who's in charge, then?" Taylor asked. "You?"

"That's right."

"Wow." Taylor shook his head. "So...we're still doing this, huh?"

Paisley squeezed in beside Po, which caused the shelter of branches to bulge outward. It hadn't been big enough for three of them, really, and Po was already looming over Taylor and Darshim where they sat, pretty close to standing on their feet. The thing certainly wasn't big enough for four, with three in SERAPH suits. Paisley didn't say anything—he just glared at the Nibiran.

Po turned his own gaze back to Darshim, too. "We found Omal." A light of hope was ignited in her eyes, and Po was sorry to extinguish it. "He was already dead. It looked like Janus tortured him to death."

Her features fell, her lips trembling violently, which was quite a sight on a Nibiran.

"I'm sorry, Ara."

"It—" With that, she broke down, burying her face in her hands and weeping.

Po and the others waited awkwardly for her to compose herself.

"Ara...I need you to pull yourself together. I know it's hard. Trust me. But we all need to stay strong, now."

Gradually, the trembling and sobbing subsided, and she pulled her damp face away from her palms. "Yes," she said. "It's just...I...." She reached with both hands into the shallow pool to her left, scooping out the gelatinous orb in which her young grew and cradling it against her. "I loved him so very much."

"I know. And we did what we could to try to get him back for you. We kept up our end of things. Now, we need you to do the same. We need you to tell us where To'sheth Rin is, and we need you to take us there."

"Yes," she said again. "Of course. I will keep up my end of things. I've been thinking about a plan for that."

Paisley opened his visor. "Of *course,* she says." He turned to spit on the wall of the shelter. "She's just *so* ready to help. Her lover just died, but hey, that's all good. Anything to lend a helping hand."

Po shot him a look. "She's clearly upset about that."

"How do we know we can trust her, Po? How can we *possibly* trust her? Look at what she just sent us into."

"Emery was willing to trust her." Po turned to Taylor. "Did she make any attempt to get away?"

The other Marine shook his head. "I even, uh...I accidentally dozed for a bit," he said sheepishly. "When I woke up, she was sitting exactly where she'd been before."

Po snorted, then turned to Paisley again. "If she'd intentionally sent us into danger, I doubt she'd be keen to wait around here for any survivors to get back. She would have slipped away at the first chance, which Taylor here apparently gave her."

"You really believe it, huh?" Paisley said, his eyes wide and full of fire. "You really believe she isn't about to lead us into another trap."

"What you say is illogical," Darshim said.

"What did you just say to me, frog-dog?"

"What you say is illogical," the Nibiran repeated. "*Nibiru* is the trap. And you led yourselves into it."

Chapter 25

"So where is he?" Po said, not seeing much point in letting the ensuing silence to drag on after Darshim's statement. "Where is Rin?"

The Nibiran's eyes rested on the fleshy orange sphere she cradled in her arms, apparently not as motivated as Po was to break up contemplative silences. "He's in Morati Firth," she said quietly.

"Is that supposed to mean something to us?" Paisley asked.

"It is another city state, one whose relationship with Gomorate has been strained for centuries. The two have had an unsettled peace for nearly two decades, but Morati Firth has always been more willing than others to defy the Gomorati, because of their location."

"Their location," Po repeated. "What about their location makes them so gutsy?"

Darshim's eyes rose to meet his. "Morati Firth lies under the waves."

That brought a groan from Taylor. Paisley spat again, this time on the ground near Darshim's feet.

"He's in one of your underwater cities?" Po said.

"That's correct."

"How sure are you?"

"Dead sure. Or I wouldn't have made this deal with you in this first place."

"How deep is the city?"

"It's over a kilometer under the ocean."

Po closed his eyes. *How can we possibly be expected to get to Rin there?* As he'd done so many times before, the Janus leader had outthought the Marines once again.

His breathing was accelerating, and he gritted his teeth, his fingers flexing at his sides. "You knew all along it was impossible to get to Rin, and yet you strung us along this far? With three of our Marines dead because of it?"

"But it is not impossible."

"Explain."

"Don't you know the Gomorati Army wants To'sheth Rin dead just as much as you do?"

"I doubt that," Po said grimly. "But go on."

"The water protects Morati Firth from humans, and it poses a significant challenge to Nibirans when it comes to mounting a large-scale assault. But we are capable of withstanding much higher underwater pressure than you. A distance of even two kilometers would not be beyond our reach, so long as one had somewhere to take a breath once one swam that far—and so long as one took one's time when returning to the surface, to avoid the deleterious effects of decompression."

"What are you suggesting?" he asked slowly. "That we ask some GA to go down and kill Rin for us?"

Darshim shook her head. "Even if I gave them Rin's location, Gomorate isn't likely to send soldiers there. That would too readily be considered an act of war by the Morati. But I *do* think they'd be prepared to lend you submersibles while *you* get the job done. Especially if they were painted to resemble civilian craft, leaving a chance Morati Firth would never realize Gomorate's involvement."

Po studied the Nibiran's face as he contemplated her words, and she continued after a few more seconds:

"There's a coastal military base positioned specifically to respond to threats out of the Firth, which has four submersibles that operate out of there. The base is walled and well-guarded. I believe they'd also be willing to equip you for the mission as you need, and to help you prepare."

"*You believe,*" Paisley snarled. "Remind me what that's worth, again?"

This time, Darshim met his eyes levelly. "I can't see that you have any other options at your disposal. But you're welcome to disregard my offer to act as liaison between you and the GA. Try to access Morati Firth on your own, if you'd like."

"The GA is riddled with spies," Po said. "What are the chances Rin stays in the dark about our mission, once we bring an entire GA base in on it?"

"Our bases *are* capable of going into lockdown. But this seems like a matter for discussing with them once we arrive."

"How far is the base from here?"

"Just over six hundred kilometers."

Paisley swore. "Abbato, tell me you're not considering this."

"Well, she has a point. What other option *do* we have?"

"Surviving. Returning to Gomorate and regrouping with the rest of the Corps. You're asking what options we have other than walking right into a trap."

Po returned his gaze to Darshim's face. "I don't think that is what I'm asking."

"Use logic," Darshim said, her eyes still locked on Paisley. "You found me in a grimy cell with my child." She lifted the egg a couple centimeters. "They murdered my love, Omal. And Janus has been terrorizing *my* people much more than they have yours."

Paisley's eyes were narrowed, his lips a rictus of disgust. But Darshim continued.

"I have lived for years among them, fearful every second I would be caught and eviscerated alive by their butchers, just as your Marines were. To survive, I had to get into the mindset of an insurgent, but I could never truly forget my reality, and my fear. I have had a gun planted in my back and told that I had been found out, and that I would now be killed. I lived only because I recognized it as the type of random loyalty test to which they subject all their members.

"Do you know the reason I was finally caught? It is because I was caught transmitting the details of their plan to attack Valta—the second-largest town in the region controlled by Gomorate. A town where you have several units stationed. And because of what I did, that particular plot was thwarted."

"All sounds like lying to me," Paisley said. "Lying, with just enough sugary truth to make it taste sweet. From someone whose job it is to lie."

"That's enough," Po said. "Gunny trusted her, so we're trusting her. Paisley, I want you to keep your opinions to yourself."

The other Marine's narrowed eyes darted to his face, and at first Po was sure he'd have something to say.

But he didn't. He merely turned on his heel and left the shelter, ripping out half the entrance as he did.

***

They still had a long way to travel on dwindling supplies, and it was slow going from the outset.

Darshim assured them that they'd be out of the jungle in five days, and onto the open plains of the continent's southeast. That would probably let them move a lot faster, along with putting them out of enemy territory at last.

But in the meantime, they were forced to pick their way carefully through the largely untamed jungle, ever-paranoid of running into an enemy patrol and blowing their presence...and likely the mission.

If it became known among the Nibirans that a platoon—even a diminished platoon—of Marines was at large in the region and headed toward Morati Firth, To'sheth Rin would almost certainly hear of it and know what they were up to.

Their pace was further slowed by Ara Darshim's need to stop regularly to soak her egg, to prevent it from drying out, which would apparently cause complications. Possibly even death.

At least, that's what she claimed. In the meantime, Po could almost taste his men's impatience as they took turns looking out for the Janus force that would stumble on them and ruin everything while Darshim was watching her egg lie at the bottom of some pool or stream. There was plenty of muttering about it over the platoon-wide channel, and his new command privileges let him know that there were also plenty more private conversations happening. He could guess what the topic might be.

They moved only when Gnara was down, so they'd at least have the jump on any patrols they did encounter, as well as all the other advantages conferred by their suits' sophisticated sensors. During Nibiru's day, such as it was, Po found himself reviewing the phrases in Nibiran which Navarro had sent him. He'd been resistant to the idea at first, largely because of its source, but eventually the logic of what the other Marine had said caught up to him.

It *would* be better to have the ability to say at least a few words to the Nibirans in their native tongue. At the very least, he knew the attempt to speak to them in their own language would create good will. Besides, if Navarro himself hadn't actually known Nibiran back in Shackleton, he never would have overheard those Janus sympathizers talking. And then they never would have uncovered the hidden launch facility where they were keeping nukes ready to rain down on Earth.

So, familiarity with the enemy's language obviously did have its benefits.

On their second night of travel, it was raining as they picked their way carefully down into a valley that wound through the land like a snake.

Without warning, Paisley shouted, "Janus!" just as they were cresting a small rise.

Before anyone could react, they were on top of them—Nibirans at camp, plenty of them asleep, others sitting in silence beneath fabrics stretched between trees, and still others moving along the perimeter. But somehow, they looked as surprised as Po felt. Their patrols hadn't spotted the Marines coming.

"Open fire!" Po shouted over the platoon-wide.

His Marines' training proclaimed itself in the way they instantly had weapons up and shooting, spreading out from each other and efficiently selecting their targets based on each man's implicit zone-of-fire. Within seconds, what Nibirans were left had capitulated and were on their knees speaking frantic words in their language. Po didn't know nearly enough of it yet to understand what they were saying, but if he had to guess, he'd say they were begging to surrender.

"You know we can't let them live," Paisley said, eyes on Po's like a hawk's.

Zanth appeared on Po's other side. "He's right," the Emplor affirmed.

Oh. Now you're here.

"You have no way to safely take prisoners." The alien looked almost happy as he said it. "You can't risk one of them running off and blowing this whole thing wide open."

Pressing his lips together, Po raised his own rifle and shot the nearest Nibiran. Paisley got the next, and Taylor and Patrice took care of the remaining two.

Po lowered his rifle, feeling suddenly queasy, as if those had been the first aliens he'd killed during this war. Ara Darshim walked past the line of Marines, gazing around the camp in bewilderment, her egg nestled in its sling at her side.

She knelt beside one of the fallen Nibirans, plucking at his sleeve. "Shine a light here."

Reluctantly, Po stepped forward, activating the light built into his suit's right forearm. The beam fell on an insignia borne by a patch stitched onto the alien's shirt.

"These were GA. Not Janus. They could have helped us. There was no need to kill them."

Willing himself not to move, but feeling suddenly helpless, Po's eyes drifted to Paisley's featureless visor.

"We came on them suddenly," Po tried to explain, suddenly aware of why he'd felt nauseous as soon as he'd taken the shot. Somehow, he'd known as soon as he did it. "There was no time to—"

"They fell to friendly fire," Paisley said. "Happens sometimes in war, sadly. While we're here, we should see what they have for resupply."

He stepped over one of the soldier's corpses, and after a couple seconds, other Marines began to follow suit. Soon, everyone was searching the downed Nibirans and their camp for what they might take with them.

Ara Darshim rose shakily to her feet, still looking at Po, one hand caressing the lump that was her egg.

But Po had nothing to say. He walked past her, continued past the others, and stood on the far edge of the camp for some minutes to stare into Nibiru's deepest night.

Chapter 26

Something was bothering him as he bedded down to try to catch some shuteye in Gnara's first faint glow. Something other than the fact that he'd obviously known, on some level, that those Nibirans were GA. His brain hadn't caught up to his gut in time to stop the slaughter. But somehow, he'd known.

Another thing tugged at the edges of his frayed consciousness, nagging him, until at last he was able to pin it down:

It was about Paisley. The Marine had shouted "Janus" before he could possibly have seen the Nibiran camp. Po felt sure of it, and when he replayed the footage, he was even more sure.

The Marine couldn't have heard them in advance—no one else had. The Nibirans had clearly been trying to be just as quiet as they'd been, and the heavy rain would have drowned out any sound they might have made.

But Paisley had known they were there. And he'd shouted "Janus." Not "Nibirans"—"Janus."

Would it have made a difference if he'd used the more general term, the one which included allies as well as enemies? Po would never know. But he did know Zanth had appeared to egg him on as the soldiers were on their knees begging for mercy.

But no one had pulled the trigger for him, had they?

No. Po had done that all on his own.

Even if they *had* been Janus...was it really true they couldn't have managed to take them prisoner? Sure, it would have been a risk. But was killing them truly the right thing to do, even if they had turned out to be the terrorists Paisley had named them?

Somehow, he managed to get to sleep. In his dream, he was standing outside Eremus, waiting for the Marines' assault on the city to begin. This time, though, Eremus had a sun overhead, to shine brightly down onto it, just as it was said to do on Earth.

The sunlight seemed very fitting. This was a thrilling time for Po, after all. His first real campaign, surrounded by his brothers and all their terrible weapons of war. The collective power the Corps was about to bring to bear on this city surged through him in the form of excitement and anticipation. They were about to avenge the Marines who'd died in Cycler 3, victim to the insurgents' brutal attack. Swift justice was about to be visited on To'sheth Rin's minions.

"Whoa," Zapletal said. Zapletal, who was dead, but didn't know it yet. "Check that out."

"Check what out?" Po asked as he turned around.

It was the horizon—the one in the opposite direction of the city. It was being blown toward the sky in its entirety, with great chunks of terrain hurtling into the air toward the brilliant sun, only to arc and come crashing down into the chaos of disintegration and confusion.

"Looks like it's getting closer," Krik said, sounding annoyed. "And I haven't even had a chance to blow my paycheck at the MCX yet."

The explosion of earth and blue sand continued, as if all the C4 in the universe was buried under the desert landscape and was being detonated in succession. The phenomenon didn't take long to draw near the four regiments arrayed outside the city, waiting to attack it. Soon, APCs were flying, Torres tanks were being tossed into the air, and Marines in their armor went with them, arms and legs flailing.

The ground erupted under Po's feet, and it was his turn to be flung into the air. The earth opened beneath him, releasing a burst of unbearable heat that began to cook him alive in his suit as someone shrieked nearby.

"*No!*" that desperate voice pleaded. "*Please!* Someone help!"

Po sat up on the jungle floor, the dream evaporating as he groped for his M37C.

The dream evaporated...except for the shrieking.

"Po!" that voice called. "Stop him, please!"

Still groggy, Po found his rifle and gained his feet to see Paisley marching up the hill toward the cliff that was just a couple dozen meters from their camp.

"He has my baby!"

With those words, everything snapped into place, and Po knew what was happening. Just as Paisley was nearing the edge of the cliff and raising the egg, Po barked his name and raised his rifle.

The other Marine froze. "What," he snapped.

"Put it down."

"Oh, I'll put it down all right. I'll put it down before it kills us. I'm finished with risking our lives for a frog-dog's spawn." He lifted the egg higher.

"Don't do it," Po said. "That's an order."

Paisley turned to look over his shoulder, and didn't seem surprised to see Po had his rifle pointing at him. He cocked his head to one side, and suddenly Po felt sure he was listening to something...or someone.

He refocused on Po. "Since when do you care so much about frog-dogs that don't even *exist* yet? This thing's holding us back, and humans stopped letting things like this hold us back a long time ago. Have you ever gotten this upset over a human fetus? Are you really going to let this *thing* jeopardize our mission, when *people* have flushed more for a lot less?"

"Put it down," Po said slowly. "Or I'll put you down."

They stood in tableau for a long time. At last, after what felt like an eternity, Paisley slowly lowered the egg to the ground. With that, he began to walk off into the jungle.

"Paisley, get back here," Po sent.

But the other Marine just kept walking, soon vanishing into the jungle's foliage without a word.

***

Should I have shot him?

The question played in Po's mind again and again as they ranged across the verdant plains of the continent's southeast, which they were cutting across toward the Gomorati ocean-side base.

He had no doubt there would be people who'd believe he should have. Desertion during wartime used to carry the death penalty, although GEA had done away with that punishment for anything decades ago. Still...Paisley had threatened to disobey a direct order and relented only under threat of death. Then he'd walked into the jungle wearing a fortune in advanced military tech. Tech the Nibirans might now get their hands on.

But the whole thing had blindsided Po, even though now, thinking back over the last weeks, he felt like he should have seen something like that coming. He and Paisley had been in such a good place after the battle for Eremus, when Po had saved the other Marine's life. He'd even started to think of Paisley as his friend, of a sort. Sure, he'd never been completely accepting of Po's command, but they'd seemed to come to an understanding.

And now, this. He wasn't sure what came next for Paisley. What was his plan? Join up with Janus? Return to Gomorate and hope no one minded that he'd defied the orders of both Po and his real platoon leader, Gunny Emery?

And what would that look like, if he did go back to Gomorate? The only way Paisley's career as a Marine could remain intact was if he came up with a lie to make it look like *Po* had done something wrong.

Or if Po and the others never came back...

...and that was the other worry. Would Paisley go to Janus and tip them off about the mission to kill Rin? Was he capable of something like that?

Should I have gone after him?

Zanth had been there to urge him to kill GA soldiers, but he'd gone missing again immediately after. He had nothing to advise, apparently, when it came to Paisley. All Po could do was go with his gut, which said to press on with the mission as quickly as possible.

There wasn't much cover available as they traversed the plains, but thankfully there also wasn't much in the way of opposition. Janus' efforts all seemed to concentrate around Gomorate's two largest towns, Gomorate itself and Valta.

That also serves to distract from Rin's true location. Clever.

Even so, Po kept his Marines on alert, with their audio's sensitivity turned up and their AIs set to warn them of anything aberrant. Even the tall, emerald grass rustling against his suit's legs sounded loud, almost like rushing rapids, which was odd given he couldn't feel the blades of grass through the armor.

They traveled only when Gnara was down, though the region was still hot even at night—the plains were low-lying, and therefore closer to Nibiru's active molten core.

"I want you to know something," Ara Darshim said to him on the second afternoon of their crossing.

Reluctantly, Po opened his visor and met her eyes. They needed Darshim enthusiastically on their side, and making her talk to a featureless, polarized visor probably wouldn't contribute to that.

Then again, the alien looked plenty enthusiastic, to Po. Her eyes shone as they met his. A few of the other Marines turned curious looks toward them. They were separated from the conversation by a few meters, but their helmet's sensors would let them listen in if they wanted to.

"What is it?" he asked.

"I intend to do everything in my power to ensure the safety of your men. And I will spend myself in achieving this mission's success. I will go to war for you, if I need to. The authorities at the base we're headed for will heed me, because I will *make* them heed me. They will give you everything you need."

"Well...thanks, then, Ara. We appreciate it."

She inclined her head. "Because you saved my child's life, when it might have seemed easier to let him be killed...because you did that, you will never have a more dedicated ally than I will be. I promise you that."

Po never knew what to say in the face of such earnestness—such fervor. Most times, actually, he lacked much to say, but times like this especially left him without words. The truth was, he'd rather be fighting terrorists right now than receive what Darshim was sending him. That open expression of respect, wonder, even reverence...

It made him want to hide, or die. He knew he didn't deserve for anyone to look at him like that.

"If I'd let it die, I doubt you'd be as cooperative as you're being right now," he said at last. "It was for the good of the mission."

Darshim shook her head. "I *would* still have helped you...if I could manage to pull myself together after losing my child. Rin needs to be taken out, and no one else is in a position to do it. So I still would have. But I don't think the good of the mission is the only reason you did what you did, Po Abbato."

He shrugged uncomfortably. "Well, uh. Don't mention it." *Please. Never mention it again.*

When they reached the Gomorati Army base at last, they found it surrounded by walls, as Darshim had promised—tall mudbrick walls, behind which armed soldiers patrolled along ramparts. The grass had been cut back for hundreds of meters in every direction, no doubt to thwart attack by terrorists willing to crawl on their bellies with all their gear in tow for endless miles.

There was a village off to the south, which Po assumed had been there before the base, and was probably part of the reason it was located here. The village was made up of structures similar to the cracked-egg homes he'd encountered in the desert, though these were more squat, maybe to withstand strong winds coming in off the sea.

A guard sat in a gatehouse before the great double gates of the base, and Darshim spoke to him through a narrow horizontal slit. There was a heated exchange that sounded like an argument to Po, and after a few moments he radioed someone inside. Then came another exchange between Darshim and the guard.

"They want you to relinquish your weapons," she explained to Po. "I told them that was unacceptable. If you will wait here, I'll go inside and explain to them the need to trust and accommodate you maximally. Will you trust me to go in by myself and see this thing done?"

He closed his eyes. He could send someone with her, but whoever he sent would have to be unarmed by the sounds of it, and maybe outside his SERAPH suit too. It wouldn't make much difference, then, whether he sent an escort with her or not.

He sighed. "Yes. Go ahead."

A side door swung open, just a few meters from the gate, and another guard ushered Darshim in. Po and his Marines stood arrayed on the ground in front of the base, appraising the Nibirans on the ramparts, who returned their gazes with expressions of detachment.

Chapter 27

It was a longer wait than it should have been. This wasn't how one treated allies, but the base's CO apparently hadn't gotten the memo about the Marines helping GA to defend Gomorate, or about them generally operating jointly together for months now.

When the gates finally opened to admit them, his men were still asked to wait—but on the other side of the walls, in a dusty courtyard that didn't offer much in the way of accommodation. Especially after a long journey over rough terrain, with dwindling supplies.

Ara Darshim was nowhere to be seen. Two armed Nibirans approached Po, looking just as impassive as the sentries they'd seen on the walls. One of them spoke to him in their native tongue, and his implant translated automatically.

"Please come with us."

Who needs Navarro? Po thought sardonically. He nodded, then gestured for them to lead the way.

"Platoon Leader," Crotty said over the wide channel. "You want some company?"

"I'll be fine. Stay near the exit. If anything goes funny, I'll let you know."

The buildings were made of the same locally sourced material as the wall—mudbrick. He was taken through a broad, low entrance and led along a series of curving hallways, which seemed to meander endlessly without ever getting to the point.

At last, an abrupt turn through an open door took him to an office with a Nibiran sitting behind a desk, who wore the same kind of bomber-looking cap To'sheth Rin wore, except this one had a large gold-colored medallion in felt stitched to the side. Darshim sat against the far wall, facing perpendicular to the GA officer, and she nodded at Po when he entered.

"Private First Class Abbato," the officer said via the translator, rising, then sitting again as Po took the seat he'd indicated with his webbed claws. "Welcome to Naval Advance Base

Bodur. Ms. Darshim here has made very clear to me that we must offer to be of service to you and your men in every way we can think of, and very likely some ways we cannot yet think of. If we fail to do this, I'm given to understand the consequences will be very dire indeed, for Nibirans and humans both—possibly for the entire galactic supercluster, or at least that's what I assume based on the surprising degree of Ms. Darshim's fervor."

To her credit, Darshim didn't react, unless there was some Nibiran indication of embarrassment Po hadn't learned to pick up on yet.

"I have been in touch with superiors in Gomorate, and they vouch strongly for Ms. Darshim's pedigree and convictions. Therefore I am inclined to do as she says—to cooperate fully in whatever it is you're planning, which, by the way, I'd like to know as little about as possible. And so, I make myself at your service. How can I help you prepare for this thing?"

"I need this base on complete lockdown," Po said immediately. "No one leaves until our mission is complete, and no one comes in without the understanding that they'll be staying a while. And no transmissions unless authorized by you, all of them encrypted."

"That...is quite the set of requests."

"I guess it's one of the ways to be of service you hadn't thought of yet."

"That is for certain. Supposing a crisis unfolds, which requires the mobilization of—"

"Are there no other units in the area? Operating out of other bases?"

"There are five other units, operating out of two naval bases within fifty miles of this one."

"Then, call on them to respond to any crises that crop up."

"And if one arises that requires the mobilization of all seven units, from all three bases?"

"When was the last time that happened?"

"Well...never."

"Then let's hope it doesn't in the next week or so."

***

"We're going to die, aren't we?"

Po stopped in the middle of his description of Plan A and turned to Taylor, doing his best to keep his expression neutral.

What do I say to that?

He sighed. "What are you looking for me to say, Taylor? Something uplifting or something honest?"

"Well, honest, of course, Platoon Leader. But lately, I'm just wondering if Paisley didn't have the right idea."

"Paisley, the deserter? The one who defied direct orders from at least two superiors? That the Paisley you mean?"

Taylor tossed his head. "All I'm saying is, he seemed to have a pretty good idea of what we're about to walk into. And he wasn't interested."

"Tell you what, Taylor," Po said. "Why don't you stay back here at base while the rest of us go? If we survive, we can try to bring you back a t-shirt."

"No way."

"Then what are you complaining about?"

"I'm not complaining. I'm just saying...we *are* going to die. Right?"

Po closed his eyes for a long second, then opened them again to scan the assembled Marines. "Raise your hand if you joined the Marines thinking there was a one hundred percent chance you'd survive."

No one raised their hands.

"Okay. Then let's pretend we could bring back Holmes, or Zapletal, or Staff Sergeant Young, and chat with them right now in this room. Raise your hand if you think they'd tell us they had no idea *that* was what might happen to them."

None of his Marines moved.

"Or, let's say we could bring back all the men we lost when Janus attacked Cycler 3. Just for ten minutes. Just long enough to ask them if we should go get justice for what To'sheth Rin did to them, or if we should leave here right now and head back to Gomorate, in the hopes some insurgent patrol doesn't catch wind of us and take us out on our way back. Who thinks those Marines would tell us to save ourselves? Who thinks they'd advise we stay far away from Morati Firth, because it's clearly a death trap?"

Po's eyes fell on Taylor, and the other Marine spoke slowly. "They wouldn't say that, Platoon Leader. And I wasn't saying it either."

"I'm glad. Because in case you haven't noticed, this job isn't just a paycheck. Sure, plenty of us became a Marine to keep out of simjail—I know I did. But I think we've also come to realize that there's a lot more to being a Marine than getting paid and staying out of prison. And I'm not talking about helping GEA gain more power."

A few of them looked surprised that he'd speak against GEA so openly—he basically never did, out of a sense of self-preservation. But as Taylor had pointed out, what did self-preservation matter now?

"We're *Marines,* and it's our job to fight so the families we left behind don't have to. We fight to stop bad guys like Rin, to keep our loved ones safe. But it's more than that. It's like Colonel Tuffin said, way back in FOB Longhorn: the only way to truly do our jobs is to keep our *brothers* safe. Right now, we have a shot at taking out an alien who's already killed thousands of Marines, and who stands to kill a whole lot more. Next to that, what are our lives truly worth? Anyone want to tell me?"

No one did, so Po continued. "We're currently planning a mission to infiltrate a hostile power's city and kill the most notorious terrorist in the solar system. A terrorist that would have nuked Earth and killed millions, if not billions, if we'd let him. Is his compound rigged to explode the moment he detects it's been compromised? Probably. Will he have true believers ready to kill themselves if it means taking out one or two of us—like the scum that took out Staff Sergeant Young? I can pretty much guarantee he will. Then there's the fact we'll be relying on Nibiran submersibles to stay airtight long enough to get us there and back. If a Nibiran finds himself a kilometer deep in a sub that malfunctions catastrophically, there's a pretty good chance he'll be able to save himself by swimming out of there. So their equipment's safety standards don't need to be as high as *we* need them to be. If that happens to us, there's a very good chance we'll drown, because our suits aren't rated to operate that deep underwater for long enough to get us back.

"On top of that, we're going to have little more than forty minutes to complete this mission. I've been over it with the Nibiran techs again and again, and we simply will not have the ability to take enough fuel to give us any more time than that. So that's our time limit: forty minutes to infiltrate Rin's compound and get out of there with whatever useful intel we can grab."

He met Crotty's eyes, and then Zhang's, and then Taylor's again. "So, you want to ask me are we going to die? The answer is yes. We're probably going to die. And my question for you is, what difference does it make? Anyone have an answer?"

The Marines remained silent.

"That's what I thought. Now, let's get back to work."

***

As reluctant as the Nibiran base commander had seemed at first, he stayed true to his promise to accommodate the Marines in every way he could. Apparently he too saw the value in taking out Rin, just as Darshim had predicted.

With Po's go-ahead, he activated some intel operatives he had on the ground in Morati Firth, without giving them any details about why. The Marines' plan was to infiltrate Rin's compound by blowing open an airlock at the back, which was big enough to allow a private submersible to come and go. That had the dual benefit of drastically reducing Rin's chances of escape, while also putting the Marines close to where the Janus leader's quarters were likely to be: on the compound's lowest level.

But the airlock was flush with the ocean floor, and a nearby coral reef was blocking the Marines' best angle of approach. And so, the base CO sent some of his operatives dressed as city workers to clear away the reef, which grew on an unusable hillside apparently owned by no one.

The 131st Marines also needed an entirely new arsenal, since their M37Cs weren't designed to operate underwater. But the Nibirans were much more accustomed to designing everything to function amphibiously, and they outfitted Po and his men with rifles, HMGs, and even grenade launchers that could be fired underwater if needed.

Of course, Po's Plan A didn't involve fighting outside the compound...but if they had to, he wanted to be ready.

"This thing feels awful," Taylor said the moment Po handed him one of the new weapons.

"I know." There was no use in denying it—after getting so used to their fully customized and personalized M37s, the amphibious weapons felt clunky and strange in his hands. "So we'd better learn to love them fast."

They drilled intensively with the weapons, working long into the night to get as close as they could to feeling like the amphibious firearms were extensions of their bodies, just as their normal weapons did. And they made faster progress than even Po had expected. He'd forgotten just how adaptable the Marines of boot battalion were.

The base CO also contributed workers to help them build a mock compound in one of the open areas, which modeled their intended place of ingress, as well as the levels they'd have to fight through to reach Rin. One of the CO's operatives had somehow managed to get a hold of floor plans for the compound and to transmit them encrypted to Naval Advance Base Bodur.

Relying on the operatives made Po antsy. They were being kept in the dark, but surely they'd figured out what was being planned, if only in rough outline. They probably didn't know that Marines were involved. But still...all it took was one informant to put Rin on high alert.

The Nibiran commander assured him that these were his most trusted spies, all of a caliber with Ara Darshim. And as much as Po had been reluctant to accept their help, he recognized that the tasks they were performing were badly needed.

They'd need all the help they could get.

All the same, he almost had a heart attack when he learned about the base worker, a logistics tech, who was caught trying to sneak off-base.

"He claims he only wanted to visit his sick wife," the CO said to Po when he broke the incident to him. "And that he wasn't expecting to be separated from her for this long." The commander shrugged. "I have people looking into that story, to confirm it. Either way, he's being detained, and will be until all this is over. You have my assurance."

"Thank you," Po said, after taking a couple deep, steadying breaths. "What are the chances he's Janus?"

"Fairly low, I hope. But whether he's with Janus or not, we stopped him from leaving, just as we will stop anyone else attempting to leave this base. We are remaining vigilant, PFC Abbato."

Po nodded slowly. The CO seemed competent enough, and he'd given Po no reason not to trust him. But he still couldn't help from thinking that if someone *had* managed to slip away from the base successfully, then the probability was that neither of them would know about it until it was too late.

Chapter 28

Space was at a premium aboard the Nibiran sub. Po wasn't exactly a stranger to cramped quarters, having grown up aboard Psyche Station and later traveled for months aboard the S.S. *Gear Issue.* But the submersible was the closest the Nibirans had ever come to building a spaceship, and they were clearly at the very beginning of that particular technological journey.

"Man, it's tight in here," Crotty said as he slowly disappeared down a ladder that descended into the bowels of the sub.

"If *you're* saying that, then we might just have a problem," Taylor said.

"Very funny," Crotty shot back.

But Po didn't think Taylor was joking. In the SERAPH suits, the Marines were larger than any Nibiran ever was. They needed to be able to deploy rapidly from the sub, which could be challenging if they were all jammed up against the bulkheads.

Po took the ladder next, to confirm just how difficult this was going to be. He found himself going down even slower than Crotty had. His back was pressed against the bulkhead behind him, and there was barely enough room to shift his arms and legs down to the lower rungs.

But he made it to the bottom eventually, and things opened up a little when he did. He exchanged looks with Crotty through their open visors, then turned toward the submersible captain, who was waiting alone to greet him a few meters down a side corridor.

"Are you prepared to tangle with any Morati police or military units that pick a fight with us?" Po asked him by dint of the translator, without preamble. He'd already met the captain multiple times on-base, in and out of strategy meetings, and he didn't feel like wasting time on formalities now.

"We have four torpedoes, all of which have already been launched five times each during exercises. They are also thoroughly tested on an ongoing basis. But I tell you, if we enter into a fight with Morati, the chances of your returning alive are effectively zero."

We know that already. "Well, hopefully the new paint job will do the trick." The sub had been in dry dock for most of the last week, getting painted to look like a luxury civilian craft. It wasn't a perfect disguise, and wouldn't hold up under close scrutiny. But it was something. "Just get us to the compound. We'll do the rest."

"What about getting home?"

"Please God we'll have the opportunity to do that."

Po blinked. That was the first time he'd ever said anything like that, to his memory.

He met Crotty's eyes. "Don't tell Navarro I said that."

"Uh...all right."

"Take us to the first escape trunk," Po told the captain as the Marines continued to come down the ladder and assemble at its base. "Taylor, Krik—you're with us."

With that, the Nibiran led them through a warren of corridors to the first airlock, or escape trunk, as they were apparently called on a sub. Po had the alien open the inner hatch, and he piled into it with the other three Marines.

"Close the hatch," he said once they were all inside. The captain complied, which required him pushing it from the outside while the four suited-up Marines tried to make themselves as small as possible.

At last, the hatch's lock engaged.

"It's not comfy," Po observed. "But I think it's going to work."

The two subs 131st Platoon was taking to the compound had two escape trunks each, and so the fact they could fit four Marines inside one of them meant sixteen could deploy at the same time. That left only one Marine to follow behind—though, Po had decided that instead, he would have two First Squad Marines deploy together, several minutes behind everyone else. It wasn't ideal, but it was how it had to be.

The captain let them out again, and Po had the other three Marines file down the corridor, to give him room to speak to the Nibiran.

"I want to know when we're twenty minutes out from Morati Firth," he said. "We'll be waiting outside these airlocks—escape trunks—and that's when we'll get inside them and begin taking water in. I want to be ready to go the moment we touch down outside Rin's vehicle bay."

"It will be done," the captain said.

***

The journey to Morati Firth would be three hours, barring any mishaps. But mishaps seemed likely enough as Po and the rest of Second Squad stood around the bridge and listened to the sub's groaning and shaking all around them. The sub was currently diving, which caused everyone present to lean back about twenty degrees relative to the deck, with no effort at all.

Taylor inched closer to him as the sub descended. "Hey, Platoon Leader?" he whispered.

"Yeah?"

"You really think we should be outside our suits right now?"

Po frowned around at the Nibiran officers stationed throughout the bridge. They seemed calm enough, in spite of the loud and worrying noises coming from the machinery surrounding them. Then again, if something went wrong, the Nibirans would probably make it. The humans, on the other hand....

He cleared his throat, then whispered back, "We'll be able to get them on in time, if something happens."

"Mm." Taylor sidled back to where he was standing, not looking very reassured.

The Marines had essentially been living in their suits for weeks now, and while that had been reduced a little bit during the last week of training—they hadn't slept in their suits, on the Nibiran base—they were all well past being sick of wearing the things. Po had figured that the approach to Morati Firth offered a good opportunity to let his men be outside them for a while.

They still all carried their weapons, though. The Nibirans had been nothing but helpful and accommodating since they'd arrived at Naval Advance Base Bodur, and so far, the same went for the submersibles' crews. But that didn't mean Po was about to let his Marines go unarmed around aliens, any of which could still prove to be insurgent moles.

The base's CO had promised to send his remaining two subs thirty minutes behind the two the Marines were on, with extra fuel loaded aboard. Stopping to refuel over an increasingly agitated city would be far from ideal, and it probably wouldn't be a great idea while withdrawing from that city back to base, either. But it was still good to have the option—and it also meant they'd have backup transportation in case anything happened to the subs they'd come in on.

Before Taylor had whispered his concerns, Po had been thinking about his last conversation with Ara Darshim, in the hours before they'd boarded the sub.

"It's not just Marines counting on you, you know," she'd told him. "And it's not just the people back on Earth, or wherever in the system you came from. Nibirans care about this, too. We're not all Janus. Most of us hate what To'sheth Rin is doing just as much as you do. The strife they've brought to Nibiru. We all want it to end."

Po had nodded. "I just hope you're right that he's there. If we came all this way, and risked so much...lost Marines...all for nothing...."

"I understand, Po. But I'm telling you. He's there."

"Well...." He sniffed. "Thank you, Ara. For everything you've done to give us this shot at him."

"Thank *you,*" she said, then held his gaze a moment longer before leaving without another word.

Po had exhaled sharply through his nostrils. It hadn't exactly been the rousing speech Colonel Tuffin had given on the eve of their assault on Eremus, but it would have to do.

Hopefully this goes a lot better than Eremus did.

A half hour into the journey, the Nibiran captain offered the Marines the chance to use their racks to nap on the way to Morati. It was a generous offer, Po knew, because the number of racks on any sub was limited, and if the Marines were using them, then that meant off-watch crew *weren't* using them. It was an offer to sacrifice sleep for them, and it impressed Po.

Only Krikorian took them up on it. The other Marines all watched him go as one of the crewmembers led him off the bridge.

Po watched him, too. *Guy can go to sleep on the way to something like this?* He slowly shook his head, finding he had a new respect for the Armenian. *Cold as ice.*

The journey was uneventful—until it wasn't.

"I'm getting reports from our agents in the Firth that the target compound is on high alert," the captain said about an hour out from the underwater city.

Po paused, processing the information. "How can they tell?"

"There are Nibirans patrolling outside the base. Mostly concentrated on the airlock that was our planned point of entry."

Po cursed. "Do you know if they're mostly patrolling on the sea floor, or on the structure itself?"

"Mostly the sea floor, or at least according to the last update. But there are some stationed on the structure."

"How many are there?"

"Eighteen have been spotted."

That has to be most of them. Rin couldn't house a whole lot more than that inside that compound. Unless the thing goes a lot deeper than I was told.

"I do have some good news," the captain said.

"I'm here for it."

"The compound's one submersible was observed leaving two hours ago, and hasn't returned yet. Until it does, it's possible Rin has no viable means left to escape."

That would be lucky. But Po knew it might also mean Rin had left aboard the craft. *Can't worry about that now.* "Can you position us directly over the compound's uppermost level?"

"How far up?"

"Directly over, and as close as you can get us."

"They'll be firing on us."

"No, they'll be firing at First Squad. We're switching to a modified version of Plan B. I want First Squad's sub to pull ahead and drop *them* two blocks south of the compound, five minutes before we arrive. They'll draw the insurgents' fire while we blow our way in from the top." The upper level of the compound consisted of a square attached to the broader third level, which sat on the even broader second level. The ground level was broadest of all.

The submersible captain conferred in Nibiran with his counterpart aboard the other craft via radio. Soon, he had an answer. "Submersible 2 is in agreement."

Po nodded. "Good." Considering he'd been guaranteed the full compliance of both submersible crews, it didn't come as a surprise, but it *was* still good to hear. "Someone go get Krik. Nap time is over. We're suiting up now."

No one voiced any protest, and a Nibiran ran to wake the sleeping Marine. Po was getting his men into their SERAPH suits a fair bit earlier than planned, but with this unexpected development, he didn't want to risk being at anything except the maximum level of readiness.

As he went to get his own suit, he realized he wasn't nearly as excited as he'd expected to be at this moment. He wasn't nervous at all.

The moment had finally come to settle the score with the alien who'd ordered the deaths of thousands of Marines, and who'd tried to nuke humanity's homeworld. He found that he was completely cold inside. Just like Krikorian.

Maybe I should have taken a nap, too.

Chapter 29

"Your First Squad is engaging the enemy," the submersible captain said as they made their final approach to To'sheth Rin's compound.

"Good," Po answered over the channel he'd established with the bridge. He and his Marines were already in the escape trunk, which they'd filled with water. Deploying from the sub would be a simple matter of opening the outer hatch and dropping to the roof of the compound's uppermost level.

In theory.

Less than five minutes after his last transmission, the captain spoke again, this time sounding frustrated. "They have portable torpedo launchers and have fired two in our direction."

Po managed not to curse. He'd known this was a possibility, but for Rin to be this prepared, it seemed likely he'd had warning of some kind. "Can you handle them?"

"I'm launching a decoy. But considering we're heading directly for them...."

Maybe the captain was fishing for Po to tell him to deviate from his course, but he couldn't do that. If Rin was still in that compound, then he was surely thinking hard about how to get out of there with his life. And Rin's own submersible was probably already on its way back to the compound, at top speed. Every second mattered.

"One of the torpedoes is chasing the decoy out over the city," the captain reported less than a minute later.

"And the other?"

"It's about to hit us."

Seconds later, as promised, something like a giant's fist hammered the sub, causing it to shudder violently in the water and sending the Marines drifting through the water toward one bulkhead.

"How are we looking?" Po asked the captain.

"Not good."

"Can we make it to the compound?"

"Yes. But that's about all we can do."

"Your crew will need to transfer to one of the subs coming behind us, then."

"And you will need one of them to take you home."

That would *be nice, provided we survive that long.* "Let's cross that bridge when we come to it."

"I...don't understand. There are no bridges underwater."

"It's a human expression. Ah—just forget it. We'll keep the insurgents occupied so you can make a clean transfer."

"It is appreciated. We are almost in position, PFC Abbato."

"Thanks." He switched over to his squad-only channel. "Me and Krik deploy first, then Crotty and Zhang. Crotty, you got your boom-boom ready?"

"Sure do."

"Good. We'll look to secure the rooftop on our way down, then we'll cover you as you set the charges."

"Got it, Platoon Leader."

The com crackled as the captain got back in touch. "We're in position. Opening the airlocks now. For your information, two of the rooftop insurgents are already aiming up at us."

"Copy."

And just like that, it began. Po pushed himself out of the airlock with his buoyancy compensator completely deflated. He sank like a stone, and fired on one insurgent on the roof while another's rifle fire *pinged* off his boots and leg, sending pain lancing through him and promising to leave nasty welts—provided a round didn't make its way *inside* the suit.

***

Krikorian took out the Nibiran firing up at Po, and Po neutralized the other one. Long seconds later, they dropped onto the roof, activating their boot magnets and moving to the perimeter. Even with their boots clinging to the metallic surface, Po still felt like he was moving in slow motion.

Crotty descended next, at the same time Zhang came from the other airlock. The shorter Marine, who looked like a little person next to the giant Chinese, began unspooling an eight-foot charge of C4 while the other three set about taking out Nibirans on other parts of the stepped roof.

The next pair of Marines—Windham and Taylor—touched down on the surface, and then came Drobnic and Patrice, who Po had also added to Second Squad. That was everyone.

Each Marine took up a position along the rooftop's lip, firing down on targets that were also being suppressed by First Squad from covered positions in and around buildings nearby. The Nibirans didn't stand much chance...which was good. Because next, Crotty asked them to abandon their cover.

"This charge will probably blow this entire upper section apart," he told them. "The tamping effect of all that water pressing down is going to direct almost all the force downward...but we still don't want to be there for the debris blowback."

And so they all inflated their suits' bladders and pushed off, surging upward while continuing to fire down on the remaining insurgent positions, which they now needed to keep suppressed even more than they did before, since they'd essentially tuned themselves into floating targets.

Once Crotty decided they'd put enough distance between them and the roof, he blew the charges.

He hadn't been kidding. The explosion created a sphere of water that ballooned briefly outward, and the shockwave hit Po like a brick wall, in spite of how far they'd floated from the roof. Next, a cloud of dust and debris came surging upward.

"There's our cover," Po grunted over the squad-wide. "Let's get back down there."

They dropped into the cloudy water where the roof had once been, and found that they were able to fall directly down onto the next level—the charge had blown through the upper level's floor, too.

Incredible.

They found themselves in a small section of corridor which had apparently automatically sealed when water started gushing into it. The section itself was already filled floor-to-ceiling.

"Can you override one of these hatches long enough to get us through?" Po asked Crotty. He'd rather not have to keep using C4 to blow their way further into the compound.

Crotty made his way over to the hatch closest to him, and tapped at a panel, which apparently still functioned even while submerged. "Looks like it. Which makes sense—anyone trapped here in the event of a breach would need to be able to escape. If they survived the breach in the first place."

"Do it." They didn't need to worry about decompression sickness. The SERAPH suits weren't rated to hold up under these pressures for any longer than a half hour, but until then, they effectively acted as atmospheric diving suits.

Crotty did, and Po and his squad found themselves swept out of the section on a torrent of water. Po barely managed to keep a grip on his rifle. The water carried them for several meters, but the farther it surged, the more places there were for it to go—such as intersecting corridors, open doors, and stairwells leading deeper into the compound.

He struggled to his feet at last, then grabbed Crotty as he floated by, pulling the other Marine to a standing position. The others were finding their footing all around them.

"Look for a panel," Po said. "We're not getting back through the water to that open hatch, so hopefully there's another one somewhere we can control it from."

"Found it," Crotty said within seconds. The hatch they'd come through closed, and the torrent of water subsided.

"That was...messy," Po said, eyeing all the places the water had found to flow down further into the compound. "If they didn't know we were coming before, they must now. But we need to move fast either way." He grinned. "You know what the means," he added, meeting Taylor's gaze through his de-polarized visor.

Taylor rolled his eyes, but answered nonetheless. "Means we gotta go slow. Cause slow is smooth."

"And smooth is fast," Po confirmed. "Let's move."

***

"Bad news, platoon leader," said First Squad's leader over a two-way channel as Po and Second Squad made their careful way down to the next level.

"What's up, Bozz?"

"We made it to the wall of the compound and set charges to blow a hatch, but it ended up being a false one. Just a solid wall behind it. We didn't use enough C4 to get through a wall, and now we only have enough left to blow another hatch."

"That's not bad news, Bozz. That's good news."

"Huh? I don't copy, Platoon Leader."

"They wouldn't have bothered installing a false hatch if this wasn't where Rin has been hiding out. Means he just might be here." A thrill ran through Po even as he spoke the words.

A brief silence came over the com. "Huh. Never looked at it that way. Cool."

"I'm tracking your location. Keep moving around the building, keeping tight to the wall. If we have an opportunity, we'll let you in ourselves."

"That I copy, Platoon Leader. Bozz out."

Po and Second Squad exited the stairwell onto the compound's second level, and ran straight into the first resistance they'd faced inside the compound. It was just a couple Nibirans taking shots at them from behind a door they'd opened into the corridor to use as concealment.

Second Squad wasted no time.

"Frag out," Krik said, giving the bomb an easy underhand toss, to land at the insurgents' feet.

The Marines were pressing forward even as the grenade was going off, swiftly coming up on the wounded, disoriented Nibirans and putting them both down as they tried to swing their weapons around.

"Whoa," Taylor said. "Ease up. Their families are here."

"Seriously?" Po stepped forward and peered into the chamber whose door the insurgents had been shooting at them from behind. Sure enough, there were two female Nibirans cowering against the far wall, one clutching two small aliens to her chest and the other holding three.

They let their families live here with them. Despite the danger. Po's lip curled in disgust. "Taylor, watch them while Crotty restrains them. Catch up when you can."

"You gotta be kidding me," Taylor said.

Po snorted. "You really think so?" He motioned for the others to follow, without another word.

***

The Marines were cutting a warpath through the compound as they fought through to the ground level. *The seabed level, I guess you'd call it.*

Every one of them knew that the house was probably rigged to blow, and that Rin would trigger it the moment he decided he'd lost. And so, despite the talk about going slow to go fast, the Marines of Second Squad were taking risks they wouldn't have otherwise—and Po didn't try to stop them.

Especially when those risks involved running across the enemy's line of fire to usher mothers and children to safety. Po's heart swelled when he saw his men putting their own wellbeing on the line to protect noncombatants.

Would a Janus member have done something like that? He knew the answer, and it made him glad to be on the side he was. Working for GEA didn't exactly fill him with pride, and the Marines were far from perfect. But it was vastly preferable to being one of Rin's terrorists.

As they pushed through the compound, their numbers dwindled, and soon it was just Po, Krik, Zhang, and Drobnic pushing through the bottom level. That was the inevitable result of Marines lingering behind to tie up the insurgents' families, and to make sure each room was properly cleared to avoid Janus coming at them from behind.

Then they came to the outer airlock First Squad was waiting outside of. Po was able to open the exterior hatch using the control panel—the thing required no security clearance to operate, probably for greater ease of use for the compound's inhabitants.

It would still take several minutes more for the thing to drain the water it had let in and to admit Bozz and his men into the compound proper, but it brought peace of mind to know reinforcements were on the way.

In the meantime, Po had entered a state of flow. His movements were like clockwork—efficient and purposeful. They won the last firefight to take the ground level, which necessitated more room-clearing. Po assigned Zhang and Drobnic to it, leaving just him and Krikorian to push to the first sublevel.

The lights were switched off down here, and soon they were stalking through darkness. This was where Rin was said to sleep, according to intel. Was the dark meant to make them think no one was here, or did the Nibirans hope the slight degradation in the Marines' sight would work to their advantage? If so, it had been a dumb move. Their suits' night vision was almost as good as seeing by halogens.

Po didn't expect to encounter much resistance down here either way, figuring the Janus leader had already sent most of what he had at them. But if he'd rigged his compound with explosives, then now would be the time he'd detonate them. If they were to have any hope of survival, they needed to move fast.

Ara Darshim's words rang in his ears, from one of many briefing sessions. "I have it on good intelligence that Shiv Horan has joined back up with To'sheth Rin in these last weeks," she'd told them. "And if that's correct, he'll be Rin's last line of defense. "Horan is young, but he's like a brother to Rin, and he's his staunchest loyalist and defender. He will give his life to protect his leader, if it comes to that."

Sure enough, as he and Krik approached the one area they hadn't checked yet of the bottommost sublevel, a Nibiran poked his head out of a doorway.

That'll be Horan, Po realized. *Why isn't he shooting at us?*

Then, it struck him: Horan didn't know the outcome of the fighting above.

He thinks there's a chance we might be fellow Janus, come down to update him.

Somehow, he knew what to do without thinking about it. He selected one of the limited Nibiran phrases Navarro had sent him to learn, opened his visor, and deployed it.

"*Shiv, come here,*" he hissed in his best Nibiran accent. "*Shiv,*" he whispered again, "*come here.*"

A confused-looking alien poked his head back out of the doorway, and Po already had his shot lined up. He fired, and the head cracked backward.

Shiv down.

He and Krikorian swept through, kicked the insurgent's fallen body to make sure he was dead, then advanced on to the final room.

Po was first in, and it was he that saw Rin rising from the couch. The Nibiran looked terrified. He held an assault rifle in his hands, already pointed toward the door, and he opened fire as soon as he saw Po.

His shots went wild, glancing off Po's side before trending up toward the ceiling.

Po's didn't. His first round took Rin in the face, and his second and third went into his neck. The Nibiran fell backward, arms flinging out to the sides as he crumpled to the floor in a twisted heap, to move no more.

Po walked over to the body and nudged it with his foot, confirming the kill.

"That was for Staff Sergeant Young," he told Rin's inert form.

With that, it was over.

Chapter 30

"Rin is neutralized," Po said over the platoon channel. "Begin sensitive site exploitation, and get it done fast."

Within a couple minutes, First Squad was there with him, and the rest of Second caught up soon after that. Together, they searched Rin's room and the surrounding area for anything of value—mostly papers and drives that might contain intel on Janus' future moves, along with who knew what else.

"Is anyone hurt?" Po asked, his eyes on Bozzelli.

The First Squad leader shook his head. "Not a single casualty."

Po closed his eyes and breathed, "Thank you," not totally sure who he was directing it at.

"Uh, you're welcome," Bozz said.

They took Rin's body back to the ground floor, to the vehicle bay, whose airlock they'd cycled by the time the GA subs came to exfiltrate them. Po had ordered the tied-up woman and children left for the Morati military to find. He didn't know how involved they'd been with Rin's business, and he didn't want to know. 131st Platoon had done what it came to do.

The ride back involved some of the tensest moments of the mission yet. Po was sure every one of them was convinced that Morati submersibles would rise from the underwater city as they left, to torpedo them to oblivion—or that some weapon emplacement would draw a bead on them and do the same.

Neither happened. And as they drew farther and father away from Morati Firth, a reality unfolded that none of them had expected. It became more and more solid with each passing moment:

They had survived, and they were *going* to survive.

They'd killed the most wanted being in the system.

And they'd lived to tell about it.

Po felt both triumphant and unsettled. He wanted to let himself go—to celebrate the win as much as the others were, as they began to pound him on the back and shake his hand.

But something inside him was bracing itself, and he couldn't stop the same question from repeating over and over inside his head, as if on a loop.

What's next?

Epilogue

Gomorate was barely recognizable upon the return of the victorious 131st platoon.

Po remembered remarking on how much their initial defense of the Nibiran capital had changed it...but that was nothing compared to this. The city had been utterly transformed. Few buildings had escaped any effects from Janus' second attempt to take over the capital, and based on what he'd seen, he estimated at least half of them had been reduced to rubble. Most of the rest bore scorch marks, and many of those had suffered the collapse of up to half their floors.

Shortly after disembarking the AC-900 that had brought them back, Po had been informed that he would soon be subject to multiple debriefing interviews, so that the Corps could establish a clearer idea of what had happened in the underwater compound, and what Po and his men had observed, along with their impressions of the GA personnel and facilities they'd encountered.

To'sheth Rin's body had already been positively IDed twice now—once by the Nibirans at Naval Advance Base Bodur, and once by Corps specialists here in Gomorate. One more examination would be done, and after that, they'd burn the body and scatter the ashes over the ocean. The Nibirans weren't keen to host a gravesite that would inevitably become a target for further insurgent activity. Po couldn't say he blamed them.

The intel they'd harvested from Rin's compound was being analyzed, a process that had started the moment they'd gotten back. Po could understand that, too. The back-to-back assaults on Gomorate had been unexpectedly brutal, and he could understand an eagerness from anyone who'd been through both to find out what Janus might do next, and quickly.

As for Po's reception since getting back to Gomorate...the enlisted men all heartily congratulated him, with many a handshake, fist bump, and back-pounding. But for the most part, the higher-ups seemed more reserved. Colonel Coleman had shaken his hand firmly while looking him in the eye, but the rest of the officers mostly seemed to be waiting for what the reaction would be from the even-higher-ups—not to mention from GEA.

His first night in the city, he had trouble sleeping, and he expected that to continue. The two nights he'd spent at the Gomorati Army base waiting for the gunship had been mostly sleepless, too.

Everything that had happened since the attack on Cycler 3, and everything he'd done...all the constant going, then waiting, then fighting...it was beginning to catch up with him in a way it hadn't before.

Killing To'sheth Rin was supposed to bring closure. He'd envisioned it as an end of some sort. But it didn't feel like one now. The future was still unclear, with everything up in the air, everything in motion. He may have acted as a lance corporal during the raid on Rin's compound, but he was still just a PFC, and even if he'd been promoted already he doubted his superiors would be telling him much more than they were.

On his second day, he visited the field hospital where Gunny Emery was recuperating from delayed abdominal hemorrhaging caused by the RPG blast, along with a broken femur, severe burns, and debris that had been extracted from all along the right side of his torso. The gunny was sleeping when he came in, so Po just sat for a while, happy enough for the rare peace and solitude it afforded him.

He'd already visited Navarro and Gomez. Navarro was doing well...and so was Gomez, all things considered. But he *had* suffered a moderate brain injury, and the doc said it could take up to nine months to recover from it. That meant nine months out of commission.

I wonder what that'd be like.

As for Paisley, he hadn't shown up in Gomorate, or anywhere else as far as Po could tell. He was officially a deserter, now, recognized as such by the Corps. With everything else going on, he didn't know whether any Marines could be spared to go looking for him. But it *was* a worrying thought—the simple fact he was still out there, but also the potential for him damaging the Corps, whether by outright treachery or simply by falling into the wrong hands, with everything he knew along with the technology he carried.

Emery woke up, saw him, and gave a faint grin. "Abbato. They process your promotion yet?"

"Not yet, Gunny."

"It's coming. You better believe it's coming. I know what you did out there. You can consider yourself a lance, Marine."

"Thanks." Po sat with his forearms resting on his thighs, and his hands dangling between them. He stared at the floor. "Gunny," he began and sighed. "Look, I...I'm really sorry about Staff Sergeant Young."

"I'm sorry about him too, Abbato. But why do I feel like you're apologizing?"

He shook his head. "I should have had my boys check that house better. We rushed through there, and we missed—"

"You rushed through because you were on your way to *save* the sergeant, and his men."

"But I led him to his death."

"Cut that out. I watched your implant footage of what happened, Abbato. We were all rushing through Karakata, and we were losing men left and right. The longer we'd have taken to get out of there, the more of us the Nibirans would have killed. If it hadn't been Young, it would have been someone else. If he was here, he'd tell you the same thing."

Po nodded slowly. Emery's words didn't do much for his aching conscience, but they made a certain sort of sense, he supposed. *If only I could believe them enough to help me sleep a bit more.*

"Hey," Emery said. "You think you're the only one who's done stuff in war that you'll carry with you the rest of your life?"

Po met the gunny's gaze with raised eyebrows. This was realer talk than he'd been expecting. Then again, this was one of the things he liked most about Emery.

"War is a disaster, Abbato. Not just this war—any war. It's always a complete disaster. Anyone who gets themselves involved in a war can expect it to be the messiest, most psychologically damaging thing they'll ever do in their lives. And you're not done yet. So, expect to carry some baggage with you, and the more you fight, the more you can expect to accumulate. I'm not saying it's right, and I know this probably doesn't come as much of a comfort. But it's also the reality."

"Yeah. I get it, Gunny." He swallowed around the hard lump that had suddenly formed in his throat. *Change the subject,* he told himself, and he did. "When do you think we're getting off this planet?"

Emery shrugged to the best of his ability, in his bedridden state. "The ships to clear away the orbital debris should be here within weeks. After that, it'll be at least another month or two before it's safe for ships to land and launch again from Nibiru. But that still leaves the question of what effect Rin's death will have on the insurgency, and of what else GEA thinks we're going to accomplish for them here."

"Have you heard about anything from the intel we hauled out of Rin's compound?"

Emery's gaze drifted toward the door, and he hesitated. "Not sure if I should tell you this or not. But screw it. I know Young trusted you with this kind of thing, so I will too. Besides, it'll probably get out soon enough. Until then, just keep it to yourself, all right?"

"What is it?"

"There are clear indications, all throughout that intel treasure trove, that the Emplor are the ones who supplied Janus with the missiles and launch facilities on Maw—the ones that took out our satellites and ships. And the thinking goes that *all* of Janus' advanced weaponry came from them too, even though a lot of it's of human make. How the Emplor got our stuff in the first place, *I* sure don't know. But the talk now is that GEA wants to move on the Emplor."

"Whoa." Po tried not to think of Zanth, because if he did, his distress would surely show on his face.

"Yeah," Emery said. "Obviously, they'd need to tread very lightly if they're going to do that—at least at first. We still have no idea what the Emplor are actually capable of. But things are turning, and there are prominent elements in GEA that now recognize the need to address the Emplor's influence and power with our species."

Po's heartbeat was accelerating. Zanth had once pointed out that not all Emplor were aligned with each other, but the fact he'd accepted so much help from the alien was suddenly making him feel nauseous.

What would it mean to fight the Emplor? The Nibirans were one thing. Sure, they'd almost turned at least part of Earth into a nuclear wasteland. But what might the *Emplor* be able to do?

"You all right, Abbato?"

"Yeah, I only...." He offered a smile that felt tepid on his lips. "Guess this is just what we signed up for, right?"

"This is *exactly* what we signed up for." Emery reached up and patted Po's shoulder.

With that, they sat in silence for a time. For his part, all Po could think of was Nicky back in Psyche, completely vulnerable to the first alien power that might care to take out the vital mining station.

And with that, all resentment he felt toward his sister for not writing him fell away.

I won't let them hurt you, he thought fervently. *I won't.*

Acknowledgments

Thank you to the Marines and other veterans who allowed me to interview them one-on-one in order to get the details of Marine life as accurate as I could. They include Dan Abbott, Chuck Chambers, Richard Hakala, Bill Paradis, Steven Reneau, Dennis Whalen, and one other veteran who requested to remain anonymous.

Thank you to my Alpha Team, who have been reading this book since its earliest stage and who've provided substantial feedback along the way, which helped me develop the story with my readers' desires foremost in mind. They are Sheila Beitler, Gwen Collins, Richard Hakala, Colin Oliver, and Jeff Rudolph.

Thank you to my ARC/proofreading team, who helped eliminate scores of spelling and grammar issues. I take full responsibility for any mistakes that remain :)

Thank you to Tom Edwards for creating such stunning cover art, as always.

Thank you to my family - Mom, Dad, and Danielle - your support means everything.

Thank you to the people who read my stories. I couldn't do this without you.

Printed in Dunstable, United Kingdom